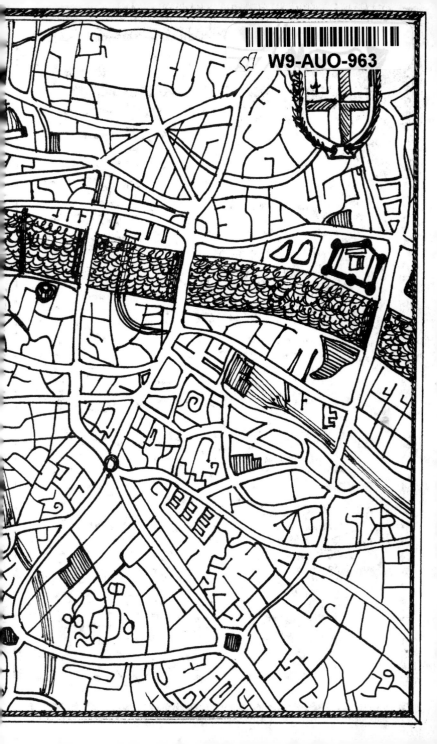

Neil Flambé

and the
BARD'S BANQUET

Also by Kevin Sylvester

Neil Flambé

and the
BARD'S BANQUET

KEVIN
SYLVESTER

SIMON & SCHUSTER BOOKS FOR YOUNG READERS
New York London Toronto Sydney New Delhi

SIMON & SCHUSTER BOOKS FOR YOUNG READERS
An imprint of Simon & Schuster Children's Publishing Division
1230 Avenue of the Americas, New York, New York 10020

For information about special discounts for bulk purchases, please contact Simon & Schuster
Special Sales at 1-866-506-1949 or business@simonandschuster.com.
The Simon & Schuster Speakers Bureau can bring authors to your live event.
For more information or to book an event, contact the Simon & Schuster Speakers
Bureau at 1-866-248-3049 or visit our website at www.simonspeakers.com.
Book design by Laurent Linn and Tom Daly
The text for this book is set in Goudy Old Style.
The illustrations for this book are rendered in pen and ink.
Manufactured in the United States of America
1214 FFG
2 4 6 8 10 9 7 5 3 1
Library of Congress Cataloging-in-Publication Data
Sylvester, Kevin.
Neil Flambé and the Bard's banquet / Kevin Sylvester.—First edition.
pages cm. — (Neil Flambé capers ; 5)
Summary: Fifteen-year-old celebrity chef Neil Flambé
is summoned to England to solve a Shakesperian mystery.
ISBN 978-1-4814-1038-0 (hardcover)
ISBN 978-1-4814-1039-7 (pbk.)
ISBN 978-1-4814-1040-3 (eBook)
[1. Mystery and detective stories. 2.Cooking—Fiction.
3. Shakespeare, William, 1564-1616—Fiction. 4. England--Fiction.]
I. Title. II. Title: Bard's banquet.
PZ7.S98348Ne 2015
[Fic]—dc23
2013042087

FIRST
EDITION

This book is dedicated to all my friends at the University of St. Michael's College—especially the Muggeridge clan—who would spend hours in pubs talking about great books.

"If this were played upon a stage now, I could condemn it as an improbable fiction."

—William Shakespeare, *Twelfth Night*

PROLOGUE

SIT DOWN AND RELAX IN PROPER STYLE

The proper way to make tea and scones according to Neil Flambé

Scones are a staple of English cooking. They warm you up on a cold day. Yours won't be as good as the ones I make at Chez Flambé for Sunday high tea . . . but you might as well try. Good luck. You'll need it.

INGREDIENTS:

1 cup flour
2 tablespoons sugar
1 tablespoon baking powder
Dash of salt
1 stick (5 tablespoons) unsalted butter, chilled
1 cup heavy cream
¼ cup dried raisins, cranberries, or currants (optional)

with notes from Larry! ← me!

COOKING INSTRUCTIONS:

1. Preheat oven to 425° F (220° C).

2. Mix together the dry ingredients in a bowl.

3. Cut the butter into small chunks and then mix together with a pastry knife. Keep mixing until the whole mixture resembles small crumbs.

   You can do this in a food processor. Add the butter and pulse the blades until it looks like small crumbs. Don't tell Neil! He's old-school.

4. Add the cream and dried fruit (if using). Mix together with a wooden spoon or spatula until the mixture forms a sticky dough.

   make sure its mixed well. Too dry or too wet and you'll end up with something resembling a hockey puck!

5. Take about a ¼ cup of dough and work it into a rough ball in your hand. Place it on the baking sheet. Do this with the rest of the dough, then brush a little cream on the top of each ball.

6. Bake in oven for 12 minutes.

7. After you take the scones out, let them cool on a rack while you make tea.

8. Break each scone in half.

9. Serve with clotted cream and your favorite jam. Cream
   first.

Don't be a doofus. The jam clearly goes on before the cream. Anyone who says otherwise is nuts!

If you don't have clotted cream, or Devon cream, or similar,
Larry says you can make something similar by whipping
about a cup of cream in a blender (not with a mixer) but
stopping before it turns to butter. But that's because Larry
is a goof.

(HA! I may be a goof but I'm still right!)

CHAPTER ONE

TWO BEES OR NOT TWO BEES

Neil Flambé's head hurt.
Of course, he'd just been hitting it with a frying pan, so that made sense.

What didn't make sense— to Neil, anyway—was the antique jar of honey that sat on the kitchen counter, facing Neil with a suspicious attitude.

Lord Lane of Liverpool had uncovered a case of the honey during a recent building demolition—or, more precisely, his workers had—and he was asking fifteen-year-old super-chef Neil Flambé to cook him a meal using the ingredient.

The problem wasn't the honey. Neil could have cooked an amazing meal with the jar itself, if that's what Lane had wanted. The problem was the scroll of paper suspended inside the jar.

When the case of honey had arrived, Neil's cousin

Larry had held one jar up to the light to get a closer look inside. The sunlight had revealed a note that said, or seemed to say, *help*. A cry for help, even from the distant past, was the last thing Neil wanted to hear after months of globe-trotting battles and mystery solving.

"Are you done banging your head?" Larry asked, smiling and walking over to Neil. "A little dramatic, even for you."

Neil moaned. "I want to be a chef, not a private eye."

"Private nose."

"Whatever! The point is that I just want to run my restaurant."

"And do your homework on time."

"And do my—wait, *no*, just run the restaurant, in peace for a change. That would *be nice*!" Neil bellowed, lifting himself off his chair. The movement made his head throb again. He sat down and rubbed his temples and moaned some more. "I'm done with solving crimes. Tell Lord Lane he can have his honey back and can find someone else to cook him dinner."

"Chill, cuz! I only said that the note *looks* like it spells 'help,'" Larry said. "There's a whole roll of paper in there. Maybe it says 'help is on the way' or 'honey will *help* cure your gout' or something like that."

"I don't care," Neil said. "Dinner is off."

"Have I mentioned that Lane is practically royalty?"

Neil actually snorted. "Royalty? Look at what Japanese royalty almost did to us!" The Flambés had just returned from a scary few weeks in Tokyo that had almost killed them in a number of different ways. For a while, Neil had been sure Larry *had* been killed.

"Did I mention that he's rich? You could buy some nice new frying pans to hit your head with!"

Neil hesitated for a moment, then shook his head. "Nope, I still don't care."

"And did I mention that I already accepted the down payment for the dinner?"

"What?" Neil said, straightening up. "You didn't ask me first?"

Larry grinned sheepishly. "It was sort of a last-minute kind of thing. He's already in town for some play or something. And I thought you'd be intrigued. He could have asked any chef, but he chose you. He clearly wanted the best. That's you, isn't it?"

Neil had to admit this was true. His ego started to wake up, fighting with the pain and exhaustion and beating them both into submission. Neil stole a glance at the jars of honey. The honey glowed like gold in the sunlight.

"All right, look," Neil said finally, standing up and wagging his finger at Larry. "I'll cook this meal, but we don't use *that* jar of honey. It stays closed. Deal?"

"Deal," Larry said. "We just hand it to him after dinner and then forget it ever passed through our kitchen."

"Right," Neil said. "And if Lord Lane wants to know why some long-dead Victorian guy needed help, then he can find out himself."

"Deal times two," Larry said.

Even Neil suspected this wasn't going to be the end

of the story, but he stashed that suspicion in the back of his much-better-all-of-a-sudden head and started to actually think about planning his glorious meal.

"Okay, honey is an amazing ingredient in any number of dishes." Neil walked over to the counter and examined the unopened jars. They were made out of glass, with each top sealed with a ceramic lid coated with a thick layer of beeswax.

"Let's see how this all tastes, and then I'll make Lane's taste buds implode."

Larry rolled his eyes. He carefully took the jar containing the note and placed it on a high shelf. "Stay," he said, pointing angrily at the jar.

Neil took a knife and carefully began prying the top off one of the remaining jars.

"Honey can last for centuries without going bad," Neil said, "as long as it's properly sealed."

He carefully cut a slit around the lip of the jar and then gingerly maneuvered the blade between the lid and the glass. He needed to be very careful. Old glass was fragile, and he didn't want to be stuck figuring out what was a crystallized bit of golden honey and what was a shard of glass.

He cracked the seal. The pungent aroma of honey swelled his senses.

"Wonderful." Neil smiled. He took a deeper sniff. "And weird." He sniffed the honey again. It smelled, there was no other word for it, *pure*. He could detect the powerful aromas of numerous flowers, and just the faintest trace of smokiness. "Definitely weird."

"What's weird?" Larry asked.

"Well, from what I know about Victorian London, it was a pretty dirty place. There were lots of factories and stuff, burning a lot of coal. I should smell that in this honey."

Larry gave a gasp of astonishment. "You *have* been doing your homework!"

"Well, actually, I have b—" Neil was just about to accept this pat on the back, when he was interrupted by a derisive laugh from the kitchen door.

Isabella Tortellini made her way into the kitchen. Her left arm was still in a sling, a result of a bullet wound she'd suffered in Japan. Neil noticed that even her sling seemed to be made of some exotic and wonderful fabric.

"Ah, speaking of honey, here's your very own sweetie!" Larry said with a chuckle. "And so stylish! You should get shot more often."

"*Sei un buffone!* You are such a clown," Isabella said.

Neil felt his face redden, a little with embarrassment but more with pleasure. Isabella was definitely his "sweetie" (just as Larry was definitely a clown).

Larry smiled. "I believe you were about to suggest that our young chef is lying about doing his homework?"

"Homework?" She raised an eyebrow and looked at Neil, who squirmed.

"Actually, Isabella was telling me about the origins of modern perfume making the other day. For a book report . . ."

Isabella glared harder.

"Okay, an *overdue* history assignment on the Industrial Revolution."

"Exactly!" Isabella smiled. "See, the truth is always *meglio*, better."

Neil continued. "Perfumes helped the rich and not-so-rich cover up the smells of city living and coal dust. It was kind of ironic that the factories allowed them to make enough to satisfy demand, while also making the smells that needed covering."

"Ironic, or smart business?" Larry said. "I always say, never trust a perfume maker. *Ouch!*"

Isabella had very deftly used her one good arm to grab and twist a tea towel and whack Larry on the rear end with the tip.

"I am sweet like honey, but I also sting like *un'ape*, a bee," she said, touching her forehead with her finger. "Remember that."

"More like a *vespa*!" Larry said, sidling a step away.

"*Sì*, more like a wasp," she said, smiling.

"My arm is almost healed, then watch out! See, I do not need a bodyguard all the time!"

"Speaking of which, where is the human tank?" Larry asked. Jones, Isabella's friend and bodyguard, was usually hovering close by.

"He is in the car. We are leaving for France tonight for a very big perfume convention. I will return very rich."

"Well, at least I'll know *one* teenager who's successful!" Larry expertly ducked the spatula Neil flung at him.

"Anyway, Neil, you were explaining about *il miele*, the honey?" Isabella said, gliding over and giving Neil a kiss on the cheek.

Neil smiled dumbly for a second, then continued. "Well, I'd expect that this honey would smell way more, I don't know, dirty or sooty."

Larry laughed. "And you say you don't like mysteries!"

Neil put the honey down abruptly. "I don't. *This* is about cooking. Flavor undertones, hidden things like smoke or soot, can affect the type of dishes I can cook with honey. This honey doesn't have any of those. It's incredibly pure."

"So. What *do* you have planned?" Isabella said, leaning closer to him. She loved watching Neil work.

Neil felt a thrill as he stared into her chocolate-colored eyes. "Um, uh . . . well, there are a few standard things. Lane is British, which means he'll probably love meats, pastries. I'm looking at some simple recipes and fresh ingredients."

Neil's mind was racing now as he began to construct combinations of flavor and texture out of thin air. His hands flew around as he mixed the imaginary ingredients.

"I'll start with an appetizer that plays on the idea of crumpets, with honey-glazed cakes. It's more of a baklava but with an infusion of Earl Grey tea. Not too sweet, just sweet enough to set the tone for the evening."

"British with a twist," Larry said.

"That sounds *fantastico*." Isabella smiled.

Neil raced on. "Main course? Honey-glazed ham, but deconstructed as a kind of almost bacon-flavored meat pie—or! Or maybe as a kind of charcuterie plate!" Neil was speaking more quickly with each possibility. "Then dessert will be a selection of cheeses, but with honey-baked toasts, some honey ice cream, and then a honey trifle."

Larry jumped to his feet and clapped his hands. "And you didn't once mention fish! What are we waiting for? Let's start prepping!"

Isabella landed a quick kiss full on Neil's lips. "Wonderful," she whispered.

Neil's headache was now completely forgotten.

CHAPTER TWO

SHAKE AND BAKE

Neil expertly drizzled a fine pattern of honey over his plates of crispy, butter-fried pastry. The lines were so thin and airy they seemed like they might float away if the slightest breeze came through the back door. That was exactly the impression Neil wanted.

"Honey can be an overwhelming taste," he told Larry as he laid down the first line. "Too much, even one glob out of place, and the balance of the dish is completely thrown off."

Neil Flambé never let that imbalance happen.

Never.

"It smells like a candy shop in here!" Larry yelled happily as he peeled potatoes. "Who can make the buns rise? Pringle them with stew!" he sang, mashing up the words to the tune of "The Candy Man."

Gary, the bike courier and part-time kitchen helper,

joined in. "The candied ham! The candied ham can!" Gary had recently stepped in to help cook at Chez Flambé, during Larry's ill-fated trip to Japan. Gary had proven so good—especially with fish—that Neil had kept him around for the busier nights.

"Please be *quiet!*" Neil yelled as he attempted to concentrate on his honey pattern.

Larry stood stock-still, a shocked expression on his face. "Neil Flambé said . . . *please!*"

"Mark today on the calendar!" Gary said, chuckling.

"*Shut up!*" Neil yelled. . . . "*Please!*"

"Twice!" Larry yelled, leaping up and giving Gary a high five.

"Even the 'shut up' sounded polite!"

"I think the chef is in love!"

Neil shook his head sadly and turned his attention back to his meal. "Note to self: earplugs," he murmured sadly as he continued the delicate work. Larry was right about one thing: The kitchen smelled wonderful.

The ice-cream maker was gently churning a perfectly blended honey confection.

The honey-glazed ham was braising on low heat in his oven, the honey browning and mellowing as it mixed with the fatty meat, the cloves, and other spices.

The ham itself had been bought—for a hefty price—from Neil's hefty mentor, Angel Jícama. It was worth the money. Neil knew it would be better than anything you could get at a butcher shop, even a great one. Angel had that special, magic touch. Neil would eventually slice the cooked ham so thin it would melt on the mouths of his guests like a fine pancetta.

A tiny rush of cool air slid under the kitchen doors from the dining room. The draft was a sure sign the front door of their dilapidated building had opened. The guests had begun to arrive.

Neil put the last gossamer thread of honey over the pastry. He took a step back and smiled. He was ready.

Zoe and Amber Soba, Neil's waitstaff, peeked their heads in through the kitchen doors.

"Showtime!" Zoe said.

Neil barely nodded his head in acknowledgment.

"Is Lane's daughter, Penny, out there?" Larry said, smoothing the front of his chef's jacket. "I haven't seen her in ages."

Zoe shook her head. "Sorry, lover boy. Lane says she's accepted some research assignment on bugs or lizards or something in the middle of a jungle somewhere. Even he doesn't know where she is."

Larry's shoulders sagged, and he scrunched up the front of his chef's jacket again.

Zoe's twin sister, Amber, peeked her head into the kitchen. "Menus have been delivered. Don't blow it!"

Neil narrowed his eyes and growled.

Larry and Gary exchanged a chuckle behind him.

"I think the best chance for 'blowing it' comes from the sous-chefs," Neil said, walking over to the stove and agitating a frying pan filled with caramelized onions.

"Hey, I'm only here because *you* said *you* needed help!" Gary said with a look of mock disgust.

"Then stop cracking jokes with Captain Coffee over there and actually *help*," Neil said.

"Coffee! Great idea, Neil! Gary, let's make coffee!" Larry cheered.

Larry busied himself with the coffeemaker as Gary began grinding some freshly roasted beans.

Neil rolled his eyes. "Fine. *I'll* get the food ready. It's safer for everyone that way." Thank goodness tonight was a set menu, no variations allowed. He sounded more annoyed than he actually felt. On a normal, busier night, he'd be ready to kill either Larry or Gary . . . or both.

Neil took the ham out of the oven and placed it on the counter to rest. Then he set out the plates for the appetizer course.

Larry and Gary got the coffee brewing and got back to work. The sound of all the chopping, slicing, boiling, cutting, and plating gave the kitchen a kind of electric buzz.

Neil allowed himself a deep, satisfied breath. He was finally back in his element, in his kitchen paradise. He loved being a chef. This was *way* better than solving crimes. He glanced up at the one bottle of honey that threatened his peace, and scowled.

Amber and Zoe collected the appetizers and took them to the dining room.

The appreciative oohs and aahs and the animated conversation wafted into the kitchen.

"Music to my ears." Neil smiled as he pushed some silky boiled potatoes through a ricer, giving them the exact creamy texture that would balance the meaty ham.

Tonight was going to be another crowning, and lucrative, success.

"I prefer my music with more drums." Larry laughed as he quickly sautéed some green peas with butter and garlic.

"That's because your head stops working if it's not banged around by loud noises," Neil said.

"Ha-ha," Larry said. "This from the guy who spent all week cranking a fry pan off his noggin."

"Can I do anything?" Gary said. He'd finished cleaning some pots and was now sitting on a countertop rocking his legs back and forth.

Neil began slicing the ham. "Yes," he said. "For the dessert topping I need exactly two cups of honey. Not a molecule more or less. The honey is still a little crystallized, so you'll need to heat it a bit in a double boiler to liquefy it. I need it nice and silky so I can pour it into the trifle with the crumbled chocolate."

"Yes, sir!" Gary said, leaping down from the counter and prepping a pan of water on one of the stove tops.

Neil heard Amber and Zoe gathering the plates.

He knew, from experience, that this was the best moment to make his appearance. The crowd would be happy and attentive. Their first glasses of wine would leave them mellow and settled.

Neil put his knife down and smoothed the front of his chef's jacket.

Larry made a drumming sound on the counter with his hands. "The great star prepares to make his grand entrance. Should Amber get the spotlight ready?"

Neil ignored him and walked up to the kitchen doors. Amber and Zoe began bringing in the dishes, smiling and giving Neil pats on the back and relaying the various compliments the diners had asked them to convey.

Amber offered up . . .

"Delicious."

"Delectable."

"Fantastic."

"Fabulous."

With each word, Neil seemed to grow taller.

Zoe, as she passed through the doors, added . . .

"Wonderful."

"Stupendous."

"Repulsive."

Neil did a double take. "What? Repulsive? Who said repulsive?"

"I made that one up," Zoe smiled. "We don't want you getting too cocky."

Neil took a deep breath and then pushed open the kitchen doors.

"I'm surprised he can fit his head through there," Larry called, just loud enough to be heard over the swinging hinges.

The diners heard it as well, and turned to see Neil, who was actually scowling for a moment as the insult lingered in the air.

Neil made a mental note to put a laxative in Larry's next coffee. The idea cheered him up and the smile returned to his face.

Lord Lane was seated at the head of a large table. A group of five men and women were seated around the table.

Lane spotted Neil and leaped to his feet. He strode over to Neil, his hand extended. "That was an exquisite use of that honey. I knew you were the perfect chef for this job. 'Some pigeons, Davy, a couple of short-legged hens, a joint of mutton, and any pretty little tiny kickshaws, tell William cook.'"

Neil took Lane's hand, but as happy as he was with the compliment, he was completely confused by the string of words Lane had added to them.

"Thank you and . . . um, sorry," Neil said slowly. "Was that last bit German? Or . . . French?"

Lord Lane looked at Neil as if he didn't quite understand him. "You were supposed to say, 'Doth the man of war stay all night, sir?' It's the next line from the play!"

"Play?"

"*Henry the Fourth, Part Two!*" Lane gave Neil a slap on the shoulder.

Neil still looked perplexed. He suddenly felt an incredible urge to hightail it back to the kitchen. His mood was further confused by a bright flash from outside the front window. Neil looked over and saw a photographer taking photos.

Paparazzi? Snapping pics of an English lord having dinner? Possibly . . . The British press were notorious for their rabid pursuit of celebrities. Or was it something else . . . ? *Forget it!* Neil told himself. *No more mysteries!*

Lane's silky voice snapped Neil back to reality. "Shakespeare," Lane was saying slowly. "You've heard of him?"

Neil was distracted by another flash. What was going on? He looked outside as a large man in a trench coat got into a dark car and drove away. Lane was still talking.

"You seem perplexed, lad. Well, perhaps you don't study Shakespeare here in the colonies anymore?" Lane asked, a mischievous smile playing on his lips. "He's actually quite good."

"I know who Shakespeare is," Neil said. "I just haven't read that particular play." Neil hadn't read any Shakespeare plays, in fact. He was more interested in unlocking the secrets of pepper than of poetry.

"Well, you should try, dear boy! Or perhaps, like so many of *your* generation, you are more enamored of video games and loud music?"

Neil never liked it when someone accused him of being "just a kid." Lane hadn't said that exactly, but Neil still felt as if he were being mocked.

"Lord Lane is quite a champion of the theater," said a woman to Neil's left. "He has supported many productions, and actors."

Lane smiled. "Well, let us rather say that I have been blessed with numerous good friends who have made names for themselves on the stage. And the study of Shakespeare can make one, quite simply, a much better person. Much better, in fact, at whatever one calls one's job."

Neil smiled, but he felt incredibly ill at ease. It wasn't that Lane was judging him, exactly. Or was he? Neil couldn't say what it was . . . there seemed to be a kind of implied suggestion that Neil wasn't doing all he could with his life. He shuffled uneasily. The conversation had so quickly shifted from his area of strength, cooking, to his great weakness, school.

Neil gave a small, nervous cough and turned back toward the kitchen doors. "Well, I just came out to say hello and I hope you enjoyed your starter . . ."

"Very much so, old boy!" Lane called, making his way back to his seat. "And we await the second act with keen anticipation!"

Neil felt the confidence begin to return. He'd just been congratulated on the food. Good. Things were swinging back his way. He turned around. "The main course will be ham, but no ordinary ham! I have infused the salted meat with honey. The ham will be sliced razor-thin and served over a spiced potato and sweet potato compote."

There were numerous oohs and aahs.

Neil gave a short bow and turned back toward the kitchen.

"Exit, pursued by a bear!" Lane called out just as Neil reached the doors. This was followed by more laughter. Neil frowned and pushed the doors open.

Larry saw the look of confusion on Neil's face. "Everything cool, cuz? You look a bit weird . . . weirder than usual even."

Neil seemed to be staring into midair. "Does 'exit, pursued by a bear' mean anything to you?" he asked.

Larry smiled and said in an English accent, "Of course! It's Shakespeare, old bean— a stage direction from one of his plays, *The Winter's Tale*. You were supposed to write an essay on it last term, weren't you?"

Neil shuddered as he remembered the incredible pile of homework that sat on his office desk. He had promised to complete it all on time. His parents had issued a number of threats should he fail. He felt a headache creeping back.

"At least they like the food," Neil said quietly as he walked back to the ham. He looked around and didn't see Gary, although he could smell freshly opened honey.

"Gary, where are you? How goes the liquefying?" Neil said.

"Um, actually, Neil. You know how you said 'two

cups of honey, not a molecule more, or less'?" Gary had a weird tone to his voice, a voice that seemed to be coming from around Neil's feet. Neil looked down and saw Gary on his hands and knees, sweeping shards of broken, sticky glass onto a dustpan.

"Gary, what happened?" Neil said, doing his best to quell the rising panic in his chest.

"It was an accident," Larry said, walking up behind Neil. "The jar was so brittle it actually started to crack as soon as Gary picked it out of the water. There must have been an air bubble in it that expanded or something."

"Or something," Neil said, irritated. He rubbed his temples. "Gary, how much honey were you able to get from the jars?"

"Um, about a cup and a half," Gary said, trying to sound hopeful. "But that's okay, right? It's *almost* two cups."

Neil rubbed his temples. "No . . . no. Trust me, the whole balance will be thrown off if we don't use precisely what I said we needed. I didn't *estimate*. I determined *exactly* what was needed for the dish."

"So, what do we do?" Gary asked.

Neil lowered his head and rocked back and forth. He just wanted to be a chef. He didn't want to even come close to any more stupid mysteries. The one remaining jar of honey seemed to be calling to him from the top shelf.

"We could use a different honey to top it off," Larry suggested.

Neil just shook his head and walked over to the shelf. Neil Flambé didn't know the meaning of the word 'compromise,' and it wasn't just because he never did his English homework. No. Perfection was what he had planned, and perfection was what he would achieve.

That only allowed one choice.

He reached for the jar of honey. Opening the jar would open up a range of possibilities Neil wasn't going to think about right now. He just knew that he needed the incredible liquid that surrounded the mysterious note.

CHAPTER THREE

STAGE AND ONION

Neil Flambé wiped a bead of sweat from his forehead. His nerves, as always when he cooked, had been taut and raw. He was like a gymnast who had just performed a perfect routine, and now the stress that he'd pushed to the back of his mind flooded forward.

Larry slapped him on the back. "Nice job! But let's hope that last jar of honey isn't like Pandora's box."

Neil reacted to that with a blank stare. "More Shakespeare?"

"Very good. Shakespeare does refer to Pandora, but it's originally a Greek myth."

Neil just blinked. Ancient Civilizations was one more subject Neil ignored. Larry explained.

"Pandora was told not to open a box. So of course, duh, she opened the box. What idiot told her not to open a box? Seriously! People!" Larry shook his head.

"What happened?"

"All the evils of the world flew out."

Neil didn't like the image.

Had opening that final jar of honey opened up a

Pandora's box of problems? He looked over at the note, which was now sitting on a silicon baking sheet between two pieces of sturdy plastic wrap. After opening the jar Neil had gently laid the paper, still sticky, onto the sheet. It was about the same size as a page from a paperback novel and had lots of writing on both sides.

Neil had done his best to not look at the paper at all. Whatever secrets it contained were better left to someone else. Still, he found himself actually fighting to look away. Luckily, the dessert couldn't wait.

But for the rest of the evening, Neil was aware of the ominous note—which lay on the counter like a warning.

Now that dinner service was over, it was time to accept the accolades and pass the Pandora's note on to someone else.

Neil walked into the dining room and was greeted with a series of loud cheers. "Huzzah! Huzzah!" sang the various guests.

Lane didn't get up from his chair but gave Neil a magnanimous smile and opened his arms. "I am directing a virtual hug toward you, young man. Excuse me, but I'm afraid I am too stuffed to even give a feint of standing up to proffer the true article."

"You feel faint?" Neil said.

Lane chuckled. "No, dear boy. *Feint*, not *faint* . . . oh, never mind. That was a meal that was as good as I had anticipated, better in fact. 'He hath eaten me out of house and home; he hath put all my substance into that fat belly of his.'"

"Shakespeare?" Neil guessed.

Lane nodded. "The boy has been doing his homework!"

Neil flinched. It was time to change the subject, although it wasn't necessarily a better subject.

"Lord Lane, I have something to give you." Neil hesitated, dreading what might happen next. "But I'm not sure exactly what it is."

"What? *More*, dear boy? After you have already given us all satisfaction and indeed a sense of inner peace?"

"Um, well . . . it's a bit odd: a note of some kind. It's in the kitchen." Neil gestured to the doors. "It'll be easier to explain by showing you."

"'Nay, but make haste; the better foot before,'" Lane said, standing up and bowing to his guests. "I shall return. 'The spirit of the time shall teach me speed.'"

Neil assumed this was more Shakespeare. The guests seemed to understand. They nodded and went back to discussing, Neil assumed, how full and happy they were.

Neil led Lane into the kitchen.

"So, what is it you have discovered, my dear boy?"

"There was a note—I mean, there is a note. It was hidden in one of the jars of honey." Neil gestured toward the counter. Larry had smoothed the note out and stepped aside.

"Perhaps it's a coupon of some sort?" Lane stayed in his casual pose as he said this, leaned against the counter, and even yawned. But he trembled slightly. Or was Neil imagining things? Lane examined the note quickly and gave a shrug.

"It appears to be some gibberish," Lane said, waving his hand dismissively.

"Good," Neil said. "Should we throw it out?"

Lane definitely trembled now, but quickly recovered his composure. "Um, when I say it is nothing, I do not mean it has no value. I simply mean that it has some interest as an artifact, an antique, but the content of the note is just twaddle."

"I don't know," Larry said. "It looks like a poem or something."

Neil growled, but Larry ignored him and went on. "There's a whole series of numbers, letters. And some picture of a key that looks like a fish. Weird. Cool, but weird! I love old stuff!"

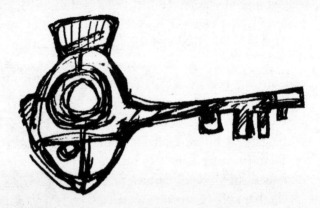

Neil thought he saw beads of sweat on Lane's forehead. What the heck did this note say? Neil fought the urge to look, but now found himself drawn to the note.

It was all written in a scratchy hand, in pen and ink. There was even a crude drawing of what looked like an old-fashioned key at the very top. Whatever it was, it was certainly not a coupon.

Lane chuckled. "As I say, it seems to be some silly scribbling. Perhaps it's a shopping list."

"There's some stuff on the other side," Larry said. "I saw it when we took the note out of the jar."

Neil wondered for a second if he should strangle Larry. This whole discussion was leaving Neil feeling agitated, the sense of foreboding now starting to spread up from his toes.

Larry was now turning the note over. "See, there's

the word 'help' we saw through the glass, but it's only part of a longer bit. 'Help comes to thee, Master Shakerags, for you will have need of this key. For thy witless head be empty, a brainless orb, and in need of a mappe, indeed, to complete thy journey.' What does that even mean? Cool!" Larry was beaming.

Neil growled again. Maybe throwing Larry into the deep fryer would be more efficient?

Lane smiled weakly. "It is just a scrap of paper that somehow, years ago, found its way into a bottle of honey—wonderful honey as our young chef has clearly demonstrated. It's an accident, likely a bit of a poster that hung in the workplace and was blown into the machinery, like a shard of glass in a bottle of beer."

Lane reached over and rolled up the sheet. He gave a quick bow toward Neil.

"Master Flambé, I thank you again for a wonderful meal and the gift of this strange piece of paper. Perhaps, as Larry suggests, it does bear some more scrutiny, but I doubt this. I will, if you indulge me, keep the baking sheet and recompense you extra on the bill."

Neil just nodded. Despite his best efforts, he felt a million questions going through his head, and he didn't like any of them. He didn't care whether the note was an old poster or a million-dollar bill. He just wanted it out of Chez Flambé so he could go back to being a chef. He was done with mysteries.

Neil followed Lane out into the dining room.

"My friends, I am tired and must head to bed. Thank you all for joining me for a wonderful meal." Lane pulled out a credit card and handed it to Zoe.

The rest of Lane's entourage seemed disappointed that the night was so rapidly coming to a close. But they each gave Neil a handshake as they left through the front door. Neil didn't see any waiting paparazzi.

Lane put on his raincoat. He walked back up to Neil and shook his hand. "I would appreciate it if you kept word of this note to yourself. I am sure it is nothing, but until I return to England, it's best if we keep any talk of this amongst ourselves."

"Fine by me," Neil said.

"Thank you." Then Lane gave Neil a low bow and walked out the door and into a waiting limousine.

Neil collapsed in a chair.

"Wow, that was close!" he said, giving out a long, low breath. "Let someone else solve the stupid mystery."

Larry leaned close to Neil and patted his head. "It's okay, chef boy. I took lots of pictures of the note before you and Lane came into the kitchen. I'll print some copies tonight."

Neil was up in a flash, chasing a laughing Larry through the kitchen doors. The sound of the violently swinging hinges was soon followed by the sound of clattering pots, pans, and cutlery.

Gary turned to Amber and Zoe and chuckled. "Exit, pursued by a crazed chef."

CHAPTER FOUR

"DART NOT SCORNFUL GLANCES FROM THOSE EYES"

Neil parked his bike in front of Chez Flambé and then unlocked the front door, or tried to. The lock, like everything else in this dumpy part of town, was run-down and rusty. It required numerous attempts to get the key to actually turn, and that was on a good day.

Today was not a good day. It was cold and damp outside. Neil just couldn't shake the mystery of the honey, no matter how hard he tried. The dinner had been days ago, but he was still having dreams about being doused in honey, then chased through his kitchen by a bear.

There was also the extra level of stress from his parents. They had read the riot act to him, yet again, the night before. He was still a teenager and a student, and if he didn't start catching up with his homework, they were going to pull the plug on his restaurant and blah blah blah.

As Neil finally succeeded in opening the door, on the thirtieth try, he heard a rapid series of clicking noises behind him. He looked over his shoulder. A black car was just pulling away, the tinted window on the driver's side closing. More paparazzi? Lane wasn't even at the restaurant today.

Neil felt a tingle in his fingers. Was he actually missing the action of a good mystery? *No.* He shook his head. He walked inside.

A loud noise from the kitchen stopped him short.

THUNK

THUNK

Then, all of a sudden, Larry's voice. "Nooooo!"

THUNK

THUNK

"I warned you! This one's going right for the heart!" said a man's voice. It wasn't a voice Neil recognized. Had another of his enemies decided to attack?

THUNK

THUNK

"*Stop!*" Larry yelled. "You're killing me!"

THUNK

Neil looked around in a panic for something to help him defend his cousin. He grabbed a butter knife from the nearest table and rushed into the kitchen.

"*Get away from my cousin!*" Neil yelled.

Larry and a large hairy man turned to look at Neil, who stood before the still-swinging doors, holding the

34

butter knife in front of him. The large man was also holding a kitchen knife in his right hand and seemed poised to throw it, or thrust it, at Larry.

"Put down that knife!" Neil said. "Or I'll . . . I'll . . ." He was suddenly struck by how ridiculous, and unthreatening, he actually looked.

After a second of shocked silence, Larry doubled over, laughing. "Or you'll what? Butter Enrique to death? Or maybe smother him with an olive tapenade?" Larry was laughing so hard he was grabbing his sides. "Ouch! Put down the knife, cuz. You look ridiculous."

"What? Who? Enrique? What?" Neil said, his arm faltering. "You . . . I thought you were being attacked!"

"Um. No," Larry said. He turned to Enrique. "Final throw, *compadre*. This one's for all the marbles."

Neil watched as Enrique lifted his hand and threw the knife straight across the length of the kitchen. The flight ended with a loud *thunk* as the knife stuck into a large block of wood.

Neil noticed with sudden alarm that the wood was actually his new four-hundred-dollar maple cutting board. It was hanging from the wall, and someone had drawn a series of circles on it with food coloring.

Enrique's throw stuck deep into the wood, but well above the small red bull's-eye. The knife quivered. It was one of his handmade Japanese sushi knives . . . also worth hundreds of dollars.

Larry made a mock grimace and slapped Enrique on the back. "*Ohhh!* Bad luck, Enrique. So close, but I win by two points! Better luck next time."

"*Sì,* next time, amigo," Enrique said unhappily, handing Larry a small stack of bills.

Neil watched, dumbfounded, as Enrique walked out the back door. Then he started to shake with rage. "You were playing darts *with my chopping block and my knives*?!" He bellowed, *"Are you a total idiot?"*

Larry waited for the pots to stop rattling, then smiled. "Not a total idiot. You should thank me, actually."

"*For what?* Trying to *ruin* me?" Neil raised up his arm again, the butter knife poised for attack. Larry started to laugh but sidled away, to the opposite side of the counter from Neil.

Neil followed him. "Do you know how much those knives *cost*?"

"I know it'll cost a lot to replace the shattered glass in the windows if you don't stop yelling," Larry said, starting to pick up his pace to stay ahead of Neil.

"What were you thinking?" Neil yelled.

"I was thinking of our restaurant. Enrique is the new veggie delivery guy. You want the best and freshest stuff delivered here before it goes anywhere else, right?"

"So?" Neil said, stopping for a second.

"Well, I challenged Enrique to a game of darts. If he wins, we pay him extra for the privilege. But if I win, which is a sure bet—I trained with Annie Archer, remember—he delivers here first *and* gives us a discount. I'm undefeated so far."

"You've done this before?"

"Yeah, three or four games so far. Maybe five."

"And what about the gaping holes in my new chopping block?"

"It's a chopping block. It's supposed to have holes, isn't it?"

"You're an idiot," Neil said, shaking his head.

"And we only dinged up a couple of those knives so far."

Neil's face started to burn.

Larry went on. "Enrique shot a bit wide the first few times and hit a cast-iron pot. But I figure with the money we're saving, we can get new knives."

"*Ahhhhh!*" Neil said, resuming his pursuit. Larry's laughter got more intense as Neil's anger seemed to grow.

"You know what I really think is bugging you?" Larry called back over his shoulder. "I think you miss the thrill of the chase, the lure of a good mystery. You're going stir-crazy! Maybe a coffee would help your nerves?"

"Coffee?" Neil suddenly stopped and grinned. "*Yes! Coffee!*"

"What do you mean, 'yes, coffee'?" Larry said, looking suddenly worried. "You don't even drink coffee."

Neil gave an evil laugh and rushed over to Larry's coffeemaker. He unplugged it and held the butter knife up against the mesh filter. "Aha!" Neil said. "Maybe a few holes would help your coffee taste better?"

"You wouldn't!" Larry said, smiling but less assuredly.

"You can use that money Enrique gave you to buy a new one," Neil said.

"You monster!" Larry said, starting toward Neil.

"One more step and the coffeemaker gets it!"

Just then there was a knock at the back door. It was Sean Nakamura, inspector for the Vancouver Police Department. Nakamura walked in, followed by two women in dark suits and sunglasses. They had the distinctive look of security officials.

Nakamura stared at Neil, and let out a chuckle. "Um,

Nose, you might want to put down that butter knife. Although it's nice to see things are back to 'normal' around here."

"What are you doing here?" Neil asked, dropping the knife on the counter. Larry ran over and hugged his coffee-maker.

"I'm just a chaperone this time," Nakamura said, gesturing toward the two women. "These women have something they need to talk to you about." Nakamura leaned in close to Neil and said in a low voice, "And I know you're swearing off detective work, but this is coming from *very* high up, so I suggest you listen."

Nakamura stood up straight and nodded at the woman on the right, who marched up to Neil. She was carrying a blue briefcase. She set it down on the counter, clicked the clasps, and lifted the lid. Then she stepped away silently and gestured for Neil to take a look.

Neil didn't like this one bit. He was pretty sure whatever was inside that case was going to have him taking more precious time away from Chez Flambé.

He looked at Nakamura, who just shrugged and nodded toward the case. *VERY high up*, he mouthed, jabbing his finger toward the ceiling to further emphasize the point.

Neil walked over slowly and peered inside. Sitting on a bed of plush purple velvet were a blue cell phone, a stack of British fifty-pound notes, and an envelope with his name written on it in flowing pen.

There was a tag attached to the envelope by a large glob of melted red wax. The wax showed a woman with a crown, wearing flowing robes.

The note simply said, *Read Me*.

CHAPTER FIVE

CROWN ROASTED

Neil took a knife and carefully slid it between the folds of stiff white paper. The seal cracked as Neil lifted the flap and pulled out a letter.

He gulped as he noticed the large crown at the top of the page. He scanned down to the typed words.

Dear Master Flambé,

You are the last person known to have spoken with Lord Aloysius Lane. He returned to England after dinner at your restaurant. He was by all accounts as silent as a stone following that evening. We have spoken to his companions from that night, who say he was very rattled by some private discussion with you in your kitchen.

Now Lord Lane has gone missing.

"Missing?" Neil said. Neil looked at Nakamura, who merely nodded. Neil turned back to the letter.

Neil Flambé and the Bard's Banquet

It has come to our attention that he came into possession of an interesting artifact during this dinner: possibly a piece of paper. Further, that you have seen this artifact and smelled this artifact. Do not deny that you have a powerful nose. Our sources are very clear on this.

Neil looked up and glared at Nakamura, who seemed incredibly focused on a speck of dust in the air outside the back window.

This combination of proximity to Lord Lane and the paper makes you uniquely capable of solving this mystery. Inside this case you will find enough money to cover your expenses during a one-week stay in England.

There are also two first-class tickets. One for you and one for Lawrence.

Neil snorted. *Lawrence!*

It is crucial that this be top secret. To provide a cover story for your work, at the end of your week here you will give a command cooking performance at Buckingham. A Royal Warrant awaits if your cooking is as enjoyable as we are led to believe. And a Royal Warrant can be beneficial to business.

We await your imminent arrival.

There was no signature.

Neil wasn't 100 percent sure what a Royal Warrant was, but he knew what money was. He also knew he always needed more. Running a restaurant, even a successful restaurant, was a constant race away from bankruptcy. He looked up from the letter at the kitchen of the dump he was forced to use, the restaurant Larry had won in a poker game.

In a better location, Neil could charge more for his wonderful food to cover his costs, maybe even make a small profit. The only way to achieve that goal was to keep this place going long enough to make some savings. To do that he needed to cook, not travel the world. Neil shook his head.

"I refuse," Neil said firmly. He threw the letter back into the case. "I'm a chef. I've done too much of this stuff, and I want to stay here and cook. There must be detectives in England who can find Lane."

The woman marched up to Neil.

Neil flinched, half expecting her to pull some ninja-style chop across his neck.

She merely reached past him and took the blue cell phone out of the case, flipped it open, pressed a button, and held it up to Neil.

Neil frowned and shook his head.

She lifted her right arm in a chopping motion, and Neil took the phone and held it up to his ear. A voice was coming from the receiver.

"Hello, hello. Is he there? Will someone please answer the phone! Harry, is this thing even on?"

The voice seemed familiar.

"Um, hello?" Neil said.

The woman's response was sharp. "Neil Flambé, we do not find it amusing to be kept waiting. This is a matter of incredible importance to our nation. If I have been roused from my afternoon tea, it is clearly because you need some more persuading."

"Wait, is this the, the Qu—?"

"Of course it is! Don't be dense. Now listen to me, young man. Your family, despite their obvious French pedigree, made the choice to escape to Canada. That makes you *our* subject. Do you intend to be a loyal subject?"

Neil said nothing. He was too shocked.

"Young man, have you gone deaf? We asked you a direct question, and we are accustomed to receiving a direct answer, directly."

"Um, sorry, Your Majesty. Yes, no . . . well, look. I barely spoke to Lord Lane, and I only saw a glimpse of the paper."

"Well, I'm afraid that our scientists have done a forensic test on the honey that surrounded that paper, we received some shards from your garbage, and it is much older than the glorious age of Queen Victoria.

One might say it hails from an earlier, equally glorious Queen's reign."

"Um, sorry. Who might that be?" Neil said, history being yet another subject he barely paid attention to in school.

"Elizabeth, you idiot!" said the Queen, exasperated. "Honestly! I believe it is time that we ended this charade. You will come here and help solve this mystery. There is one more incentive to be thrown into the mix."

"I can't think of anything else that would make me change my—" Neil stopped. The Queen was gone, replaced by an instrumental version of "Bohemian Rhapsody."

Just then, the phone in Neil's office rang. Larry ran over and picked it up. Neil could hear the unmistakable tone of his mother and father. They didn't sound happy. Larry held the earpiece farther and farther away from his ear as they got louder and louder.

"Yes, I'll tell him," Larry said, hanging up the phone. He shook his head from side to side, and massaged his ears. "That was your *loud* parents. The school just called, and they are demanding all your homework by the end of the week, or you'll be suspended."

Neil looked at the cell phone in his hand. The song had stopped.

"What's this other incentive?" Neil asked slowly, guessing what was coming.

"It is easily within our power to issue a letter excusing you from homework for the remainder of the term. Would that be of interest? Or are you adept at running a restaurant while also doing three hundred quadratic equations and an essay on the use of cactus imagery in T. S. Eliot's *The Waste Land*?"

You monster, Neil thought, but said nothing.

"We will expect a glorious meal in approximately one week, with a side dish of solved mystery."

"Who is going to run Chez Flambé while I'm chasing—"

There was a click, and the call ended. The security woman came over and took the phone from Neil. Then she bowed her head slightly and exited out the back door. Nakamura gave a quick nod and followed her.

Neil was too dumbfounded to speak.

"So, London this trip." Larry sighed. "Why do we keep ending up in countries that like tea so much?"

Neil shook his head slowly back and forth. He'd tried his best to avoid getting back into the detective business, but he'd been pulled right back in. Still, was part of him secretly excited? He couldn't deny the tingle in his fingertips . . . and nose.

Neil looked at the money and the tickets. "So who's going to keep this place going? Gary? I can't ask Angel again."

There was another rap at the back door, and Angel Jícama walked in. He stopped, stared at Neil, and then rolled his eyes. "Say hello to your replacement chef."

"I thought you were sick of filling in," Neil said.

Angel sighed. "I got a very persuasive phone call."

"Did she promise to take care of all your bylaw violation tickets?" Larry asked, smiling.

Angel nodded and walked over to the counter, unpacking his knives and laying them out carefully. "And there were other . . . incentives." Angel shuddered.

"More stuff from your mysterious past coming back to bite you on the butt?" Larry grinned.

"Let's just say there's an embarrassing file that dates from my time working as a chef in Manchester."

"That will now be destroyed?"

Angel nodded. "If you two are successful."

Neil let out a low whistle. "That is one spooky woman."

CHAPTER SIX

FOGGY AND GROGGY

Neil stared out the window of the train at the gray London morning. They were passing over the river Thames before heading back underground on their way to the far south of the city.

It wasn't raining, exactly. It was more like a constant misty drizzle that hung in the air and eventually stuck to the windows. Once there was enough moisture, the mist would form small drops, leaving streaks down the glass before finally succumbing to gravity.

"Lovely weather," Neil said sadly. "It must take an hour for the water to actually hit the ground."

The weather outside matched the mood in Neil's heart. Sure, he'd escaped a month's worth of homework and would be certain to grab a Royal Warrant in a few days (how could Neil Flambé *not* wow the royal family?). But he missed his kitchen.

And Isabella. She and Jones were in France, and she'd said she would try to fit in a trip to London, but it was far from certain.

He and Larry had been in London for two days already, and all Neil had caught was a slight head cold. They'd gone to Lane's gigantic stone country house. It was empty. It looked, and smelled, like Lane had never even made it back there from the airport. Neil had sniffed around his office, his club, even his car. No trace of the honey.

The trail, like the weather, was cold.

"There certainly is a lot of Cynthia Paine," Larry said. A book of English slang lay open on his lap, almost every page adorned with a sticky note. "That's cockney for rain." Larry took a sip of his coffee. He grimaced. It wasn't bad, but it wasn't the high-octane brew he made for himself back home. Still, the weak coffee and weather didn't seem to dampen Larry's natural enthusiasm for exploration.

"Oh! Here's a great word. '*Gongoozler*, noun: a person who stares for a long time at boats and other stuff on canals'! Man, I thought I spoke English, but apparently not!"

Neil ignored Larry as best he could and tried to concentrate on the tiny bits of evidence they had so far. Larry had, cleverly, snapped more than a few high-resolution pictures of the honeyed paper. "Just in case the Nose gets back on the case," Larry had said.

Neil pulled out his phone now and opened up the photos.

He zoomed in on the image of the fish, and it certainly looked to him like a key, with a fish-shaped bow. Neil knew the top of the key was called a bow because it was one of the first words Larry had recited on the flight over.

Neil hadn't slept much.

He read the poem that was written under the key.

> Turn thine bow upon the lock.
> It windes the arms of yonder clock.
> Point thee to a finer robe
> As merry Drake goes round the globe.
> Where, hidden, sits the stolen jewel?
> Prithee, search thy tasteless gruel.

Then there was a series of tiny letters and numbers.

> iviiiii
> iii
> iviiii
> iiivi
> ivi

Poetry was *not* Neil's thing. He preferred recipes, written down in identifiable chunks, with each line containing a specific amount, instruction, or ingredient. The poetry was in what you *did* with the recipe, or at least what Neil did, which was to take the same building blocks that everybody had available and then create the Taj Mahal.

But this just looked like more homework.

Then there was that other bit on the back.

Help comes to thee, Master Shakerags, for you will have need of this key, for thy witless head be empty, a brainless orb, and in need of a mappe, indeed, to complete thy journey.

"What the heck does that even mean?" Neil said out loud.

Larry looked over at his cousin. "Don't be such a mungo."

Neil didn't even care what that meant, which didn't stop Larry from offering a definition. "A mungo is someone who steals things from a trash bin."

Neil frowned. "Sounds more like you than me."

"Ha! It's such a great word! I think I'll rename one of the alley cats Mungo when we get back!"

"Can we please focus on this stupid mystery?"

Larry closed his book and smiled. "I knew you missed the adventure. Face it, we're like Sherlock Holmes and Dr. Watson. The game is afoot!"

"I'm just a chef; I'm not Sherlock Holmes!" Neil said.

"I never said you were." Larry smiled. "Holmes is a genius, who solves crimes using the power of his brain. I think I know which one of us is Holmes." Larry pointed at a finger at his own brain.

"Watch it, that finger might be loaded. Your head certainly isn't."

"I deduce that you are feeling antsy. Fine, Watson, let us consider the evidence before us."

"That's what I've *been* doing!"

Larry ignored him. "We know that the honey is old, very old. 'Shakerags,' according to my mesmerizing dictionary, is an insulting term denoting 'a disreputable, shabby person.'"

"But since the honey is old, very old, maybe it's a reference to Shakespeare?" Neil recalled how much Lane loved Shakespeare, and how shaky his hands had been as he'd read the back of the paper.

Larry nodded. "Possibly, Watson. Drake was also alive around that time, assuming the reference in the poem is to Sir Francis Drake. He went around the earth in the late fifteen hundreds. It was a huge deal at the time."

"And the numbers are a code of some kind. Which leads us where?" Neil said.

"Well, the honey is old, so we assume the paper is old. There's something about a stolen jewel, some guy named Drake, and possibly a reference to Shakespeare. And we have a missing Lord Lane."

The loudspeaker on the train interrupted their conversation. They'd reached the Elephant and Castle tube station. The station was at the heart of the south end of

London, where the original honey jars had been found in a demolished factory.

They got off the train and walked up the slippery steps and back out into the drizzly day. Neil felt a chill and hitched his collar up as high and tight as possible. The view did nothing to warm him up.

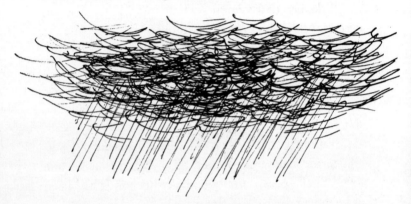

There was a shabby pub just outside the station exit. Its walls were covered with graffiti, most of it rude. There were cracks—or possibly bullet holes—in at least two of the large windows.

Tall apartment buildings and what looked like an old shopping mall were covered in grime, and funneled a cold wind down the street.

Paper and garbage clogged the gutters, allowing the drizzle to accumulate into mucky gray pools.

Neil looked at Larry, who was grinning. "What's so funny?"

"It's just like home!"

"Sadly, that's true," Neil said. The area looked eerily like the part of Vancouver where Neil tried to make

Chez Flambé a going concern. "What was a rich guy like Lane doing with a factory in this part of town?"

Larry shrugged. "Urban renewal, maybe? I read that this part of town is pretty rough."

"You needed to read that? And you're supposed to be Sherlock?"

"Ha-ha. Let's just get to the site of Lane's factory and see if there's anything worth checking out." Larry pulled out his phone and typed in the address. He pointed. "Thataway, Watson."

They walked for a few blocks, passing numerous fish-and-chip shops, tiny parks, and run-down churches. Neil looked around nervously, but no one seemed to pay them much attention. After a few minutes they arrived at a bank of plywood barriers, with a chain-link gate.

Through the gate they saw a giant hole in the ground. Bulldozers and construction crews were gathered around. Many of the workers were on break, sipping tea and eating small cakes. Neil sniffed the air. "Honey and dried fruit scones . . . with Devon cream," Neil said. Then he looked at Larry and pointed at his nose. "And the tea is a mix, mostly Darjeeling. Most of the workers seem to have added a splash of milk."

"See? Who needs brains with a nose like that?" Larry smiled. "Is the honey old or new?"

Neil sniffed again. "Definitely new. Highly processed, a hint of preservatives and exhaust fumes."

"Well, let's join the construction workers and do a little digging, shall we?"

Neil nodded.

Larry walked through the gate and up to a man who was covered in mud but gracefully sipping tea from the lid of his thermos.

"Hello, my fine fellow. A bit early for a lunch break, no?"

"It's time for elevenses, ain't it?" said the man, taking another sip of his tea and sighing happily. "Lunch ain't for another hour or so. Name's Danny, by the way, and me blokes might not agree about the 'fine fellow' bit."

"Danny. Lovely. I'm wondering if you can tell us anything about this location. There was, like, a big old factory here, right?"

The man took a bite of his scone and looked at Larry with a sideways glance. "This about the honey what we found?"

Larry nodded.

"The honey weren't liquid gold, were it? It were just honey?"

Neil nodded this time. "Amazing honey, once I cooked it, of course, but just honey. Why?"

"It's just that you're the third person what's asked me about it today."

CHAPTER SEVEN

EYE OF FRUIT

Danny the foreman poured another cup of tea and seemed to warm into his storytelling. "I can't tell you much about them. The first man was a copper, or so he said. Tall bloke, with a beard. He walked with a red umbrella, which in my, ahem, *limited* experience, isn't usually standard issue for a copper."

"And the second . . . bloke?" Larry said. "Was he a copper?"

"Seemed more like the opposite, I'd say. Huge guy. Knuckles scraping on the ground type."

"Maybe Jones has an English cousin?" Larry smiled.

Neil shuddered. "And what did you tell them?"

Danny took a bite of scone. "Same as I'll tell you. It weren't just an old factory. Once we knocked down the brick, we found an old stone foundation hidden underneath this end." He pointed to the nearest part of the hole. "There were honey in there; and a few other things."

"What other things?" Neil asked, surprised at the eagerness in his voice.

"Well, there were an old fork and some buttons. And rotten old oak kegs what must have held beer, and more than a few cups and mugs and things. The honey were actually hidden in a slot in the stone, covered in thick soil, almost solid like brick. That honey could have survived an earthquake in there."

Neil thought for a moment. "It sounds like a pantry, maybe the basement of a house or even a restaurant. The honey was pretty well protected. They wanted it kept safe."

The man nodded. "My thinking exactly. Of course, this area hereabouts has never been what I'd call a particularly upper-class part of town. And honey wasn't exactly an everyday sort of commodity in these parts, in good Queen Victoria's day, or a long time afore, nor after."

Neil nodded and turned back to Danny. "You seem to know a lot for a construction guy."

Danny shrugged. "You spend enough time digging around this city, you become a bit of an expert in old things what's been buried underground. I also take a lot of interest in the history of me city and me country.

People think ordinary types can't be interested, or interesting. But some of the smartest people I know don't teach in university. They work in holes in the ground and then head to a pub. Anyway, lads, elevenses is over. Time to get back to work."

He gave a wave, and he and the other workers climbed back into the machines.

"Danny! One other thing!" Neil called after the foreman. "Why were you tearing down the factory in the first place?"

"Lord Lane's company makes a proper habit of it. He tears down old buildings and puts up theaters." Then Danny stepped into the cab of an excavator and revved the engine. He waved for Larry and Neil to head back out the gate before they got knocked over or buried.

"Well, helpful but not *too* helpful," Neil said as he closed the gate. "We already knew the honey was old. And we already knew Lane owned the building."

"Yet more proof I'm the Sherlock in this duo," Larry said as they walked away from the noise and back out onto the sidewalk.

"Oh, please do illuminate us," Neil said sarcastically.

"Well, Watson—or should I say, Witless—we now know that it was odd, at least to Danny, to find honey in this part of town. It wasn't, as he said, the sort of luxury you'd normally find in a slum. We also know the part of town isn't the greatest, and apparently never has been."

"I could have told you that two seconds after walking out of the subway."

"Ah, but why was the honey so carefully packed away? Did it originally contain the stolen jewel from the note? Was there more honey buried somewhere else? And if you're going to send a coded note to someone, presumably the best way to do that is to *not* hide it in a wall somewhere."

"Fascinating. But I don't feel any closer to figuring out what's going on. Danny didn't say anything about why the honey might have been buried here, just that it was odd. He also said Lane was planning to build a theater. Not sure what that has to do with anything."

Larry stopped in the middle of the street. "Speaking of theater, I need a coffee."

Neil scratched his head. "What does theater have to do with coffee?"

Larry shrugged. "What *doesn't* have to do with coffee?" He began walking back toward the lone café they'd passed on their way to the hole.

Neil trailed behind, running the confusing list of evidence and clues through his brain. "I think we need an expert," he said.

"First the coffee," Larry said, marching over to the nearest café. "Then I know just the person to call."

"Who?" Neil said. "Another girlfriend of yours?"

Larry smiled. "Not yet! It's actually somebody a certain Isabella Tortellini suggested we look up."

"Isabella?" Neil was confused. Larry handed him a small envelope.

Neil sniffed it carefully. It smelled like Isabella's lavender perfume. He smiled.

Isabella had written, *Open only in case of un' emergenza*, on the outside. Larry had already opened it, apparently, because the flap slid apart easily.

Neil glared at Larry. "What was your emergency exactly?"

"Hey, I was drinking a coffee and the steam just sort of loosened the glue," Larry said.

Neil opened the envelope. Inside was a hand-drawn map, with the words "The Rose" written over the address for a college campus in London. There was a picture of a rose next to that. Neil noticed that Isabella had made sure the rose had plenty of thorns.

CHAPTER EIGHT

SMELLS AS SWEET?

Rosalind "Rose" Patil smacked herself on the forehead. "You cabbage!" she yelled. She walked over to a large whiteboard on the wall of her office and began erasing a complex chemical formula. Then she grabbed a marker and began frantically rewriting.

Neil Flambé sat in a chair by her desk. He and Larry had arrived at her office ages ago, and Rose had greeted them with what Larry sarcastically called "English cheer."

"Oi! Sit down and keep your gobs shut, if you know what's good for ya!" Then she'd pointed at the chairs and continued writing a formula, the one she was now erasing.

Neil Flambé was no fan of being ordered around (*giving* orders was his forte), but he'd sat down. He'd felt obligated. Rose was a friend of Isabella's. She was a fellow perfume maker and—according to Larry's reading of Isabella's note—somehow an expert on Shakespeare. It seemed an odd combination to Neil, but he'd already met a foreman who knew more history than a textbook (Neil assumed so anyway, rarely having cracked a textbook).

Larry, on the other hand, had seemed instantly smitten. He sat sipping his coffee as he gazed at Rose doing her work.

Neil had actually dozed off—he was still fighting some jet lag and the cold—but the reference to cabbage shook him out of it. "Cabbage?" he whispered to Larry.

"Slang for stupid," Larry said. "But sung like a symphony by that glorious daughter of York."

"Shakespeare?"

"Sort of," Larry said, not taking his eyes off Rose.

Rose continued to stare at the board. "That'll do," she said at last. She tossed the marker in the air, then expertly kicked it before it hit the floor, sending it spinning into a nearby garbage can.

Neil gave a small cough to get her attention.

Rose spun around. "Are you lot still here?" she said.

"From where thou art why should I haste me thence?" Larry said.

"Pshaw! Sonnet fifty-one, eh? Don't try getting clever on me. Isabella warned me about you, you scruffy imp. Now, what can I do to help you, and how much is it worth to me?"

Neil was totally rattled. "Um, maybe we made a mistake? You are Rose Patil, right?"

Rose looked at Larry and jerked her thumb back at Neil. "Sharp one you got there. Passed right by me name on the door, and did I *not* just mention that Isabella had warned me you lot might show your ugly mugs hereabouts?"

Neil coughed again. "How exactly do you and Isabella know each other?"

Rose just winked. "There's a lot more to that girl-friend of yours than you can smell with that magic snout of yours, me old numpty."

Neil looked at Larry for help. Larry stared at Rose, but was able to whisper, "'Numpty' is another term for idiot," out of the side of his mouth.

Rose crossed her arms. "Now, enough of this pleasant chitchat. Let's get down to business. I realize that you are here for my help. Since you both smell like a couple of mingers—"

"Smelly people that haven't bathed in a while," Larry translated.

"—you're clearly not interested in perfume, although you should be! I'll wager that you need a little help in the Shakespeare department, or I'm a treacle tart. And that's a reference to what I'm having with my tea in about"— she looked at her watch—"two minutes. Go."

Neil nodded. "Lord Lane has disappeared. We gave him an old note that we found in some honey. The honey was very old. Bottom line, we think Shakespeare is involved in Lane's disappearance."

Rose smiled. "Well, that would be rather miraculous, given that the Bard has been dead since sixteen hundred and sixteen!"

"Good one!" Larry said.

"Stuff it, you moke," Rose said, frowning at Larry, who just smiled even more. "As for the mystery, as you can see, I'm very busy. I'm in the middle of an important experiment." She gestured proudly at the whiteboard. "I'm recreating the actual scents that Shakespeare's wife might have worn."

Neil looked at the diagram and couldn't make fish heads or fish tails out of it. "Are you, um, close to doing that?"

"Are you having a laugh?" Rose said, looking peeved.

"He had his funny bone surgically removed last week, actually," Larry said, helpfully. "It was already pretty tiny."

Rose ignored Larry (who beamed). "It's as plain as day. That bit I just added completes the formula for a columbine and oxlip cologne." She got up and walked over to the board. "Don't tell me I have before me a chef who can't read a chemical formula!"

"I'm afraid I tend to work by actual smell, not the formula stuff so much," Neil said, feeling a bit embarrassed and unsure why.

Rose appeared shocked. "Well, I am gobsmacked! You don't do your math homework either, I suppose?"

Neil felt like he was being interrogated and struggled to get the conversation back, or at least within a hundred imperial miles of, on track. "Look, I've already got plenty of people who are 'gobsmacked' over my performance at school. I need to figure out the stupid poem and this stupid code from the note before—"

"Code? Poem? Why didn't you blokes mention that when you got here? Let me see this poem." Rose's mood completely changed.

Neil handed her his phone and called up the photos of the poem and the list of letters and numbers.

Rose scanned them, her eyes growing wider and wider by the second.

"Oh ho!" she said finally. She ran over to her computer and began typing furiously, her eyes darting from the photo on the phone to her screen. "Oh ho!" she said again, more loudly. Then she ran to her bookcase and thumbed through some ancient-looking leather-bound books. Neil half expected her to yell "eureka." She'd clearly discovered something.

Rose snapped a book closed and stood for a while, thinking. She ran her fingers through her hair, a serious look on her face. Finally, she walked over to Neil and handed him back the phone. She cocked her head and stared at him for a few seconds before speaking.

"Before I agree to help you and your baker's dozen over there . . ." Rose nodded at Larry.

"It means cousin," Larry said.

"Before I say yes to helping, I would like a low-risk, up-front agreement."

"Low-risk for who?" Neil said, not quite sure what Rose was talking about, but curious to see what had gotten Rose so excited.

"Whom," Rose corrected him. "And it's low-risk for

both of us. You get my expertise for free. But if we are successful, I receive twenty-five percent of the worth of this jewel what's mentioned in the poem."

Neil frowned. "I'm not sure what's going on with this jewel thing. All I know is that I've been, well, *commanded* to find Lord Lane."

Rose threw her head back and gave a loud laugh. "Commanded! I know who that sounds like."

"She was very persuasive."

"She give you that line about a Royal Warrant?"

Neil nodded. "She said it would help me make a bundle."

Rose scoffed. "That might help you if you're some desperate punter. But it won't be bringing the throngs to your restaurant just because you've got a sticker with her name on it glued to your front door."

Neil fidgeted in his seat. "Well, I'm not really after the jewel."

"Then you're an idiot. It's simple. If I help you find it, then *we've* got all the leverage in this situation. I'll bet it's worth a finder's fee that'll make even the Queen shake. Or maybe we could keep it . . ." Rose said this last bit almost to herself. "Anyway, you want my help, that's the deal."

Neil considered. The Queen hadn't exactly said that Neil couldn't keep whatever else he found, in addition to Lord Lane. And he definitely needed expert help if he was going to find anything.

"What about finding Lord Lane?" he said.

"Look, if Lane and this parchment of his went missing at the same time, I'll wager they are still together. Either he's hot on the trail and doesn't want to be followed, or someone else is, using him as a hostage, maybe. Wherever you find the jewel, you find Lane. If he finds it first, you may never see him again. If someone else finds it first, you can be sure you'll never see him again."

Neil tapped his fingers on his knees, thinking.

Rose continued. "Would it help if I told you that, if I'm right, what we are looking for here is so big it could set up you and your friends with enough bread and honey for life?"

Neil looked confused, again. "Bread and honey?"

Rose leaned in close before Larry could explain. "That's money, dearie. Cold, hard cash." She rubbed her fingers together.

Neil looked over at Larry, who was nodding up and down. Neil found himself nodding as well.

"Good," Rose said, clapping her hands. "Then there's no time to waste."

Neil stood up as well. "Where to first?"

"The kitchen, sweetie," Rose said, smiling. "I'm off to boil some water and warm some currant scones."

"I'll help!" Larry said, following Rose like a puppy on a leash.

Neil gave a deep sigh and sat back down.

CHAPTER NINE

FULL CIRCLES

Will Kemp is our man," Rose said, walking back over to her whiteboard. She drew the face of a bearded man with an arrow pointing at his head.

Neil was sitting in his chair, nibbling on a surprisingly delicious scone. "Will who? He doesn't look familiar. Have I met him? Was he with Lane at the restaurant or something?"

"I don't think so. He died five hundred years ago," Rose said.

"Sorry, I'm confused," Neil said.

"That's why you need me," Rose continued. "I'll give you the short version. Kemp was a friend of Shakespeare—well, for a while, anyways. He was actually an actor in Shakespeare's troupe, famous for playing comic roles."

"Like Falstaff?" Larry asked.

Neil was now even more lost. "False what?"

Rose shook her head. "You may know how to flip a burger, but you are a sad excuse for a fully rounded human being."

Larry spat out a mouthful of tea and struggled to catch his breath while also laughing.

Neil glared at Rose. "Did you just call me a burger flipper?" There was no disguising the annoyance in his voice.

Rose waved her hand at him dismissively. "Flipper, flopper, or whatever—just pay attention, chef boy."

Neil actually growled. Larry leaned over and whispered, "Now I know why Isabella drew the thorns on that rose!"

Neil nodded, still growling.

Rose had drawn some more faces on the whiteboard. She pointed to a large man with a mustache and beard. "Falstaff is one of the most famous comic characters in Shakespeare. He was a big oaf of a man, charged with helping to train Hal, the future Henry the Fifth."

"Yeah, sounds like a barrel of laughs," Neil said.

"Maybe you should actually read the plays sometime, you great big dolt. He is hilarious. He makes all sorts of double-meaning jokes, and gets all the laughs in some pretty serious plays."

"So this Kemp guy played Falstaff?" Neil said.

"Not such a dim bulb after all!" Rose cheered. "Kemp played a lot of the funny characters in old Billy's plays. Dogberry, the goofy cop in *Much Ado About Nothing*, Peter in *Romeo and Juliet*, and Bottom in *A Midsummer Night's Dream*."

"There's actually a Shakespeare character named Bottom?" Neil said.

"Not all of Billy the Bard is ye olde this, thees and

thous, and princes and princesses. If you had tuppence for every fart and bum joke in Shakespeare, you'd be richer than Lord Lane."

Neil thought for a bit. "So what does all this have to do with our note?"

"Well, I'm not a hundred percent certain, but it seems likely that this note of yours was written by Kemp as a bit of a rude gesture to Master Shakespeare."

"Because of the Shakerags reference? We thought about that too."

Rose nodded. "Shakerags was actually a pretty

common insult back then. On its own it doesn't point to Kemp."

"You said they were friends and worked together."

Rose looked at the picture she'd drawn of Kemp. "They did, and did very well—so well that they decided to build a new theater together. They called it the Globe, partly in honor of Drake's voyage around the world a few years before."

Neil's eyes opened wide. "There are references to Drake and a globe in the poem!"

Rose nodded. "But even before the theater opened, they split. Shakespeare killed off the character of Falstaff, and he even included a swipe at Kemp and his comic style in his play *Hamlet*."

"I know that one!" Larry said, excited. He quickly did a search on his phone. "'And let those that play your clowns speak no more than is set down for them; for there be of them that will themselves laugh, to set on some quantity of barren spectators to laugh too.' Basically he calls comic actors hams who want to steal the spotlight from everyone else."

Neil stared at Larry. "Wait, you knew about this already?"

Larry shrugged. "Studied it in English class. *Hamlet*."

Neil wondered for the thousandth time in his life how someone who knew so much could be such an underachiever. "Larry, you never cease to underwhelm me," Neil said.

"Underwhelm! Someone's been reading a dictionary."

"Ha-ha."

"Or perhaps you are just basking in the genius of Rose! Hark, what light from—" Larry's speech was interrupted by a marker thudding off the side of his head.

Rose glared at him. "Put a lid on that teapot, and maybe get a shave and a haircut before you try sweet-talking me."

Now it was Neil's turn to laugh, but if anything, Larry seemed even more smitten than before.

"Back to the lesson," Rose said. "Kemp and Shakes had a falling-out over the Globe or something that happened around the same time. No one is quite sure. All we know is Kemp decided to strike out on his own."

"He started his own theater?" Larry asked.

Rose shook her head. "Nope. He actually decided to dance all the way from London to Norwich. It took him twenty-three days."

Neil gave a quick laugh. "You have got to be kidding me. Dance?"

Rose nodded. "And he didn't just dance. He morris-danced. It's a kind of folk dance with music, ribbons, sashes. He even wore bells on his legs."

"I repeat: You have got to be kidding me."

"He wrote a book about it, including a dedication to all the 'shakerags' who had insulted him and lied about him."

"Just like the letter!" Larry said.

A smile spread across Rose's face. "That's why I think Mr. Kemp is the man behind our note. And I think he took his sticky fingers and stole some jewel from his old friend Billy the Bard. The question is, *what* jewel, and what do the numbers and letters mean?"

Larry gave out a low whistle. "Wow, this is big! I knew we'd come to the right place! Rose, you are awesome! Isn't she, Neil?"

Neil didn't answer. His mind was racing. He had come to Rose's with almost no information, and now his head was starting to form some theories. It was actually kind of—he hated to admit it—exciting.

Neil's thoughts were suddenly halted by the sound of a door being smashed to bits from the outside, followed by Rose yelling, "Exit window! Stage right!"

CHAPTER TEN

THE GAME IS AFOOT AND A HALF

Neil hit the ground running. Which didn't do much good, since he'd tripped over the windowsill and landed on his face. His flailing legs smacked the bushes but didn't get him any farther from whoever was currently busting through the splintered remains of Rose's door.

Larry lifted Neil by the shoulders.

"Nice dive. You bust your nose again, perchance?"

Neil felt his nose. "It's fine."

"Then run! If we don't get a move on, we're dead ducks."

Rose was already way off in the distance. She had somehow managed to grab a leather satchel before heading out the window and was still able to run incredibly fast.

"It is a distinct advantage, when escaping, to know where you are going," Larry explained between breaths. "Jones told me that once. And it doesn't hurt to have a set of very athletic, and cute, legs!"

Neil just rolled his eyes. He'd seen Larry fall in love this fast before, but never with someone who was so clearly *not* interested in Larry.

BOOM!

There was a loud bang from the building. Neil spun his head back and saw smoke pouring out of the window.

Rose gave a loud "whoop!" and pumped her fist in the air. "Aha! Weren't expecting my top-notch security system, were ya?" she yelled.

"Perfume formulas are worth that much?" Neil said to Larry.

"I think there's more to Rose than we suspect."

Neil considered this. Rose was also a friend of Isabella's. *How much more to Isabella is there than we suspect?* Neil wondered.

Rose ran into the parking lot. She pulled some keys from her satchel and clicked a button. An engine revved somewhere, but Neil couldn't see the car.

"Hurry up, you two!" Rose called as she ducked in between two large cars. Neil thought for a second she'd disappeared down a hole, but then he turned the corner and saw Rose climbing into the smallest car he'd ever seen. It seemed to have only three wheels.

"Is this a clown car?" Neil said, incredulous. "You can't fit three of us in there!"

"Fine. Then you stay here. Larry and I will escape

and tell everyone how bravely you died defending yourself from having to scrunch up your knees."

"If Neil does stay here, does that make this a date?" Larry smiled.

Rose scowled. "Change of plans. Neil can come. We leave the drooling duffer here."

There was a shout from somewhere behind them, and Neil sucked in his breath and dove into the back-seat. "Ouch!" He banged his head on the low ceiling. He scrunched up his legs just in time as Larry jumped into the passenger seat, slamming it back hard.

Rose gunned the engine, and the car shot out from between the larger cars and out into the road. It was actually a perfect getaway car, despite the cramps Neil could feel in his leg muscles. They were able to drive in spaces that would have stopped larger cars.

Rose took full advantage of this as she quickly began weaving in and out of the smallest alleys and roads she could find. "No way anyone in a big car can find us now," she said happily. "Anyone actually get a good look at the apes who smashed my door?"

Neil and Larry shook their heads. "Nope."

"They were loud, I can tell you that," Neil said. "And at least one of them had a tikka masala for lunch. That came through loud and clear. And some kind of weird cheese, maybe a Gouda."

"Well, if they were after my formula, they'll be sadly disappointed. The security system automatically sprays the whiteboard with cleanser and disables the computers."

"Is that a normal level of security for a perfume maker's office?" Neil asked.

Rose gave a slight cough and changed the subject. "There's one other thing about Will Kemp that I haven't told you. He died about three years after his split with Shakespeare."

"Did Shakespeare kill him with a quill pen?" Neil chuckled.

"What are you laughing at, you porridge brain? Shakespeare was a very adept swordsman. Most actors at the time were. Everyone carried at least a knife."

Larry looked back at Neil and pointed at Rose. *She is awesome cool*, he mouthed.

Rose quickly swerved the wheel, which shook Larry's attention back to the front.

"You drive like I do!" Larry smiled.

"Just keep an eye out for any cars that might try to dart in front and crash us," she said. She stole a quick look in the rearview mirror. "All I can see is your ugly ginger head, chef boy. Get down!"

Neil ducked down as much as he could. "So *did* Shakespeare kill Kemp?"

"Nature did. Kemp died of the plague. A huge bout wiped out about a third of London in 1603. He'd come back from his dancing and some travel, and had just started acting again. But he never achieved the fame of his Shakespeare days or his dancing. Then *poof*! He was dead."

Neil had seen more than his fair share of horrible things, a by-product of life as a human bloodhound and detective, and he also remembered something from history class about the plague. It took something pretty dramatic to pull him out of his school-time daydreaming. The plague would make the victim break out in boils; then the boils would get infected. It was swift and painful and highly contagious.

Wee dye.

"Horrible," Neil said in a low voice.

"You got that right," Rose said, making yet another unexpected turn. "There was nothing the doctors could do. Sometimes, if you got the plague, they just nailed the door to your house shut, trapping you inside so you didn't come out and infect anybody. You'd die alone, and in pain."

"Where are we going?" Neil said, suddenly needing to talk about anything else. The thought of Kemp being locked up in his house made him feel claustrophobic. He rolled down a window and greedily breathed in the cooler air.

"I'm sure Kemp wrote the letter. Those references and echoes are too close to be a coincidence. That's one other thing about Kemp. He liked codes. He even wrote a poem to the city of Norwich—a kind of tribute poem at the end of his dance—and hid his own name in the text."

"We're heading to Norwich?" Larry asked.

Rose took one hand off the wheel and snapped her finger on the side of his head.

"No, but we're heading somewhere close to here where I can get access to my files." They had pulled into an alleyway behind some older buildings in what seemed to be London's theater district. Rose slowed the car and looked in the mirrors. "Coast seems clear," she said. "I know a good café around the corner from here with computers."

"Do they serve coffee?" Larry asked eagerly.

"Ugh, I hope not. I hate the stuff. It tastes like motor oil."

And with that, the spell was broken.

"And you seemed so . . . perfect," Larry said quietly, his face suddenly fallen.

"Stop your whining, you great big git! We've got work to do!"

Larry smiled. "Oh well, almost perfect is still pretty good."

"*Stop!*" Neil yelled suddenly.

Rose slammed on the brakes. "What in the Queen's knickers are you on about?" she yelled.

But Neil was too busy sniffing the air to answer. He'd smelled something, something that was too bizarre to explain.

"Larry, let me out!" Neil said.

Larry had seen Neil the bloodhound in action before and quickly got out of the car and slid his seat forward. Neil squeezed through the door and out, sniffing the air and turning his head to catch the direction of the mystery scent. Except the scent itself wasn't a mystery—just what it was doing here in London.

Rose leaned over the passenger seat and called through the open door, "What are you on about?"

"What is it?" Larry said, stepping aside to let Neil back down the alleyway.

Neil sniffed again. "It's really faint, but I smell my cooking—*my* cooking and, I think, Lane's honey!" Neil started to run. He could smell his signature dry rub for pork and ham, his potatoes, and underneath it the subtle hint of centuries-old honey.

There was an open door a few feet away. He ignored the competing smells from the garbage cans and followed the main scent. He reached the door and sniffed the cool air that was slipping through.

Neil stepped inside, carefully. It took a few seconds for his eyes to adjust. Through the gloom he could see dozens of ropes hanging from the ceiling. Ladders and scaffolding led up to platforms that were strung with hundreds of lights.

Neil realized that he was backstage in a theater, but a grimy theater. There was dust on everything. The red curtains were tattered. He could make out the places where the fabric was worn so thin he could see through to the other side. He sniffed again. The smell was close. There was a dark lump at the edge of the worn wood stage.

Neil gingerly walked between the curtains. The entire theater was illuminated only by the red exit lights. It looked haunted. Neil had the creepy feeling that he was being watched, but all the seats were empty, so he suppressed it. Still, he'd been in enough tight spots to know that he should be careful.

He walked over to the lump. It was almost big enough to be a person. Was it a body? As he got closer and closer, the smell got stronger and stronger. His eyes adjusted.

Just then he felt a hand on his shoulder.

"*Ah!*" Neil screamed and spun around, swinging wildly.

"Whoa, cuz! It's just me," Larry said, ducking. Neil had been so engrossed in his search that he hadn't noticed Larry following him.

"Next time say something before you grab me!" Neil shouted.

"That's a first. Usually you're telling me to be quiet!" Larry walked over to the side of the stage and flicked a light switch.

"Cool! A theater!" Larry said. "This is some ancient stuff, though. I don't know who owns this dump, but they really should think about upgrading!" Larry ran his fingers over the curtains. "Yuck!"

"Maybe you could focus on the really interesting

thing on the stage?" Neil walked over to the lump and felt a sense of relief. It wasn't a human body, but just a pile of clothes.

A cloth raincoat sat on top of the pile. Neil leaned in close and took a deep sniff. It was infused with the smell of the meal Neil had made at his restaurant a week before. He flipped the jacket open and searched the inside pockets, but they were empty. "It looks like the jacket Lane was wearing after the party," Neil said. He lifted it up and placed it to the side.

There was a yellowish suit coat and pants underneath. Neil sniffed, but they didn't smell like his food. They actually smelled like sheep and old pee.

"Harris Tweed," Larry said.

"Who?" Neil asked.

"Not who, what. That kind of fabric is known as Harris Tweed. You can tell by the yellow color and the thickness of the wool. It's a pretty old style. It's worn a lot by members of the House of Lords."

"Lords, such as Lord Lane?"

Larry nodded. "Fun fact: The yellow color was made using old pee as a kind of binder for the dye. When it rains, the suits actually smell a little like a bathroom that hasn't been cleaned in a while."

"That's your definition of a fun fact?"

"Sure!"

"How do you know this stuff again? I'm guessing it's a girl."

"Actually, it's from a friend of mine named Graham Rowe-Saville. He's a nut for British fashion."

Neil made a point of examining the scruffy

sweatshirt and jeans Larry was wearing, part of his perennially scruffy overall appearance. "He clearly never got around to giving you any advice, or maybe he did and you didn't listen?"

"Are you kidding? It takes hard work to look this *authentic*."

Neil shook his head. "'Authentic loser' is not a look I'd pay to see in a fashion show."

"Fine. This from a guy who thinks chef's jackets are like tuxedos. Hey, you want to know how they get the brown color for—"

"*No.* No, thanks. I'm good." Neil stood up. He was suddenly struck by an odd thought: how similar an actor was to a chef. Both were given the same ingredients as everyone else—words, arugula—but were able to transform them into something real, better, bigger than the sum of their parts.

"I'd love to fight a duel in a theater," Neil said, apparently out loud, because Larry reached over and gave him a shake.

"Duel? Are you nuts? We've finally landed in a country where you don't have any enemies, and you want to fight a duel? Remember the last duel you fought in Japan? How'd that turn out?"

"Um, I won."

"You almost got killed! Like five times!"

"I *won*."

Larry shook his head, incredulous. "You're more thrill-obsessed than I thought!"

Neil just rolled his eyes. "Let's get to work. Where's Rose? In the alley?"

"Naw, she couldn't keep the car back there. A truck—known as a lorry over here, by the way—was coming up and she needed to move. She said she'd meet us out front."

"Cool. We know one thing for sure. The suit and the jacket and the smell of my cooking all point to the fact that Lord Lane was here."

"And he changed his clothes," Larry added.

Neil and Larry scrounged around backstage and found a box to put the jacket inside.

Neil leaned down to pick up the Harris Tweed. That's when he noticed the blood.

CHAPTER ELEVEN

AS YOU SPIKE IT

You think Lane was killed?" Rose asked Neil as they sat together in the car, waiting for the police. A soft rain had begun to fall, tapping like the fingers of little hands on the roof.

Neil shrugged. "I don't know for sure. The police will run some tests on the clothes and blood."

Neil could hear the sirens in the distance growing closer. "I do know the clothes were his."

"Because of the smell?"

"Yes." He paused. "There was a clean slice in the back of the jacket when I picked it up."

"Looked like something a knife would leave behind," Larry said.

Neil nodded.

"Maybe the same blokes who smashed down my door also took care of His Lordship?"

"And how do we know they aren't still around?" Larry said, peering in the passenger-side mirror.

Rose turned the ignition on the car. "Better safe than sorry."

"If Lane was killed," Larry said, "then why remove the body and take all his clothes off?"

"Dunno," Rose said. "Maybe it was easier to dump him on the banks of the Thames if he was naked?"

Neil was absorbed in thought. Larry's question was a good one. Why strip a dead or wounded man of his clothes? Who had beaten him up so badly, or shot him or stabbed him in the first place?

One thing he was sure of, this case was getting more dangerous by the second.

Neil stared out the window. Something caught his eye. The poster in the window of the ticket booth wasn't old and worn, like the theater, but seemed brand-new. Neil wiped the fog off his window and peered at the print.

There was a picture of a skull in a crown and the words—in large print—

MACBETH

Shakespeare's greatest play

Starring Cullen Skink, star of stage and screen, in the title role!

Tickets on sale now for a limited run!

See scheduled shows below

Neil looked closely at the dates. Opening night was scheduled for the next night, and the show was on for the whole month.

"Seriously? Someone is actually putting on a play in

this dump?" Neil said. "Maybe they're going for Larry's 'authentic' look."

"Ha-ha," Larry said. "Not that I know what you're talking about, but ha-ha anyway."

"I'm looking at that," Neil said, pointing out the window at the poster.

"Who'd buy tickets for that?" Rose said. "This looks like a place for a proper mugging, not a play."

The sirens got closer and closer.

"Anyway, we'll see what the coppers have to say about all this soon enough," Rose said. "And don't mention the booby traps at me office if you can avoid it."

Suddenly the air was filled with the sound of shattering glass. Then there was a loud crack from somewhere behind them, and the passenger-side mirror disintegrated into a thousand shards.

"Get down!" Rose yelled. She gunned the engine and the car shot off.

"Why are the police shooting at us?" Neil yelled, ducking back down into the crevice between the backseat and the front.

"Time for questions later! Hold on!" Rose yelled. She could barely see above the dashboard and was honking her horn to clear any pedestrians from their path.

"Look out, you gabblers!" she hollered.

Larry looked at her. "Gabblers? That's a new one on me."

"I just made it up!" she yelled over the sound of the roaring engine and the screeching tires. Neil dared to peek over the top of the seat and wished he hadn't. Rose was barreling out into a giant circle of traffic, heading the wrong direction. Two red double-decker buses were headed straight for them.

"Look out!" Neil yelled.

Rose gave the engine even more gas and swerved right toward the nearest bus. It swerved away at the last second and the tiny car snuck between the buses, shooting out the other side. Rose slammed on the brakes and they came to a sudden stop.

There were still sirens coming from somewhere behind them.

"That was awesome!" Larry was beaming. "What's next?"

"Just watch!" Rose said, grinning maniacally. She gunned the engine and spun the car sharply to their left. To Neil's shock and horror, they now sped toward a large stone staircase. Rose gave a loud "huzzah" and they hurtled down the steps.

Neil's head banged against the roof of the car despite

his seat belt, and his teeth chattered. The car shook so much he was worried it would fall apart.

Rose rolled down her window and yelled for people to get out of the way.

"Are we on a *sidewalk?*" Neil said as the tiny car jumped the last step and zoomed alongside the river, scattering shrieking pedestrians before them.

"No cop car can fit on this bit of pavement," Rose yelled over the noise.

"You should race Formula One!" Larry said.

"More like a demolition derby," Neil said, his teeth rattling.

They passed by an enormous Ferris wheel, and then Rose took a sharp right turn underneath a train bridge. It looked like a forest of concrete, with walls—big, thick, graffiti-covered walls.

"Can we slow down?" Neil called out as they swerved

in between the pillars, nearly hitting at least three skate-boarders.

"Soon, dearie. Almost there," Rose said. She swerved between two pillars, sending yet another skateboarding graffiti artist flying away, swearing, and then straightened out the car.

Neil could see a narrow beam of light under the far end of the tunnel. It was a ramp of some kind, not much wider than the car. Rose hit the ramp at top speed. The front of the car bounced a foot in the air and landed with a thud.

"This is so cool!" Larry said, laughing even more.

The sides of the car scraped the concrete walls, sending sparks flying. "Where's the gas tank on this thing?" Neil asked nervously.

"It's not on the *side* of the car, now, is it?" Rose called. "We'd be little itty bits if it were."

The car careened up and up and then seemed to be flying. They landed with yet another thud in the middle of a walled parking lot, and Rose slammed on the brake sagain, sending the car sliding sideways. They stopped just before a pair of large metal doors.

Rose turned off the ignition with a satisfied sigh. "Well, I think we can safely assume we've lost whoever was trailing us."

"Nice work!" Larry said, jumping out of the passenger-side door. "Let's do it again!"

Neil didn't need a super nose to smell the burning rubber. He undid his seat belt, shaking the whole time, and climbed out of the car. He wanted to kiss the ground, the first unmoving thing he'd had under his feet in what seemed like days.

"Where are we?" Larry asked.

"The loading dock of the South
Docks Historical Society. I'm a card-
carrying member. In fact, I'm the only
card-carrying member." She squeezed herself in between the car and the doors and
started to punch in numbers on a keypad on the wall.

The building was concrete and steel. No windows.
It was tucked into an alley between the train bridge and
a row of other, equally ugly buildings. There was a street
nearby. Neil could hear cars, but he couldn't see them.
You'd have to know it was there to find it.

Rose saw him looking around. "It's the back of the
National Theatre building. It looks like a loading dock,
but it's actually a false front—or false back, to be more
accurate. It's one of my satellite offices and the place
where I do a lot of my actual Shakespeare research."

"Who are you?" Neil asked, his eyes narrowing. "I
mean really."

Rose didn't answer but opened the doors.

"I think she's Aphrodite," Larry said, laughing.

"Keep that up, you bonehead, and I'll aphro-bitey
your head off."

"She even likes puns!" Larry beamed at Neil, who
just rolled his eyes.

The doors swung open, and Rose waved for Larry
and Neil to head inside.

"Now, to get to work."

CHAPTER TWELVE

GOOD LOCK

I . . . V . . . I . . ." Neil called out the letters as Rose typed them into her computer. After they'd locked themselves inside the "office," they'd started thinking about the notes again.

"With two attacks in one day let's assume there are other people after the jewel and that time is of the essence," Rose had observed.

Neil wished he could call the Queen and ask her a few questions about her royal police officers and why they were taking potshots at bystanders in a bizarre small car. "I know some strange police officers, but none who shot at me for no reason."

"Those weren't coppers," Rose said as she stared at the computer. "Coppers don't carry guns."

"Seriously?" Neil said. He hadn't actually seen who'd been shooting at them, but the bullets had arrived around the same time as the sirens.

"They use clubs," Larry said, sipping his tea reluctantly. "Do people really think this stuff tastes good?"

Rose threw a cricket ball, which Larry expertly

ducked. "Oh no. I spilled some of the tea. I think it's eating away at the floor."

"British bobbies—police—don't carry guns, at least not the sort of bobbies who respond to calls about bloody clothes in condemned buildings. Now, let's keep to the task at hand. Is there any more Kemp code?"

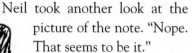

Neil took another look at the picture of the note. "Nope. That seems to be it."

"Okay, let's see what we get," Rose said. She hit enter and the computer began quoting texts of Shakespeare at her. "There's got to be some pattern." Hundreds of lines of text scrolled down the screen. "Ugh," Rose said.

"You're sure these letters are references to Shakespeare's plays?" Larry said, leaning over Rose's shoulder and looking at the screen.

She nodded and glared at the computer, as if she were trying to force it to give her the answer she was looking for. "Seems logical as a starting point at least."

"Why logical?" Larry said, pouring the remainder of his tea into a potted plant.

"Pay attention! Kemp makes all these insulting references to Shakespeare and then sends him a note, or intends to send him one, with clues to recovering some jewel that's 'stolen.' He wanted Shakespeare to search his own, most personal, most *visceral* expressions of himself for the answer. He wanted him to suffer." She smiled. "It's a brilliant way to taunt a genius."

"You are both beautiful and slightly warped," Larry said, noticing that the plant was actually plastic and the tea was leaking out of the bottom.

"But why do you think the references are to Shakespeare plays?" Neil asked, trying to follow along.

"I think the 'tasteless gruel' is the bit that's important here, obviously."

"How is it obvious?"

"Well, think about it for a second, you daft punk! Kemp and Shakes had a falling-out. Shakes attacks Kemp in his plays, so Kemp attacks him back, calling his plays tasteless. He says 'search *thy* tasteless gruel.' That's a pretty clear hint, to me, that Billy Shakes is supposed to examine his own work for answers. The letters correspond to scenes and acts in the plays, I think. Now we just have to figure out which ones."

"Seems to make sense," Larry said, leaning back in his chair.

"But for some reason he never got to send the note to Shakespeare," Neil said.

Rose nodded. "You said the honey was found packed in the basement of a tavern?"

Neil and Larry nodded. "That's what the construction guy told us anyway."

Rose went on, as the text continued to stream onto her computer screen. "And this tavern is not in a great part of town."

They nodded again, but Rose wasn't really talking to them anymore. She seemed to be thinking out loud. "So maybe Kemp is down on his luck. He steals something from Shakespeare. I don't know, maybe he plans to ransom it? Maybe he plans to keep it to cover debts from building the Globe Theatre."

"He does mention Drake and a globe," Larry said.

"Kemp likes codes, as I've said, and he was a clown, a comic, and a jester . . . so maybe he gives Shakes a sporting chance to find it first."

"By leaving him clues?" Neil said.

"Or he *meant* to leave him clues," Larry said. "But then he gets the plague and, well . . ."

Rose nodded. "Kemp gets nailed inside his plague house and quickly realizes, as the pus begins to ooze from his scabby flesh, that he will never see daylight again."

"You are a scary woman. Impressive . . . but scary," Larry said, giving a dramatic shudder.

Rose ignored him, again. "So Kemp hides the key in a jar of honey and then shoves it in a wall. He expects it to be found after they come for his body. But someone either doesn't see it or doesn't want to touch anything that's been left behind by a corpse, so they just seal the wall up."

"And the clue stays buried for hundreds of years," Larry said, giving out a low whistle. "Good thing he chose honey instead of ketchup or barbecue sauce!"

"But why put the note in honey at all? Why not just put it in an empty jar?"

"You're the chef, chef boy. You got any ideas?"

Neil shrugged.

Rose turned her attention back to the screen.

"Do you see any pattern yet?" Neil asked, watching the screen fill with lines of text.

Rose scanned the screen with her finger. "Well, there's a repeat of the word 'wretch' in three of the scenes that match the letters, assuming the *ii* refers to act one, scene one."

"Wretch?"

"I don't know if that means anything, but it could be another insult. But quite a few of the scenes also mention kings, castles, swords . . ."

"In other words, we could be here for hours looking for something," Neil said, under his breath, or so he thought.

"Oh, I'm sorry," Rose said, annoyed. "Is this too taxing for your super-brain? Why don't you go for a stroll and come back after I've solved the problem myself?"

"Or maybe I'll solve it," Larry said, grinning.

"That's as likely as a ferret being named to the House of Lords."

Neil headed for the door. "A walk might be a good idea. I'm supposed to be cooking at the palace in a few days, so I should probably get a look at the culinary offerings of London." Neil opened the door and stuck his head out, peering both ways. The coast seemed clear.

"I'll be back in a few minutes."

"Be careful and don't let any great ape with a gun kill you," Rose said, staring at the screen.

"Your concern is touching," Neil called back over his shoulder.

"I don't give a toss about you; I just need to keep this place a secret!"

"Hmph," Neil said as he quietly closed the door. Neil needed to get away. He needed food. He didn't need to eat food, necessarily, but he needed to be surrounded by it. Neil without gourmet food was like a fish without water. He could flop around for a bit, but it wouldn't take long for him to croak. He missed Chez Flambé.

He cleared his mind and his nasal passages and closed his eyes. He sniffed. His nose would lead him to food. It always did.

Neil knew he was a genius at many things, and one of them was using his brain to pick out the best information his nose was sending to him.

There were many smells assaulting his nose at the moment—moldy leaves, metallic drizzle, dust, gum of various vintages stuck to the sidewalk—but piercing through them all was the unmistakable scent of food.

"Cheese!" Neil said. Somewhere, within range of his nose, there was a very good cheese shop. Neil snuck down the narrow curving alleyway between Rose's hidden office and the building next to it, and emerged onto a busy London sidewalk.

He looked back and noticed that the angle of the buildings was so odd that it was almost impossible to see the gap between them.

Everyone seemed so busy on their cell phones or hiding under their umbrellas that they didn't notice the ginger-headed teenager who seemed to join them from nowhere. *A very good hiding place*, Neil thought. He made sure to memorize the gum pattern on the sidewalk so he could find his way back.

The cheese smell was coming from a very humble pile of buildings down the street a short way away. As Neil got closer, he could differentiate the smells.

British cuisine got a bad reputation, but if there was one thing they could make better than anyone else, it was cheese. Just a few steps away waited pungent Stilton, cheddar, Red Windsor and Red Leicester, Caerphilly. Neil reached the door.

WENSLEYDALE'S—PURVEYORS OF FINE CHEESE said a sign over the shop. Neil walked in. The smell was almost overwhelming but amazing. He instantly imagined a thousand possible dishes he could make with the cheeses, each of which would knock the crown off any monarch.

"Hello, my good man," said the young woman behind the counter. "Can I get you some cheese?"

"Um, *yes*," Neil said, unable to contain his enthusiasm. "Let me take a few samples of those cheeses under the counter, the really ripe ones."

The woman looked at him askance. "Under the counter? How do you know what's under the counter?"

Neil could have kicked himself. His nose was powerful, but part of its power was that only a few people had any idea it was so sensitive. "Um, well . . . it's like any store. The really good stuff is always hidden away. Any chef knows that."

She looked at Neil suspiciously. "And you would be one of those? A kid like you?"

Unwittingly she had put Neil back in control. Calling him a kid was always a good way to get him to focus. "Yes, a kid like me who happens to be a chef. Would you like me to suggest a few cheese combinations that will make your head spin?" he said.

She held both hands up. "Whoa! No need to get your back up. I'm only twenty myself. But just out of curiosity, what would you recommend? My head could always use a good spin."

Ten minutes later Neil was behind the counter, helping Brie—her name, as it turned out—present the cheeses in a more logical way.

"People think you can only have one cheese at a time," Neil said. "But it's like any food. Mix them together and the combination can become more powerful than each cheese on its own. It's a miracle in your mouth!"

Brie laughed. Not at Neil, like most people in his experience, but actually at his joke!

Wow, Neil thought. *Maybe there is a little Larry inside my brain after all?* He felt a happy grin forming. This was new territory for him, and he kind of liked it.

"Look, Mr. Chef, in return for your master class on fermented curd, why don't you pick a few cheeses that 'go together like magic in your mouth' and we'll call the day even?"

"Sounds good," Neil said, and shook her hand.

Neil chose some *fromage castor de Venezuela*, some amazing Camembert, and a strong sage Derby. Brie wrapped them in crinkly white paper.

"Oh, speaking of miracles," Neil said as he turned to go, "you don't by any chance have any coffee?" In fact, Neil had smelled the coffee among the other aromas, but he didn't know if it was for sale or just for the staff.

Brie smiled. "This is your lucky day! I've never been much of a tea drinker, and I always keep some fair-trade beans on hand for discerning customers. I'll go get some," she said, walking through a curtain and into a back room.

Neil perused the shelves while he waited. Something caught his eye on a large shelf of cookbooks and cheese and wine guides. It was a thin red book, with the title *Shakes and Bakes: Recipes from the Elizabethan Era.*

"Shakes and bakes," Neil said slowly. "Elizabethan recipes." This was sparking something in his brain, but he wasn't quite sure what yet.

Neil reached for the book and noticed two things at once.

One, a slight breeze snuck from the back room under the curtains, and two, that breeze carried a smell of tikka masala.

From behind the curtain Brie screamed. A man laughed.

Neil heard a thud as if someone had dropped a heavy sack of rice on the floor. Every cell screamed *run*, but Neil couldn't. Brie was in trouble. And whoever had attacked her was probably after him, or Rose, or all of them. He'd brought this trouble here. He had to do something about it.

Neil grabbed a cheese knife from the counter and ran through the curtain. A mountain of a man, with short hair and wearing a suit that looked like it might rip at any moment, was hovering over Brie's still body.

The man turned to face Neil. A giant scar ran down his face, and his scowl stopped Neil in his tracks. Neil held up the knife and waved it in front of him.

"Well, lookie here," the man said, standing up so straight his head seemed to touch the ceiling. "It's that kid what was with Rosie and the barmy blond guy."

"What do you want?" Neil said. Did the man know who Neil was? Was he coming to kill him? Had Brie gotten in the way?

"I need you to pass along a message."

"To?"

"Rose, you git. Your babysitter or whatever she is. I'm not sure why she'd let a brat like you hang around with her, but you can at least take a message back."

"I don't know where she is," Neil lied.

"Tsk, tsk, my little nosey parker. I think you do. Now, I could just take you and keep you hostage and let her find me, but I'm too busy at the moment to deal with another kidnapping."

"Another kidnapping? Did you kidnap Lane?" Neil asked.

A look of confusion or maybe anger passed over the man's face, and was quickly replaced by a twisted grin. "Now, don't ask too many questions, kid. You're liable to get yourself into all sorts of trouble."

"Kid?" Neil felt his anger rise. He waved the cheese knife in front of him and jabbed the air.

The man laughed loudly. "A cheese knife? I've got bits of those swimming in me veins from when I was a baby. You don't scare me none."

"I can butcher a pig in five minutes, and that might just come in handy if you don't turn around and leave right now."

"Don't get cute," the man said, reaching out faster than Neil thought possible and grabbing the knife.

Then he grabbed Neil by the collar, leaning in close. "I'm no little piggy, and you ain't taking me to no market."

Neil tried to break free, but the grip was iron tight. Neil took a swing; the bag of cheese he was holding smashed into the side of the man's head. The bag erupted with a white shower of gooey and smelly cheese. It dripped down the man's face and onto his suit.

"You little crumb!" the man bellowed. "This suit cost me a thousand pounds!"

"You got ripped off—the cheese was worth more!" Neil said, just as angry.

For a second Neil thought the man was going to pummel him. But then his face contorted in a twisted grin and he gave a loud, menacing laugh. "Well, well. I almost lost it there. What my parole officer would think of that. Tsk, tsk." The man reached into his pocket and pulled out a large cloth. He kept one hand on Neil's collar.

Neil detected another, sweet odor. What was it?

"Now you listen here, cheese boy. You tell that clever Rosie that the Crayfish brothers know she's 'digging around'—make sure you say that part about the digging—and that if she knows what's good for her, she'll let us in on the shoveling . . . or there'll be a different kind of hole being dug for her, a six-foot-deep hole."

"That's a long message from such a small brain," Neil said.

"And for that," the man said, "you get a little snack." With his enormous hands, the man covered Neil's mouth with the cloth. Neil realized with a panic that the sweet smell was chloroform.

The man laughed even louder.

Neil swooned.

The room spun.

Then everything went black.

CHAPTER THIRTEEN

SERIOUSLY CHEESED

Neil opened his eyes and saw Brie's face hovering above him. She smiled. She was dabbing a cold cloth on his forehead. Did she also just kiss his forehead? Or had he dreamed that?

"The effects of that knockout stuff can be a little rough," Brie said. "I'm still woozy myself."

"That guy a friend of yours?" Neil asked, closing his eyes again to stop the room from spinning. The more he woke up, the worse he felt.

A bell tingled in the distance, or was that in his ears?

Brie snorted. "Hardly. Reggie Crayfish. He and his twin brother, Ronnie, are the local goons. They show up every once in a while to extort some cash for 'protection.' Protection from the two of them is what they mean, of course."

Neil was about to say that Reggie had been there to get Neil to deliver a message, but he stopped himself. He'd learned a long while back to not trust anyone,

even seemingly innocent strangers such as Brie. He
didn't always remember to apply this advice, and had
the bruises to prove it, but he thought now might be a
time to be careful.

There were footsteps approaching. They echoed in
Neil's waking head like blows from a hammer. What
could possibly be so loud? Was Reggie coming back? Had
he figured out who Neil really was—not just a kid but
the real detective—and decided to kidnap him after all?

Brie leaned over him again, wiping the cloth over his
aching eyelids. The footsteps drew closer and stopped.

"Ahem," came a familiar voice from the doorway.
"Well, this looks very *accogliente*, cozy." This was followed by something else in Italian that Neil was pretty
sure was an angry curse.

Neil fought the pain in his head and turned his head
sideways.

Isabella Tortellini was standing in the doorway, her
eyes narrowed and her arms crossed.

"Isabella!" Neil said, fumbling for the right thing to say to defuse the awkwardness of the situation. "I thought you weren't coming for a few more days."

That wasn't it.

"Oh, really? So you thought you had a few days to try out some other items on the menu?" Isabella said.

"What? What's wrong?" Neil croaked. "Menu? What are you talking abo—"

"Now wait a second!" said Brie, standing up. "I was just trying to help him wake up!"

"Try kissing him!" Isabella turned on her heels and marched away, her hands now clenched into tight fists.

"No! Wait! Isabella!" Neil said. He tried to stand up to follow her, but his legs wobbled and he had to steady himself on the edge of the counter. Isabella didn't stop.

Neil saw her pass the hulking figure of Jones, who opened the door to let her out. Jones was grinning. He saluted Neil and then turned and followed his charge out of the door. He never had been much of a fan of Neil Flambé as boyfriend, and Neil didn't like the look of his grin one iota.

But this was crazy. Isabella was actually jealous? Over him? Neil felt an odd mixture of confusion and excitement. She couldn't believe he'd ever be interested in someone else! Then again, she also thought he might be interesting *to* someone else! Neil was used to having his cooking celebrated, but he always had a nagging suspicion that people found him kind of abrasive. As he got older, this actually bothered him.

Maybe he *was* changing?

"Who was that?" Brie asked.

"Isabella Tortellini," Neil said, still gripping the cheese counter.

"The perfume maker? I love her scents!"

"Me too," he said. "Me too."

Neil was finally able to stand a few minutes later. He didn't walk out of Wensleydale's empty-handed. Brie quickly packaged up some replacement cheeses and even some fig compote. "Maybe this will help ease the pain," she said.

Neil just nodded. "I doubt it, but thanks."

Neil walked out slowly, his head throbbing. He smelled Jones's signature cologne—a mixture of camouflage paint and wood smoke—and ducked. But there was no punch or meaty hand grabbing for him, just a slight cough from a dark alleyway.

Neil looked around. Jones was barely visible in the shadows, leaning against the wall of the cheese shop.

Jones coughed again; then, when Neil still didn't move, he just rolled his eyes and called him over with a wave of his muscle-bound hands.

"I don't understand how you keep surviving," Jones said quietly. "Follow me."

Neil took a furtive glance around him and then followed Jones into the gloom. It was still daylight, but a combination of the gray sky and the closeness of the buildings almost made it feel like they were weaving their way through dark woods.

Neil was struck by how many narrow and winding alleys he'd already been down in his short time here. London seemed to have been built by accident. Roads met and crossed at odd angles—treacherous when you weren't used to seeing cars driving on the left. Every once in a while an alleyway would thin to almost nothing, then suddenly open into a wide stone plaza or church courtyard.

Neil wondered if a map would help, or just give the false impression that there was an actual way to *not* get lost in London.

They came to the end of the alleyway. They seemed to be alone, and Neil shivered as he entertained the fleeting thought that Jones had lured him here to pummel him, or even lecture him.

But then Neil saw that a black SUV was parked in an underpass across the way from them. Despite the closed doors, Neil could smell lavender perfume lingering on the breeze.

Neil felt Jones's enormous paw on his shoulder, urging him forward.

"And give me that cheese," Jones said. Neil gave him the package. Jones opened the trunk. He put the cheese in a fridge that was built into one side. *Where does Jones find these rental cars anyway?* Neil thought.

Jones led Neil to the side door and pushed him

inside. Neil took his seat next to Isabella, but kept one hand on the door handle. Jones slid into the driver's seat and started the engine.

Isabella reached across toward Neil, who inched away on the seat and prepared to make a run for it. Jones, to Neil's consternation, hit the gas, and the van lurched forward quickly.

Isabella was getting closer, her arm moving toward Neil's neck.

Neil shook the door handle, which remained locked. His finger fumbled for the window button.

Isabella was now right next to him, her gaze intense and her hands touching his neck.

With one swoop Isabella wrapped her arm around Neil and planted a kiss right on his lips. Then she backed away. "There. Does this help you to stay awake?" she asked, smiling.

Neil's confusion was now complete. He was speechless.

"You don't honestly think I'm that jealous!" Isabella said. "I'd like to think we trust each other."

Neil wasn't sure what to say. Neil found himself

oddly disappointed again. But also relieved. Finally he blurted out something like, "That stuff back in the shop was, that was a . . . a . . . an act?"

"Not completely," Isabella said, jabbing Neil in the ribs. "The way to a man's heart is through his stomach, or so I've heard. Stay away from pretty girls in cheese shops, *capisci?*"

"Understood." Neil smiled. "Anyway, the way to *my* heart is through my nose."

Jones gave a loud scoff from the front seat. "Some advice, chef boy: Don't *ever* put that on a Valentine's card."

"Ha ha," Neil said. He quickly explained what had happened at the cheese shop. "But what are you doing here in the first place? I wasn't out that long, was I?"

Isabella squeezed Neil's hand. "We were in France, buying some lovely aromatic oils from the Alps, but business went well. We were not so far away, so we decided to come early. We phoned Rose first, but she said you weren't there. Jones did a quick calculation of how long you'd been away and came up with a possible search radius."

Neil wasn't sure, but he thought he saw Jones flinch at the mention of Rose's name.

Isabella went on. "So I did a quick look at how many food locations would attract your nose, and a shop for *il formaggio* seemed a good place to start."

"Isabella, you are amazing, like a really well-done asparagus risotto," Neil said. For some reason, to his shock, being in England of all places had loosened his tongue. Compliments never flowed easily, unless he was talking about his own food, so this was new.

Isabella smiled. "When I walked in, well . . . I don't know this cheese-shop person, so I thought it best to give her a story to chew on about a jealous girlfriend. Besides, I needed you to follow us so that we can meet up with Rose and Larry."

He took her hand. "Are we headed back to Rose's?"

"Too risky," Jones said. "We are heading across town."

Neil sat back in the seat and smiled at Isabella. "It's great to see you."

Isabella smiled back. "We just felt it was time to come help you out, or at least see if you needed some help with your mystery."

"Surprise, surprise, you two lunkheads did," Jones said, steering them into a traffic circle and out again with expert skill.

"Anyway, Rose has made reservations for dinner. So let's all get together and compare notes."

"Dinner." Neil sighed. "Maybe they'll need some help in the kitchen?"

"Oh brother," said Jones, gunning the engine.

CHAPTER FOURTEEN

THE OYSTER
IS MY WORLD

I had a brain wave," Neil said as they wrapped up what Neil called a "passable" late dinner of braised lamb. Neil had offered to help out in the kitchen at least ten times, and had even written a recipe for a better marinade on a napkin. But the chef eventually sent back a note offering a free basket of yam fries if Neil would just sit and be quiet.

Larry had agreed instantly.

"Brain wave? Don't you need a working brain for that?" Larry joked as he grabbed the last yam fry and popped it in his mouth.

"Not that you'd have any experience," Neil said. "Anyway, before I got conked on the head, I was looking at some cookbooks."

"There's a shock," Larry said.

Rose rolled her eyes. "Cookbooks? That's your brain wave? Please, somebody call the Nobel committee—we've got a bloody genius here! Isabella, don't let this one get away."

"Rose," Isabella said. "We are here looking for help, not a fight."

Rose sat back in her chair. "Okay, fine. I'm all ears."

Neil frowned. When had Rose taken over as the boss of this whole operation again? Of course, he had to admit that he and Larry hadn't been getting very far before they'd met her, so he swallowed his criticism.

"There was this one cookbook that was all about the food from Shakespeare's time. I didn't get a chance to read it, but it got me thinking about a pattern that might tie all those numbers together."

"Go on," said Rose.

"Well, we were wondering why Kemp would hide the clue in honey and then add all that extra honey to the case."

"It doesn't make sense."

"Right. But what if Kemp was using the honey to tell Shakespeare that the key to everything was food?"

Rose considered this for a bit. "So the bit about 'taste-less gruel' was maybe one more hint that food is the hidden clue that ties all the numbers in the note—let's call it the key code—together?"

Neil nodded. "It's a start, anyway."

"Yeah, and that key he drew on the key-code paper definitely looks like a fish. Yuck." Larry shuddered.

"Are there a lot of food references in Shakespeare?" Neil asked.

"Hundreds." Rose relaxed her body position and bit her lower lip as she considered what Neil was saying. "Jones, I need a computer fast . . . *fast!*"

Jones growled.

"C'mon, Jones," Rose said. "I know you always have one in the car. Just like that time in Vienna. Remember that week?"

Jones growled again but got up and walked out the door.

Rose watched his back with an amused smile.

Neil looked over at Isabella, and pointed at Jones and then Rose. There was definitely some history between them.

Isabella just mouthed, *Later*.

Jones returned after a minute or so with a laptop and put it down in front of Rose.

Rose lifted the lid and smiled. "Isabella, tell Jones he's a peach."

Jones growled again, but Neil thought he noticed a softer tone—less rottweiler and more English bulldog.

"It's nice to see everyone getting along . . . finally," Isabella said, smiling.

"So, let's see what we get if we narrow it down to food references," Rose said. She started typing furiously. "Hmm, you'd be surprised how often Shakes mentions wine, ale, beef, spices, even eggs. . . ." She ran her finger over the computer screen. "Still seems very random. There are too many hits."

Neil seemed disappointed. As with most of his hunches he was absolutely convinced he was right. He had an idea. "Wait. You said Kemp died in 1601? We should only check the plays *before* that!"

Rose smacked herself on the head. "Idiot," she said.

"An honest mistake," Neil said.

"I was referring to you, ya dope. I told you he died in *1603* about ten times, and I already factored that all into the list. No wonder you need help so much."

Larry laughed. Neil elbowed him in the ribs.

"Okay, but how many food references can there actually be in all those plays?" Neil asked.

Rose looked at the screen. "At least two hundred."

Neil rubbed his temples again. "Shakespeare was a genius. There's no way Kemp left him a simple clue. Not if the treasure is worth as much as Kemp suggested. There has to be more."

Neil looked at the picture of the note again. Drake? Globe? Robe? What the heck was Kemp getting at? "Maybe he hid the jewel in the Globe Theatre? Why don't we just go there and look?"

Rose groaned. "The Globe Theatre that's in London today is just a replica. The original burned down in 1613, during a play. They fired off a real cannon and the sparks ignited the scenery."

"I hope they gave everyone their money back!" Larry said.

"No one was hurt. They rebuilt within a year. If there'd been something valuable hidden there, they'd have found it in the rubble way back when."

"How do we know they didn't?"

"We don't, but I don't think that's the case. The poem says 'around the globe,' not 'in the Globe.' Also, I don't think Kemp was that stupid, or at least that obvious. This key-code note is more complex than that. He wouldn't

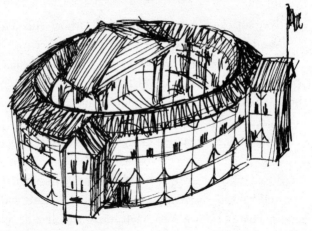

risk Shakespeare—a genius, as you mentioned—finding the jewel by accident."

Neil was silent, racking his brain for some kind of lead. Rose had said Kemp loved codes. He'd even hidden his own name in a poem celebrating his Morris-dancing journey to Norwich. He'd written a whole book about the journey and attacked his critics with a nasty dedication.

Clearly, Kemp was a man with a huge ego. Huge ego . . . huge ego . . . why did this seem important?

"*Wait*! I've got it! Huge ego!"

"We know you have a huge ego," Larry said. "You don't have to yell it so loud."

"No, not me. Kemp."

"So, chef boy, another brain wave?" Rose asked.

"Two in one day!" Larry said.

Neil nodded and spoke in a low voice. "Kemp had a huge ego. How many of the food references come from lines in the plays that might have been spoken by Kemp himself?"

Rose looked back at the list and considered. "Well,

let's assume from what we know that he played Falstaff, Bottom, and some of the other comic roles."

Rose began isolating some of the quotes, her smile growing the whole time. "Isabella, I take everything back. He isn't a complete idiot."

"What?" Neil said.

"You sure?" Jones said.

Larry just laughed.

"So what are we left with?" Isabella asked.

"Some interesting possibilities." Rose looked at the screen. "In *The Merry Wives of Windsor*, Falstaff calls someone a cabbage. And in *A Midsummer's Night Dream*, Bottom makes reference to honey, peas, mustard seed, oats. Then in *Henry the Fourth, Part Two*, Falstaff makes a reference to cheese and even radishes."

"I knew there was a pattern," Neil said smugly.

"Yes, we have a wonderful shopping list. We could make an amazing dinner!" Rose said, with obvious sarcasm. "But what the heck does it have to do with finding anything like a jewel? Did Kemp hide it in a supermarket?"

Neil frowned. "You're supposed to be the Shakespeare scholar." He slunk back in his seat, sulking.

"You're supposed to be the food expert! So is there anything you can tell me about Elizabethan food that might help?" Rose said.

Larry coughed. "If I may interject, Neil wouldn't know Tudors from toenails. But, I, on the other hand, am a lover of history. Let me have a crack at the code that 'tis hidden among the gruel of the honey-tongued Shakespeare. If I may, m'lady?"

Rose passed him the laptop.

"Let's look at those quotes again, but then cross-reference them to the letters from the key code." Larry highlighted the passages. "Interesting. In one of the plays, Falstaff makes a reference to cheese. And that play just happens to be *Henry the Fourth, Part Two*."

"So?" Neil said.

"Look at the first sequence of letters on the key code." Larry pointed to them and read, "*IVII III II*."

"Still confused," said Neil.

"Rose said right off that the letters are references to Shakespeare's plays. They tell us the act, the scene, and sometimes even the name of the play."

Neil looked at the numbers but was still confused.

Rose's eyes grew wide. "*IV* is *Henry the Fourth*!"

Larry nodded. "And if the next two *I*s are for part two, that leaves five more *I*s. That's either act three, scene two, or act two, scene three."

"Why?" Neil said.

"Roman numerals. You can only have three *I*s together before you need a *V. III* is three. *IV* is four. *V* is five. *VI* is six, and so on up to *VIII*. After that it's *I*s and *X*s and . . . *O*, just forget about it," Larry finished, noticing the look of confusion on Neil's face. "*O*, get it?"

Rose had called up Falstaff from act three and pointed the quote out to Larry, who read.

"'I do remember him at Clement's Inn like a man made after supper of a cheese-pairing: when a' was naked, he was, for all the world, like a forked radish, with a head fantastically carved upon it with a knife.'"

Larry sat back with a satisfied smile. "What, no applause?"

Neil clapped as sarcastically as possible. "So we have to look for cheese? That didn't work out so well for me last time."

Larry groaned. "Look, let me explain it again. The food is just the tip-off. The letters point to a play where Falstaff—a character Kemp played—is talking about cheese. But in that clue we end up with an actual London place to look. Clement's Inn."

"So we need to look for Clement's Inn?"

Larry nodded. "I think that's what Kemp is getting at with the first series of numbers."

"How does this tie in to all the Drake and globe stuff?" Neil asked.

Larry pursed his lips and scratched his head. "Um . . . one step at a time."

"Well, it's something to start with anyway," Rose said, yawning. "In the morning."

Neil yawned as well. He was still jet-lagged from the flight.

"Tomorrow after breakfast seems like a good time to start."

They all nodded.

"The name of that place again?" Jones asked.

"Clement's Inn," Larry said.

Jones typed the name into his phone. "Well, there's good news and bad news. The good news is that I can get us there." He stood up and walked away, calling back over his shoulder. "The bad news can wait until tomorrow."

CHAPTER FIFTEEN

THE BAD NEWS

The sun was rising on a cool but lovely London morning. Jones turned down a treelined street and parked the van in front of a thoroughly modern block of office buildings. He turned off the engine and double-checked the GPS and nodded. "Yup, we're here."

Everyone poured out of the car and stood on the sidewalk. An old church was close by, but the cornerstone said it had been built in the late 1600s, long after Kemp had died—and Shakespeare, for that matter.

Cars and buses sped by on a circular and newly paved road.

"And that's the bad news. Your chance of finding a four-hundred-year-old clue here? Zero," Jones said.

Rose put her hands on her hips and frowned.

"You are always such a pessimist."

"Realist."

"Pessimist."

"Realist."

"Duck season, rabbit season," Larry said. "Can we possibly get back to some actual detective work?"

"Well, Sherlock, where would you suggest we start?" Rose said.

Larry whispered to Neil. "See, even Rose thinks I'm the Sherlock here."

Neil just rolled his eyes. "So this is where Clement's Inn *used* to stand."

Jones nodded. "Now it's the London School of Economics."

Isabella took out her phone and read from the screen. "It was a place for lawyers to stay and work when they were in London. It had lots of beds and books."

Larry chuckled. "Sort of like having your office and the hotel wrapped into one."

Isabella nodded. "It was also apparently renowned for the wild parties they would throw."

"So what happened to it?" Neil asked.

Rose sighed. "Burned, I'll wager. That's what happened to the original church over there. That's why they rebuilt it."

"The Great Fire of London," Isabella said.

Rose nodded. "A *huge* fire in 1666. It burned down almost all of the city."

"Realist," Jones said.

"That was a short investigation," Larry said. "Well, let's go get a coffee and start looking for Lord Lane again."

Isabella scrolled down on the article she was reading. "Actually, it looks like Clement's Inn survived the great fire."

"So where is it?" Neil said, looking around. "I don't see anything looking like a five-hundred-year-old hotel."

"Well, it was actually renovated in the nineteenth century . . ."

"Great!"

"Then torn down about a hundred years ago."

Neil's shoulders sagged. "Argh," he said.

"No! This is good news!" Rose said. "I know a thing or two hundred about record keeping and lawyers."

They all stared at her blankly.

"They keep good records, and they don't get rid of them just because a building gets torn down. If the records survived the fire, then they're somewhere. We just have to figure out where."

"And how do we do that?"

Isabella continued to search on her phone. "Well. There are a few options. Clement's Inn was one of the

Inner Temple law courts. There's a library for the courts just a block away."

"We could walk!" Larry said. "With all these economics students around, there's got to be a coffee shop somewhere."

But Jones was already behind the wheel of the SUV, revving the engine.

"Or maybe driving in a stripped-down tank isn't such a bad idea."

Just as they got back in the car, Neil thought he smelled something. A faint hint of . . . ancient honey. He looked around, but couldn't see anything out of the ordinary. Just people walking busily to or from school, a few cleaners picking up garbage in the street, and some professors on bikes.

The breeze shifted and the smell was gone, if it had been there at all.

"C'mon, chef boy, time is wasting," Rose said. "Get in."

Neil closed the door and was quickly lost in thought. "I've got to make a call to Nakamura."

"You do realize it's the middle of the night there?"

"I'll speak loudly to make sure he's awake," Neil said, dialing the number.

A clearly groggy Nakamura answered the phone.

"Nose, if you were here, I'd strangle you. But you're not, so I'm just going to hang up."

"No, wait! I need you to do a little digging for us!"

"From Vancouver? Are you nuts? Wait, don't answer that; I know you're nuts."

"I'm not nuts. Oddly enough I don't have a direct number for the Queen, so I can't ask her what's going on."

"And the local police?"

"The Queen said she wanted this all done on the hush-hush. And I'm still not a hundred percent sure they didn't shoot at me yesterday."

There was a pause. "I'd say I'm surprised, but I've known you too long."

"Ha-ha. Look, we think Lord Lane might be dead."

"Go on," Nakamura said, all business now.

"I found his clothes covered in blood at a theater, but Jones read the papers this morning. He says there was nothing in there."

"That's very strange."

"It was a lot of blood." Neil shuddered at the memory. "But we don't know anything else. Was it his blood? Is he just hurt but is being held hostage? We need more info to find Lane or the jewel. Can you talk to your contacts?"

"I can think of any number of reasons to say no, like the numbers on my alarm clock. But—"

"Thanks, Nakamura!" Neil said, hanging up. "All right, Jones, let's go!"

"Got your seat belt on?" Jones asked.

"Um, no," he said.

Jones laughed and gunned the engine.

CHAPTER SIXTEEN

INN AND OUT

Rose, Isabella, Larry, and Neil jumped out of the SUV after an incredibly fast one-block trip. Jones stayed in the car to act as a lookout in case anyone was following them.

"Yes, in your giant black SUV you're very hard to follow," Larry joked. "I give it two minutes."

"I can only hope," Jones growled. Then he hit a button that slammed and locked the doors.

"Grump," Rose said. She turned on her heel and marched through the gates of the Inner Temple Library. The others followed.

Isabella leaned in close to Neil. "Jones and Rose have a rather interesting history."

"Boyfriend, girlfriend?"

"Not really," Isabella said with a cryptic smile.

Rose led the way through the front doors.

An old man sat at a large desk, poring over sheets of aged papers with a magnifying glass. Rose marched up to him. "I'd like to see the archives for Clement's Inn, please," she said. "Do you have them here?"

The man nodded and held out his hand for Rose's ID. She took a card from her pocket and held it up.

The man barely glanced at it, then waved them all through. Rose flapped the card in front of them. "Academic accreditation opens doors. Stay in school, kids." Rose walked over to a huge carved wooden door.

There was a click, and the doors opened.

Isabella and Larry gasped. The library was beautiful. An arched ceiling rose above them. Huge leaded-glass windows filtered the murky daylight into the room, illuminating dozens of carved oak bookcases filled with leather-bound volumes.

Neil was more struck by the overwhelming smells of different kinds of paper, parchment, and mold spores that floated in the air.

The old man followed them inside and pointed to

a row of bookcases at the back. An enormous stained-glass window took up most of the wall. "The record books for the old inns are back there. You'll need to wear these." He handed each of them a pair of white gloves. Then he walked back through the doors and closed them behind him.

"So where do we start?" Larry asked as they stared in wonder at the thousands of books.

"I'd suggest we each take a bookcase, and start by looking for books from before 1603."

The bookcases seemed to Neil to get even more packed as she said this. "Ugh," he said, reaching for the first book. It was a list of notable members of the Clement's Inn, since the year 1547. Neil started running his finger down the stiff yellowed page.

Coley dope

Hawtray

Ecclesthorpe

Griswold

"It's not even in alphabetical order! This'll take forever."

"Shhhhh," said the other three. "You're looking for anything in the books that might have been left behind by Kemp," Rose said.

Neil grumpily returned to the list, hoping to see a Kemp, Drake, or possibly even a Shakespeare listed somewhere. Nothing.

Meanwhile, Larry, Rose, and Isabella were carefully

stacking books on an enormous desk. "I've divided them into decades," Rose said. "Luckily, we only need to check stuff for about a fifty-year window."

Neil felt himself nodding off. This was *way* too close to homework.

He leaned his head against the bookcase. His eyes closed. His breathing grew heavy.

With a jolt, he stood up straight. There were only a few things that could make Neil Flambé do that, and 99 percent of those were food. He had smelled something.

Neil took another deep sniff. He could smell the faintest, weakest scent of onion and cinnamon coming from a book on the top shelf. There might even be a molecule of garlic.

Now he was awake. The others were still sorting the books on the table, occasionally skimming through a volume to see if there were any obvious connections to the key code or to Shakespeare or Kemp.

Neil looked up. There was a rod that ran along the top of each case. A ladder was attached, with wheels to help it slide along. Neil grabbed it and slid it into position in front of him.

Larry looked over. He knew right away that Neil had smelled something. "What is it, boy? Trouble at the old mill? Woof!"

Neil ignored him and climbed to the top of the ladder, using his nose as a guide. Larry walked over and steadied the ladder as Neil reached his fingers farther and farther to his left. Finally, he was able to wrap his fingers around what he was sure was the right book.

It was very thin, wedged tightly in a series of much

larger volumes. He almost lost his balance trying to pull it out. Larry quickly jumped up a few steps and put his hand on Neil's back.

"Thanks," Neil said.

"That's what I'm here for." Larry smiled.

Neil made his way back down the ladder and walked over to the desk. He sat down and opened the book. The cinnamon smell was especially strong now, and very fragrant. Neil almost felt like he was smelling the original cinnamon smell from the beginning of time. It was so fresh and pure.

"Wow!" he said.

"Did you find something?" Rose said, walking over.

Neil smiled. "A cookbook," he said.

"Ah. Always good to focus on the task at hand."

She frowned. "I'll just go back and do the real work, then?"

Neil checked the front piece. "It's from 1599. So I'm doing exactly what you suggested."

"Ha!" Rose scoffed. "Well, I suggest you check that book out fast and then get back to some real work, checking the legal ledgers." Then she marched back to the shelves to grab some more books.

"She's starting to get under my skin," Neil muttered.

"Yeah, isn't she's wonderful?" Larry said.

Neil rolled his eyes and turned his attention back to the cookbook.

The first recipe was for a chewet pie, with a filling of raisins, orange peel, cinnamon, sugar, and exotic spices. He was amazed. He'd had no idea the cuisine at the time had been so rich.

He read on. There were recipes for oysters and roast mutton, and dozens of recipes for special *aqua compositas*, spiced and brewed drinks with "magik propertees."

Neil started making mental notes. Maybe an Elizabethan feast was the best way to impress a monarch?

He turned the page to the beginning of a series of cheese recipes and stopped. There, scratched into the margin of the page in dark ink, was one word.

Capon.

"Capon?" Neil flipped through the pages. There were no handwritten words anywhere else.

"What the heck is that doing there?" he said out loud.

Rose looked over at him frowning. "What, found a recipe for wasting time?"

"Capon," Neil said.

"Wasting capon, how lovely," Rose said, turning back to the pile of books in front of her.

"The word 'capon' was written here in the cheese section. It's handwritten on the edge." Neil pointed at the page.

Rose took a look. "It certainly resembles the handwriting on the key-code note. Look at the swirl on that O."

"What's a capon? A kind of cheese?" Larry asked.

"Not at all. It's a type of rooster. I was just thinking of

cooking one for the Queen. It seems strange that someone would write it down in a chapter about cheese," Neil said. "At least, without any other recipe ideas."

"And I thought we were looking for a law book," Isabella said.

"Maybe that's what Kemp wanted Shakespeare to think," Larry said.

"But really it was hidden in a cookbook?"

"Yes! Remember, it was a cheese reference that sent us here in the first place." Larry beamed. "So Kemp is hiding another clue—capon—using the reference from the previous clue: cheese."

Neil thought for a second. "But it seems a pretty obvious clue. I mean, wouldn't somebody have noticed 'capon' was added in when they were looking at the book?"

Rose shook her head. "Not necessarily. Scholars and monks were always adding stuff in the margins, so this one wouldn't stick out to an average reader. We only know what it is because we are looking for it."

Rose pursed her lips. "Well, this is what we academics call a good working theory. Cheese leads to capon. Food. Food. Food. Seems you might be the right person to be on this case, despite all appearances to the contrary."

"Thanks . . . I think," Neil said.

"So what kind of a clue is 'capon'?" Larry asked. "Maybe we're supposed to cross-reference that with some rooster recipe here in the book?"

Neil flipped the rest of the pages in the book. "Weird. There's only one capon recipe. But I don't see any other words written in the margins." He tapped his upper lip, thinking.

"Maybe the clue is something hidden in the recipe that we're supposed to look for?" Isabella suggested.

Neil read the recipe. "It's pretty basic. It simply says to make a sauce with onions, oranges, and spices, and then it says to watch the clock or else the meat will get cold."

"That's a weird line for a recipe," Isabella said.

Larry smiled. "Are you sure that last bit wasn't added in later?"

Rose ran out and grabbed the magnifying glass from the old shushing man. She carefully examined the script. "It is different. The ink is just slightly darker. Kemp, if he wrote this, tried hard to make this look the same as the original."

"But why?" Neil asked. "He didn't bother to do that with the word 'capon.'"

Rose smiled. "It's a reference. *The Comedy of Errors*, act one, scene two." She called up the relevant speech on her phone and handed it to Larry.

Larry cleared his throat and put on his actor's voice.

The capon burns, the pig falls from the spit,
The clock hath strucken twelve upon the bell;
My mistress made it one upon my cheek:
She is so hot because the meat is cold;
The meat is cold because
you come not home . . .

Isabella and Rose clapped.

Larry bowed.

"Certainly a comedy, and Larry knows all about errors," Neil said, rolling his eyes.

"Ouch! Thou stabbest at me with thy wit!" Larry said.

Neil tried to connect the dots. "So the recipe book makes reference to capons. That leads to a quote that makes reference to a clock striking twelve. Kemp's key-code poem makes reference to a clock. So I guess we need to go looking for a clock of some kind?"

"Tsk, tsk," Larry said. "Jumping to conclusions. As with everything in this case, it's not so simple. This line is just telling us we're on the right track. But this quote doesn't tell us a place to look next. So it's pointing to another clue we have to find."

Neil threw up his hands. "I give up. Can I just go home and cook now?"

"C'mon, cuz, stay with me. The first clue pointed to a line from a character Kemp played."

"Falstaff," Neil said.

"He *can* be taught!" Rose said, raising her hands in the air in mock celebration.

"Sometimes!" Larry said, mimicking her. "And that Falstaff line matched the first sequence of letters from the key code."

Neil nodded slowly. "Okay so far."

"That led us here to the Inn records, where the word 'capon' tells us we're on the right track. Then that word leads us to the next clue."

Neil pulled out his phone. "Let's take a look at the key code again. The third sequence of numbers is three *I*s, which matches up perfectly with the lines from the comedy thing, whatever it was called."

Rose and Larry groaned. "*Comedy of Errors*," they said together.

"Whatever. So that means we're on the right track." They nodded. "And then we need to look at the next sequence to figure out where to look next."

"Seems right," Larry said.

"The next set of letters is *IVIIII*," Neil said.

Rose considered. "Well, the first time we saw an *IV*, it referred to *Henry the Fourth, Part Two*."

Larry nodded. "Yes. There are only four extra *I*s in this one. Hmmmm. You need at least two to refer to scene and act, which means it's either *Henry the Fourth, Part Two*, act one, scene one, or *Henry the Fourth, Part One*, act one, scene two—*IIII*."

Rose called up the script in her phone and passed it to Larry. "It's the second option."

"I know this one," he said. "Young Hal—he becomes Henry the Fifth at the end of both plays—has a whole bit where he's teasing Falstaff for eating too many rich foods and drinking too much, sleeping in."

"Sounds like someone I know, and am sadly related to," Neil said.

"Ha-ha. The lines are . . .

> *Thou art so fat-witted,*
> *with drinking of old sack*
> *and unbuttoning thee after supper*
> *and sleeping upon*
> *benches after noon, that thou hast forgotten to*
> *demand that truly which thou*
> *wouldst truly know.*
> *What a devil hast thou to do*
> *with the time of the day?*

"And in the next line Hal makes reference to a clock?" Isabella said.

Larry nodded and continued.

*Unless hours were cups of sack and minutes
capons and clocks the tongues
of bawds and dials the
signs of leaping-houses and
the blessed sun himself
a fair hot wench in flame-coloured
taffeta I see no
reason why thou shouldst be
so superfluous to demand
the time of the day.*

"So do we need to find an old clock?" Neil asked. "Big Ben?"

Rose frowned. "Big Ben is like maybe a hundred and fifty years old."

"Looks older on the postcards," Neil said.

"Put architecture on the list of things you should be paying attention to in school. And Big Ben isn't a clock; it's the bell inside the clock tower!"

Neil frowned.

Larry interrupted. "Forget the clock. I think that's a red herring. Falstaff actually says in the scene that he doesn't need a clock. He's got the stars."

"Okay, so where does that leave us?" Neil asked.

"Well, in the play, it leaves them chatting for a few more minutes."

"About what?"

Rose smiled. "Two things in particular. They discuss what Hal will be like when he becomes king. Then they sit down and plan a robbery. Hal and Falstaff also make reference to honey, and capons. It's like all the hints so far rolled into one scene."

Neil considered. "So Kemp is sending Shakespeare a message about what?"

"We know he stole something. Falstaff even implores him not to hang thieves when he becomes king, although he does exactly that in *Henry the Fifth*."

"So is the scene about robbery or about becoming a king?"

"The whole play is about how becoming a king changes you. It's all about the weight of the crown, the demands of leadership."

"So, fine, kingship," Neil said. "But where does that lead us? Where was it supposed to send Shakespeare?"

They sat silently for a while.

Finally, Larry snapped his fingers loudly. "Aha! Hal ends the scene by saying he's going to be different when he's king. And back then you only got to be king in one place. Westminster."

Rose took a second to consider and then said, "It's possible. Each clue seems to contain a red herring, but then hints at some actual place to look. Although there's not that much of Westminster left, except for the abbey."

"Let me guess," said Neil. "Another fire."

Rose nodded and held up two fingers. "One way back before Shakespeare and one back when Queen Victoria was on the throne."

Larry laughed. "Who built this city, arsonists?"

"No, lots of carpenters with lots of dry wood. But the abbey is stone, and it's pretty much the same as it's been for a thousand years."

Neil rubbed his temples. "We're sure Kemp is pointing at Westminster?"

Rose shrugged. "No, but there are a couple of other things helping us out. Hal became Henry the Fifth, one of the greatest English kings. He was buried in Westminster Abbey, the church that's attached to the palace. His grave was a big tourist attraction, even in Shakespeare's

time. So we know he and Kemp could have visited the place. We also know that it's still standing."

Larry smiled. "As you said earlier, a working theory is better than nothing."

"Let's get going," Neil said.

They reshelved the books and Rose led them back out of the library.

As they passed through the front gates, a thought occurred to Neil.

"Wait, isn't Big Ben at Westminster?"

"Zip it," Rose said, and she marched ahead toward the car.

CHAPTER SEVENTEEN

WESTMINSTER ABBEY ROAD

I feel like I'm walking on living history!" Larry beamed as he walked into the great hall of Westminster Abbey. He grabbed a guidebook from a rack in front of the ticket booth and began reading.

"'The abbey was built a thousand years ago, and has witnessed the coronation and burial of all monarchs since. It has been burned, bombed, and added to, but remains the center of faith and power in England to this day.'"

Then he looked up and lost all ability to speak. The tops of the pillars soared a hundred feet above them, and met in an explosion of intricate and interwoven patterns.

"I can't believe it's stone. It's so delicate!" Isabella said.

"Wow," Larry whispered. "Wow."

Neil was impressed too, but he was also distracted. Just as they'd passed the ticket booth, he'd smelled something familiar.

"I can smell my potatoes, or maybe my salmon. The

rosemary and dill are a little mixed up, and it's incredibly faint," Neil said to Larry, who still had his eyes locked on the architecture. Somewhere in the throng of tourists, tour guides, and security guards was someone who had visited his restaurant.

Larry didn't take his eyes off the ceiling. "The statistical probability of a tourist having eaten at your restaurant and then visited here is . . ."

"Zero?"

"No, actually it's pretty high. Look at the evidence. It takes money and good taste both to travel here as a tourist and to eat at Chez Flambé. So the customers at the restaurant are exactly the types of people who visit beautiful cathedrals far away from home statistically speaking. I'm surprised you don't smell your food every time we travel. See, that's why you study math."

Neil scanned the crowd for a familiar face, but with all the drafty old windows, hurrying people, and opening doors it was impossible to pin down exactly where the smell was coming from. And then, all of a sudden, it was gone.

Neil was now even more agitated. "Why are we here again?"

"Well, if we follow Larry's logic—" Rose started.

"Not two words that go together naturally," Neil interrupted.

"*Which* has worked so far. If we follow his logic, then Kemp is hiding clues to specific locations in his poem. The first clue led us to Clement's Inn. The clue we found there has led us through the word 'capon' to Westminster."

"I like how you always use the present tense for a guy

who's been dead for hundreds of years," Neil said.

Larry smiled. "I get it. It's like we're chasing a living person."

Rose nodded. "That's why people love Shakespeare plays. Julius Caesar was dead more than a thousand years before Shakespeare wrote his play, but for the people in the seats, it was like he was alive again onstage. That's the power of theater."

Neil sighed. "Fine, so why here in the church instead of some other building?"

Rose slapped her hand on a stone pillar. "When the original Palace of Westminster burned down, this church remained. And a few towers and smaller buildings, but they weren't open to the public in Shakespeare's time."

"But this was?"

Rose nodded.

"So there might be some kind of clue hidden here?" Isabella asked.

Rose shrugged. "It's hard to say. We kind of struck it lucky in the library with the cookbook."

"That wasn't luck, exactly," Neil said under his breath. "Remember my nose?"

Rose ignored him. "It's not likely that there are any four-hundred-year-old foods or cookbooks here, but a lot of this place is pretty much the same as it was when Kemp and Shakespeare were alive, so it's worth a shot."

They walked around, looking for anything that might have been left behind by Kemp. "Maybe graffiti or some kind of plaque," Rose suggested.

It seemed hopeless from the start. There were lots of old things, but most looked extremely clean and well maintained. They walked along the body of the church and passed a series of huge stone and iron monuments with images of kings and queens on the lids.

"Hey, look! A dead guy with a crown!" Larry said. "Another dead guy with a crown! A dead woman with a crown!"

Neil leaned against the railing and looked over at a large tomb with yet one more lid with a dead guy with a crown. He read the plaque. "'Here lies Henry the Fifth, King of England, Scourge of France.' Nice, if you're not French."

"Henry wanted to be. Read the play," Larry said.

"Wait, wasn't he an English king?"

"*Oui, monsieur*. He had his coronation right on that chair," Larry said. He pointed to a large wooden chair.

Neil walked over and examined it more closely. A faded and incredibly scuffed-up wooden chair, with a triangle-shaped back, stood on top of a golden platform, with a worn golden lion under each knobby leg.

"This chair? Seriously?"

Larry nodded.

Neil shook his head in wonder. "I guess the bottom's okay, but the top is a mess. It looks like something from our restaurant! You'd think they'd take better care of it."

"It is old. I mentioned that, right? See the slot there, between the lions and the seat?" Larry pointed at a rectangular empty space. "That's where they place the Stone of Scone."

"Scone? They cook buns on that? Is that some weird British tradition, like not refinishing furniture?"

"No. It's a stone from Scotland. They bring it back and put it in there when they crown a new king or queen."

Neil snorted. It all seemed so weird. Thousand-year-old chairs, Scottish stones. Then an idea occurred to him. He walked back over to the tombs.

"So this Henry the Fifth is the same guy who was the prince in *Henry the Fourth*, right?"

"Nice work, Einstein. And after him came Henry the Tenth?" Larry said.

"I just mean that maybe he's the clue. This place is the clue."

"How?"

Neil tapped his fingers together. "In the play,

Rose said Falstaff and the prince are talking about him becoming king. They are talking about kingship, but that's another misdirection." Neil was now thinking out loud. "Kingship is the topic, but the *place* is the clue. Hal became King Henry the Fifth over here."

Neil walked back over to the chair. "And that's where Kemp hid a clue." Neil looked all around the top and sides. He got down on his knees and looked in the cavity where the stone would have sat. Nothing.

"Try the back," Larry suggested.

The chair was set a short distance away from the wall. Neil leaned as close to the wall as he could and stared at the back. It was covered in graffiti. There were dozens of names and dates carved into the back, but he couldn't see them clearly from his angle. He waved Larry over. "There's stuff carved on the back: graffiti. Help me."

"I don't think the security guards would take too kindly to you moving a thousand-year-old piece of furniture," Larry said. "But luckily, technology comes to the rescue! Behold the Phone of Scone!" Larry looked around to make sure they weren't being watched, then slipped his phone between the chair and the wall and snapped a picture.

He held it up. "Bingo."

"You got something?"

"No, some kid named Bingo Little carved his name in 1899." Larry put his phone farther back and snapped another image. He pulled it back out and looked.

"Bingo," he said.

"The same kid?"

"No, this time I got something. Look." He held up

the phone. "Right there, next to Paul Pennyfeather, 1789, and Ralston MacTodd, 1847, it says Richard Dogberry III. 1592."

Neil stared blankly at the phone. "And?"

Larry sighed. "Rose mentioned the name to you just yesterday, for crying out loud. Dogberry was a character Kemp played in Shakespeare's *Much Ado About Nothing*. He's a kind of goofy cop, like a sixteenth-century Nakamura."

"Okay, but why the Richard bit and the date? And it's not exactly a food clue . . . unless there really is such a thing as a dogberry . . . which I doubt."

Larry thought about it for a second. "I have a couple of ideas, but I suggest we get the others and put more than my mind to work here."

"You mean mine and yours," Neil said.

"Yeah, sure, that's what I meant."

Larry and Neil tracked down Rose and Isabella, who were looking at the even more ornate ceiling of the Henry VII chapel at the far end of the abbey.

"There are certainly a lot of Henrys in this place," Neil said.

"Find anything?" Rose asked.

"We think so," Neil said. "But we need some better brains than Larry's to figure it out."

"You mean yours and Larry's," Larry said.

"Yeah, sure, that's what I meant," Neil said.

They rejoined Jones back in the car. Jones had gotten them all some takeaway fish and chips, which Neil immediately suggested could have been made better with less salt and with duck fat rather than vegetable oil. Larry beaned him with a napkin and then passed around the picture of the chair.

"Dogberry certainly seems like a Kemp reference," Rose said. "So good work on that one."

"But why Richard? That's not Dogberry's name."

"And what do the numbers mean? III. Another reference to a line from a play?"

Rose looked at the picture again and smiled. "A reference, yes. But to a play, not just a line."

"Which play?"

"*Richard the Third*. The date, 1592, is when Shakespeare wrote or at least performed that play."

"It's not when Kemp carved his name in the back?"

"The character Dogberry wasn't written until about five or six years later, so I think he was making a reference to himself, as Dogberry, but then the date is a reference to Shakespeare's Richard."

"So all we need to do is find a food reference in *Richard the Third* and we'll be on our way?" Neil said hopefully.

"Maybe we'll have to go through all the plays first," Isabella said.

"What? How many plays did Shakespeare write?" Neil whined. He was feeling exhausted.

Rose frowned at him. "Enough to create a whole

new approach to theater and about a thousand new words in the English language."

"I bet his omelets sucked," Neil said grumpily.

A barrage of napkins from everyone, including a ninety-miles-per-hour missile from Jones, convinced Neil to keep quiet.

CHAPTER EIGHTEEN

CHOP CHOP

So I've gone through *Richard the Third* and there is one, *one*, reference to eating. Richard says he'd like some strawberries." Rose pushed a pot of tea away with disgust, spilling some of the dark liquid onto the lace tablecloth, dangerously close to the keyboard of her laptop.

They'd stopped at a tea shop to go over the latest hints and clues and apparent dead ends. Neil looked up from his fluffy and delicious scone and clotted cream.

"'Strawberries' is a food reference. What's wrong with that?"

"The problem is trying to fit Kemp into the play. Richard is not exactly the biggest barrel of laughs in the universe, and he's the villain of the play, so there's no way Kemp went anywhere near playing that character. Besides, the letters from the key code don't match up with the strawberry reference. Act three, scene four. That should be *IIIIIV*, or even *IIIIIIIV* if we throw in the numbers from the title."

Isabella called up the picture of the note. "The next line of code on the key note says *IIIIVI*. That's close, isn't it?"

Rose slumped in her seat. "Yes, but close, as they say, is only good in horseshoes and hand grenades."

"Don't remind me," Jones grumbled from his seat, which barely contained his bulk. He looked a little silly in the dainty wicker, which seemed on the verge of collapse every time he breathed. "I've still got the scars."

Isabelle winked at Neil. "Details. Later," she whispered.

"Well, is there anything in scene four about eating? Dining?"

Rose ran her hand across her forehead and closed the lid of her laptop angrily. "Lots of references to wine, but pretty much zilch for food. It's like the least foodie play Shakes ever wrote."

"There has to be a misdirection in there somewhere," Larry said. "Unless the food thing is a misdirection. But why change from food clues all of a sudden?"

They were all silent. Neil spread a thick layer of strawberry jam onto his scone, and stopped.

"Or did he change?" Neil said, gazing intently at his snack. "Larry, you said the Stone of Scone was a reference to Scotland."

"The stone was originally taken from the monastery of Scone Abbey."

"How do you know all this stuff?" Neil asked.

Larry tapped his brain. "I'm just a genius."

"Wait. Didn't you and Heather MacDonald throw a Robbie Burns Day party last year?"

"Yeah, she told me all about it. But I remembered it, and if you'd been at that party, you'd know how much genius that takes." Larry turned to Rose. "Don't be jealous, Rose. Heather and I only see each other on the Isle of Skype now."

Neil expected Rose to attack Larry with at least a verbal assault, but miraculously she just rolled her eyes. "You are incorrigible," she said.

"I think you mean insane," Neil said. "Can we focus? Look, were scones actually around way back then, as a food?"

"No references in any Shakespeare plays that I can recall," Rose said. She did a quick search on her laptop. "Cakes, yes, and pies. But no scones."

"But if scones *were* around then, if you could get them in tea shops or on the street as a snack, or even at the theater, then could Kemp be making a misdirection with the words scone and stone?"

"Using one to signify the other?" Isabella said.

"A kind of Elizabethan cockney wordplay?" Rose

smiled. "I like it!" She quickly called up the script for *Richard III* and searched for "stone" in act four. "And it matches the next sequence of letters—*IIIIVI*."

"Bingo!" Larry said, looking over her shoulder. "A triple misdirection! Oh, Master Kemp, you're a scallywag."

Rose looked at the script. "In the scene, Queen Elizabeth is talking; she's the wife of King Edward, the guy Richard basically kills to grab the throne. And she's talking about the true heirs to the throne, two children who Richard has imprisoned and eventually kills. Larry, will you read these lines?"

Larry cleared his throat and read off the screen.

> *Stay, yet look back with me unto the Tower.*
> *Pity, you ancient stones, those tender babes*
> *Whom envy hath immured*
> *within your walls!*
> *Rough cradle for such little pretty ones!*
> *Rude ragged nurse, old sullen playfellow*
> *For tender princes, use my babies well!*
> *So foolish sorrow bids your stones farewell*

Rose frowned. "Not a great moment in English history, killing a couple of kids to stay king. But for our purposes, the stones she's referring to are from a specific geographic location."

"The Tower of London," Larry said.

Rose nodded. "Where the two young princes were murdered by Richard's assassins. At least that's the way Shakespeare wrote the story."

"Meaning?" Neil asked.

"Well, Shakespeare lived at a time when you needed the support of the monarchy to make it as an artist."

"Not much different from my week," Neil said.

"So Queen Betsy wanted plays that supported her claim to the throne and not someone else's. Richard the

Third wasn't her ancestor, so Shakes makes him out to be a real cruel, twisted villain."

"It's a bit of theatrical propaganda," Isabella said.

Rose nodded. "It doesn't mean Richard didn't kill the heirs to the throne, but there were plenty of others who had motives."

"But they were too close to the Queen's bloodline to implicate in the plays?" Larry said.

"And that keeps the playwright and his family with house and home and food to eat."

Neil swallowed the final bite of his scone, making mental notes about the composition of the baking powder the baker had used. "Maybe that was another little joke Kemp snuck into this clue. He has a Queen Elizabeth talk about stones, then that leads to scones, which is a joke about where Shakes gets the money for his food."

Larry stood up and tapped the top of the table. "Well, one thing's for sure, time's a-wasting! To the Batty-mobile!"

Jones didn't move. Instead he seemed to be looking at his spoon. "You know those times when everything seems to be going along smoothly?"

"Nope, not really," Neil said.

"Me neither," Larry said. "Why?"

Jones growled. "It was a rhetorical question, you idiots. The point is that the roll you've been on is in imminent danger of coming to a crashing halt."

Jones angled his spoon so Neil could see the reflection. Neil immediately saw what Jones saw, two large bulges in the curtains of the tea shop, with the toes of large alligator shoes sticking out underneath.

Neil sniffed the air. "Tikka masala and cheese! The same kind of cheese I spilled all over Reggie Crayfish." He knew the brothers were standing there, waiting for the right moment to attack.

"When did they sneak in?" Neil whispered, doing his best to stand up slowly. They were going to have to make a fast break for the door but needed a head start to get there first.

Jones slowly put down the spoon. "There must be a window behind the curtains. I had the spoon angled against my cup when we got in, and watched the curtains moving. I thought it might be the breeze, until I saw the shoes."

Neil saw Isabella tap Rose on the arm twice. Rose didn't say anything but packed up her computer, doing her best to sound nonchalant. "Well, I think I need one more swig of tea before I go anywhere." She raised the cup to her lips and said in a low voice, "On the count of three we bolt. One, two . . ."

Before she could reach three, the brothers jumped out from behind the curtain, overturning tables and spilling tea in their path like bulls in a china shop. Exactly like that, Neil thought, as the brothers rampaged toward them.

The other customers screamed and ran for the door, blocking Neil and others from making a quick escape. They'd have to stand and fight.

Rose grabbed the teapot and threw it at Reggie. The pot hit him square in the chest. "Ahhh!" he said, the hot liquid seeping into his clothes. He stopped to rip off his coat.

Neil looked to his left. Jones was engaged in hand-to-hand combat with Ronnie, exchanging devastating blows. Neither seemed to be fazed, until Ronnie pulled a handgun out from his pocket.

"Not a fair fight anymore," Jones said, grabbing Ronnie's wrist and forcing him to fire into the ceiling. They continued to struggle, Ronnie firing more shots into the ceiling. A cloud of plaster dust fell all around them.

Neil heard a yell and saw Reggie charge again. He was heading straight for Isabella and Rose.

Neil grabbed a chair and jumped into his path, holding it ready to strike, but Reggie was faster than Neil expected. He smashed the chair to the floor, shattering it like kindling.

Larry tried the same thing, but Reggie grabbed his chair in midflight and then swung it, with Larry still holding on, right into Neil. They fell to the ground in a heap, splinters of wood embedded in their clothes and skin.

Reggie smiled, then cocked his head and pointed at Rose. "You are coming with me!"

Isabella stepped in front of Reggie, grabbing something from her jacket pocket, a perfume spritzer. "Perfume? Well, at least he'll smell nice at our funeral," Larry said as he attempted to get back on his feet.

Isabella sprayed Reggie right in the face. He screamed with pain and swung wildly. Isabella kept spraying, but one of his swings caught her in the side and sent her flying into a nearby table. Cups and saucers shattered on the floor.

Rose went into a defensive stance, like a character from a martial arts movie.

The pain seemed to just make Reggie more reckless, and he took at least four swift kicks to the head without slowing down. "That's me least vulnerable part, sweetie," he said as he wrapped his enormous hands around Rose's arms. He gripped her and swung her around so that he now had his arms across her throat. Rose struggled for a few seconds but then went limp.

"Let's go!" Reggie yelled at Ronnie. He slung Rose over his shoulder and began striding back toward the curtains.

Neil and Larry jumped in his way again and lunged at him, but Reggie kicked out his legs, tripping Neil and sending Larry flying a good ten feet away and into yet another table.

"Now!" Reggie yelled, reaching the curtains and throwing them aside. There was a large patio door behind, and Reggie ran through, carrying Rose.

Neil tried to get up, but a sharp pain sent him back to his knees. Neil felt his side. It hurt to breathe.

Isabella was also moaning in pain, and Larry wasn't moving much at all.

Jones was still struggling with Ronnie, and seemed to be winning, until, with a final effort, Ronnie brought the gun down and fired a bullet into Jones's leg.

Jones fell back to the floor with a yell. Ronnie didn't take another shot. He stopped and picked up Rose's laptop, then quickly spun around and bolted after his brother.

Neil gasped for breath and stumbled over to the patio door, but he knew it was too late. He could hear the slam of a car door. The last thing he saw before he blacked out was Rose being shoved into the back of a gold-trimmed white limousine.

CHAPTER NINETEEN

BUZZZZZZZED

Neil heard a buzzing in his ear. Was he daydreaming? Was he in school, sleeping? Was it his teacher droning on about some boring history lesson or stupid Aesop fable about lizards and chickens having lunch together?

Buzzzzzzzzzzzzzzz

Was it his ears ringing? He could also hear voices, faint but getting louder. Neil forced himself to open his eyes. Larry was busily helping Jones tie up his leg in a tourniquet made out of a tea towel.

Buzzzzzzzzzzzzzzzz

"Neil, answer your phone," Larry said. "We're kind of tied up here . . . or at least Jones is!"

Neil's phone had different ringtones for all his friends. Larry's was Larry yelling "focus" at Neil. (Neil had tried to change that, but Larry had locked his phone somehow.) Nakamura was the theme from *Batman*. Angel was a Trinidadian steel-drum band playing "Blitzkrieg Bop" by the Ramones.

This wasn't one of his friends.

He rolled over to retrieve the phone, which was lying about a foot away, thrown from his pocket in the battle with the Crayfish. He expected a sharp pain in his ribs, but luckily nothing seemed to be broken. He must have just gotten the air knocked out of him.

Buzzzzzzzzzzzzzzzzzz

Neil answered the phone.

"Hello, hello. Is anyone there?" said a familiar upper-crust English voice.

"I'm here, Your Majesty, no thanks to you!" Neil said. He'd had just about enough of kings and queens, living or dead, for one day.

"How dare you!"

"No, how dare *you*! You get me over here to help find Lord Lane. Then your police fire bullets at me—"

"They did no such thing!"

"—and then I get *no help* from you or the cops when I need protection. What's so important about this stupid jewel anyway?"

"That's what I need Lord Lane to explain. Let me be frank with you, young man. Lord Lane is in some serious financial straits, due to some very questionable real estate dealings. If there have been, ahem, complications, then they are due to his dealings with unsavory characters and in no way reflect on the monarchy or the aristocracy."

"That might have been useful information to know!"

The Queen returned to her calm voice. "We did not feel that it was relevant. We were . . . we were . . ."

"Wrong?" Neil said into the phone.

"Misled by our advisors."

Neil felt a wave of exhaustion. "Look, Your Majesty, why did you call?"

"We have been informed that the police are on their way. We think it would be prudent if you were to not be there when they arrive."

"What? *What?*"

"Please don't yell. Our son may have large ears, but ours are much smaller and more delicate."

Neil rested his head in his hands. "Okay, fine. Why should we not be here?"

"Time is running out. It appears that there are many people searching for Lord Lane and the jewel from his note. The police will, of course, be forced to hold you for questioning. This would waste precious hours."

"Fair enough. But can't you just tell them to let us go?"

The Queen coughed lightly. "It would be prudent to *not* have our name mixed up in any of this."

"What? *We're mixed up in this!* Rose just got kidnapped! *Kidnapped!* I have a friend with a bullet in his leg!" Neil yelled again. *"We need help!"*

"My grandson is texting you the location of a clinic close by. Everything will be taken care of. But please leave soon." Then the line went dead.

Neil stared at his phone. *"Ahhhhhhh!"* he yelled. *"Ahhhhhhhh."* His fingers gripped the phone so hard he thought he might break it.

"Shhhh. Deep breaths, Neil." Isabella was standing in front of him, holding out her hands in a soothing "calm down" gesture. Neil took some deep breaths in through his nose. He calmed down. He could hear sirens approaching.

"We have to leave, now," he said, getting to his feet and shoving the phone back in his pocket.

"Why?" Isabella said.

"I'll explain in the car. We've got to get after those guys. Jones, are you okay?"

"Merely a flesh wound," he said. "The bullet didn't hit any bones or major arteries. I can drive."

"Whew!" Larry said. "That's good, because no one else here can figure out an English roundabout."

Isabella frowned. "Larry, you drive. Now, help me get Julius in the car."

"Julius?" Neil and Larry said together. They'd never heard him called anything but Jones before.

Isabella smacked her head. "Forget that, *per favore*."

Jones glared at them. "One crack and . . ." He pointed at his leg, and then at Neil and Larry's chests.

"Fine . . . Julius," Larry said.

Jones stood up and winced in pain, but steadied himself.

"There's a clinic nearby. They're waiting for us," Neil said.

Jones shook his head. "No time. They've already got too big a head start. I'll be fine. There's some meds in the back of the van."

"Are you nuts?"

Jones gritted his teeth. "We've got to find Rose. I promised her brother . . ." His voice trailed off.

"That's the real reason you came to London, isn't it?" Neil said. "It wasn't to help us. You knew Rose was in danger."

"I am sick of your patented stupid ego trips!" Jones said, his voice bellowing and menacing. "I spend more time cleaning up after your messes than you deserve. One day, Isabella will wise up and dump you and then we won't be around to save you."

Neil said nothing. The words had hurt. He could feel tears actually start to well up in his eyes. He held up his head and started walking to the van. Then he stopped.

"Look, if they've got Rose, that means they want her to tell them where to go next. She might, and our best bet for grabbing these apes and getting her back is to beat them to it."

"The tower," Larry said.

"If they find whatever clue is there first, then we'll

lose the trail and lose any chance of getting to her," Isabella said.

"Or Lane," Larry said.

"Finding this jewel is the fastest way to find Rose."

Neil walked out the front door. The police were just a block or so away, and the other customers had run off.

Jones rested his arm on Larry's shoulder. Isabella helped him on the other side, and together they all walked out to the van. Jones climbed into the back and opened up a plastic box full of gauze, medicines, and surgical tape.

Larry, the only other one in the group with an actual driver's license, got behind the wheel. "I'm not going to be able to drive anywhere near as fast or as dangerously as Julius—I mean Jones . . . sorry." He was chuckling as he revved the engine.

Isabella sat down next to Neil and leaned in close. "Rose's brother was Jones's best friend growing up. There was some work they did together, and it went badly. Jones became Rose's older brother. I can tell you more later, but I just want you to understand why he was so angry."

Neil nodded. "When does this stupid goose chase end?"

"I believe Rose would say, 'When we find the jewel,' whatever that is," Larry said, inching the car forward into traffic. The police were just arriving at the tea shop behind them.

"How many more letters are there in the stupid clue?" Neil said.

Isabella opened the picture and counted. "One more set. That means one more place we need to visit."

"With the jewel presumably there," Larry said, "or at least the final clue that ties all this together."

Neil was silent for a moment. He was feeling tired and frustrated. Rose was in danger. They were all in danger. He'd been away from his kitchen for days. The thrill of the chase he'd been feeling was now fading fast. London was wearing him thin, like croissant dough that had been pounded thinner and thinner until it was almost transparent.

"What if all this was just a game? Maybe Kemp wanted Shakespeare to search for this jewel, then never find it. Maybe this was a four-hundred-year-old dead end from the start."

Everyone was silent for a moment.

"It's possible," Larry said finally. "But I guess we have to act like it's not. Life's like that sometimes."

"This is getting way too pointy-headed," Jones said from the back. Whatever he'd done to treat his leg had worked. He quickly climbed over the seats and then into the passenger seat in mere seconds.

"You heal fast!" Larry said.

"Hanging around with you morons, I have to," Jones said, undoing Larry's seat belt. "Where'd you learn to drive, blondie? A supermarket? Let a pro get behind the wheel. We're losing time here."

Jones didn't even give Larry time to pull over. He grabbed him with one arm, lifted him over to the passenger seat, and then slid behind the wheel in one fluid motion.

"Wow, did you ever consider a career as a magician?" Larry said. "A sleight of hand like that could make you millions."

"Maybe. Can I cut you in half, or make you disappear?" Jones said. He gunned the engine, and they flew through the other cars like a pro soccer player against a team of toddlers.

CHAPTER TWENTY

TOWERING

Larry looked up the tower on his phone as Jones drove through London. "The Tower of London isn't really a tower. It's actually an ancient fortress, a royal residence and castle. Legend says Caesar himself founded the castle when the Romans ruled Londinium, but the current buildings date from the fourteenth century . . . some older, and some newer."

"So Shakespeare would have seen this tower?" Neil asked.

"It would have dominated the skyline for sure. There are actually a number of different towers, drawbridges set in massive stone walls, and a large grassy courtyard with a bloody past."

"Bloody?

"For centuries it was the go-to place for royal prisoners, whether they were actual enemies or just people who'd ticked off the king or queen. Henry the Eighth had two of his wives beheaded here. There's a plaque, 'nestled into a square of incredibly green grass, that marks the spot where Anne Boleyn's head was severed

in the single stroke of an executioner's sword.' Yikes!"

"Can't wait," Neil said as Jones pulled into the parking lot.

Neil, Larry, and Isabella got out.

"I'll stay here," Jones said. "If they are inside, call me. But I don't think Rose would spill any beans that quickly, so I'll look out for them here. If they do pass me first, they won't make it inside." He cracked his knuckles.

Neil, Larry, and Isabella bought their tickets and walked along a stone bridge toward the entrance.

"Looks like the sort of place you go into but don't come out of," Neil said, looking at the thick walls, turrets, and iron gates.

"I'm pretty sure the tickets I bought are for a return trip," Larry joked.

A man in a red and blue uniform bowed as they walked along the bridge and passed through the stone archway.

"Welcome, my young lads and lasses, to the Royal Palace and Fortress! I am Yeoman John Jaspers."

"We're tourists, just like everybody else," Larry said.

"Um, that's brilliant," said the yeoman. "Of course I had assumed that. From Canada, by your accents."

"Very smooth, Sherlock," Neil whispered to Larry, who just smiled.

The yeoman continued his speech. "There were numerous executions here, and not all executions went well. One time a condemned lord, James Scott, refused to pay his executioner."

"You had to pay your executioner? Doesn't seem very fair," Larry said.

"Here's why you paid. The executioner, his pockets empty of coin, lo and behold, suddenly lost his ability to aim. The first blow went *whack* into Scott's shoulder. Five more whacks later the head was finally off and displayed on London Bridge as a warning to others!"

"To pay the executioner?" Larry called out.

The yeoman rolled his eyes. "No, you great git! A warning not to cross the monarchy."

Neil felt faint. He walked away a few steps and leaned on a large cage.

CAW! CAW!

Neil started. There were live birds inside the cage. Big, black ravens. They were fighting over the remains of what smelled like rabbit.

"Well!" said the yeoman. "I see that you Canadians like to do your own tower tour!" He marched over to where Neil was standing and grabbed him by the arm.

"Honestly, son, you don't want your fingers near those nibblers."

"Weird pets," Larry said, walking over.

The yeoman smiled. "It is said the ravens were first drawn to this spot by the smell of the rotting corpses. They've been here ever since. It's also said that if the ravens ever leave the tower, the country will fall. These days there are always six captive ravens here. Their wings are clipped, but they are well fed."

"Prisoners," Isabella said unhappily.

"Not the first to be

held here, young lady," said the yeoman. "But with a somewhat longer life expectancy."

"Can we maybe skip the standard tour?" Neil said. "It's making me nauseous."

The yeoman frowned. "Fine. What would you like to see, flowers? Kittens? I think we feed those to the ravens in about thirty minutes."

"Ha-ha. Is there anything here from Shakespeare's time?"

"Subtle, Sherlock," Larry muttered.

"Hmm, let me think." The yeoman made an elaborate show of taking off his hat and scratching his scalp. "How about *all of it*!" He shook his head in disgust.

Neil frowned. "I mean weird stuff, maybe from Shakespeare himself. Was he ever a prisoner here?"

The yeoman narrowed his eyes. "Not that I know of. But if prisoners are such a hot topic among you young'uns, I can show you where we kept them. Follow me." He marched toward a flat-walled building. He stopped outside a huge oak-and-iron door.

"This is the Beauchamp Tower. You can go inside yourselves and look around. Of particular note is the first floor, where prisoners were held during the Tudor years. To pass the time before their release or—plug your dainty ears, lad—*executions,* they carved poems and drawings into the very stone!"

"Graffiti? Again?" Neil said.

"Again?" said the yeoman. "Have you been defacing the walls of our fair city?"

"No, no," Neil said quickly. "I just mean that the

English seem to like carving their names into stuff."

"Including annoying tourists," the yeoman said. Then he smiled and stepped out of the way. "Go on up."

Isabella and Larry walked past. Neil started to follow them, then stopped. Yet again, a faint smell of his own cooking wafted on the breeze, even fainter then before. It was also mixed with an odd aroma that Neil couldn't quite place. He licked his finger and stuck it in the air. The breeze was coming from the direction of the front gate. He looked over. Another yeoman was giving a tour. Neil scanned the crowd for a familiar face, or even someone he'd seen at the abbey.

Neil felt a hand on his shoulder. "Too sheepish to enter the tower? It's not haunted. . . . Of course, I'm lying about that part." And with a gentle push the yeoman guided him inside.

Neil could already hear Larry and Isabella talking excitedly ahead of him. Neil soon saw why. The walls were covered with graffiti. Poems, drawing, notes, and prayers were carved into the stone.

"They must have used their fingernails for some of these. This one says, 'Thomas Rooper, 1570.' Wow," Larry said as Neil reached the final step.

"Look at the detail on this one!" Isabella knelt down to get a look at an entire coat of arms.

Neil knelt down beside her and read the words underneath. "'You that these beasts do well behold and see may deem with ease where' . . . um, I'm not sure what that says. . . . Then there are the words 'wife' or maybe 'with' and 'brothers,' and then it just kind of ends."

Isabella said, "As if whoever carved it wanted to say more . . ."

"But didn't have time," Neil said. He knew what that meant.

Larry nodded. "Sad, but it's clearly not the graffito—that's the singular of 'graffiti,' by the way—not the graffito we are looking for."

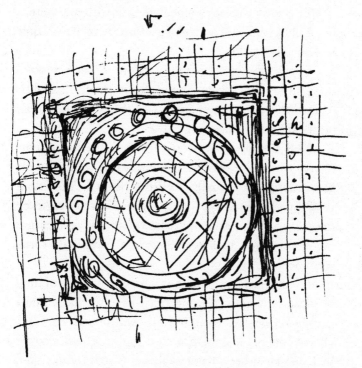

Neil stood up and looked around. There were hundreds of bits of text and images on the walls. "I guess we should split up and look for a sequence of numbers, or maybe some name from Shakespeare, maybe even a quote from Shakespeare."

Neil was also hoping that the group of tourists he'd seen, or smelled, would follow them up the stairs, so he could get a closer look, but they must have been on a different tour.

"Look, it's a zodiac symbol!" Larry said. "Drawn by some guy named Hew Draper. May thirtieth, 1561."

"Could that be Kemp in disguise?" Neil asked.

"It doesn't ring any immediate bells with me, but I'm not a Shakespeare scholar. I wish Rose were here." Larry looked very wistful.

Twenty minutes later they'd done a quick scan of everything. There were dozens of names, but none that seemed to have any significance to the code, the poem, or Shakespeare's plays.

Neil slumped down on the floor. He looked out of the window. The clouds had returned, but a shaft of sunlight was actually breaking through. He imagined for a second how lonely it must have been to be imprisoned here, knowing you were going to die, and being desperate to leave some sign behind that you were here.

He thought of Kemp, imprisoned in a different kind of place, but also knowing that the only way he was going to leave was to attend his own funeral. Neil had almost suffered a similar fate on top of an office tower in Paris. He'd been remarkably calm at the time. Neil thought about that from time to time. Maybe he'd been calm because he'd already left a legacy of great food. The world knew he'd existed.

Suddenly, Neil knew that was why Kemp had put the clue in honey instead of something else. It wasn't just a clue about food, although that was part of it. Kemp had wanted it to survive. He'd wanted someone to find it someday. He couldn't have known it would take so long, but he wanted someone to find it. That also meant that there *was* a jewel at the end of this. Neil was convinced. If Kemp had merely wanted Shakespeare to suffer, he would have burned the key code so that the jewel would remain lost forever.

So what was the clue he'd hidden here?

Neil stared out the window again. The sun had disappeared. No. A shadow had passed across the window. Neil stood up and went to take a closer look. There were dozens of ravens flying up the side of the tower.

"I thought they clipped their wings," Neil said.

Isabella joined him at the window. "Maybe they escaped?"

Larry looked too. "No. Those are just wild birds. They must have found something to eat, probably the garbage from the cafeteria."

Neil watched the black birds disappear.

"Ravens," he said, almost to himself. Then he turned to Larry. "Did Shakespeare talk about birds a lot?"

"Rose would have a better idea, but I can look it up."

"Our guide did say they'd been here as long as the tower itself. Hmmm . . . what if Kemp wanted Shakespeare to think about birds?"

"Meaning?"

"He did want Shakespeare to come here looking for a clue, but we've been thinking about the tower the wrong way."

"How do you mean?"

"Like modern tourists."

"Okay . . . and?"

"Shakespeare and Kemp wouldn't have actually been able to come inside the tower back then unless they'd been imprisoned, or were royalty."

"In other words, we actually have to take the *real* history into account," Larry said, smiling. "See, you can be a good student."

"Look at the last clue. Rose said Westminster would have been open to tourists, even back in Shakespeare's time. So Kemp had access to the coronation chair."

"And apparently so did every schoolboy for five hundred years."

"But here, Kemp wanted Shakespeare to look for something everybody could see, prisoner or not."

"But the only thing an everyday citizen would have seen here was an execution of a prisoner . . ."

". . . and the ravens who flocked here for the leftovers. Are there any raven references that match the series of numbers on the key code?"

"The next numbers are *IVI*." Larry leaned against the wall and did a quick search on his phone. "Well, yes. But this is weird."

"What?" Neil said, walking over.

"Well, the numbers match this quote from *Othello*:

Thou said'st, it comes o'er my memory,
As doth the raven o'er the infected house,
Boding to all . . .

"That's pretty dark," Isabella said.

"But it doesn't seem weird," Neil said. "He talks about ravens and a house, and we know we're looking for a final place to look for the jewel."

Larry nodded. "Yes, but what's weird is that *Othello* wasn't performed until 1604, the year after Kemp died."

"What?" Neil said. Larry called up a website on his phone and held it up for Neil and Isabella to see.

Neil read the screen. "'*Othello* was first performed at Whitehall Palace as part of the November festivities, by the King's Majesty's Players.'"

"King?"

"Yeah, Elizabeth died earlier that year, before the plague hit."

Neil ran his fingers through his hair, frustrated and confused. This was making no sense at all. "Well, are there other raven references in other plays?"

Larry checked his phone again. "Lots. Romeo and Juliet use the term to describe all sorts of lovey-dovey things. Even a character Kemp might have played, Peter, makes a raven reference. But none of them match the numbers on the key code, and that's been a consistent thing."

"Maybe it's another misdirection. Kemp might be using the *Othello* quote to point to a bit from one of those plays," Neil said.

"But how could Kemp know what was in *Othello*?" Isabella said.

Before Neil or Larry could even attempt an answer, they were all distracted by a commotion outside the tower. They ran to the window.

A group of yeomen were chasing one of their own across the lawn. The man's hat flew off as he ran up a set of stone steps, then disappeared behind a stone wall.

"C'mon," Neil yelled. He ran down the steps three at a time. The yeoman who'd given them the tour was walking angrily back toward the tower.

Neil ran up to him. "What happened?"

The man's face was as red as his uniform. "There was an imposter! He had the nerve to lead a tour! But then he called himself a beefeater, and my soldier's radar went up."

"Isn't he a beefeater?" Larry asked, catching up.

"No! Some stupid people might call us that, but no self-respecting member of the Yeoman Warders of Her Majesty's Royal Palace and Fortress the Tower of London, and Members of the Sovereign's Body Guard of the Yeoman Guard Extraordinary, would refer to himself as a beefeater."

"Although it would be shorter," Larry said.

"Call me a beefeater and you'll be shorter by about eight inches!" the yeoman said, pointing menacingly at Larry's head.

He turned back to Neil. "But the clincher was when I took a closer look at his uniform. It wasn't standard issue, if you know what I mean."

"Fake," Neil said.

The yeoman nodded. "Look at the hat, for example. The cloth is blue, but not the right blue. And the stitching!" He held it up, clearly disgusted. Neil couldn't tell the difference, but Isabella took just one look and shook her head.

"Not bad seamwork, but the cloth is a much lower quality. It's made to look realistic, but at a fraction of the cost."

"So where are you holding him?"

"Nowhere," the yeoman said, clearly angry. "He jumped over the wall and ran away."

The man waved an angry fist in the air, shaking the hat.

Neil noticed something about the hat. It smelled faintly of potatoes and pee.

CHAPTER TWENTY-ONE

GRASPING AT STRAWBERRIES

Jones hadn't seen anything suspicious in the parking lot, or anyone resembling the Crayfish brothers or Rose entering or leaving the tower. In fact, he seemed genuinely angry that he'd missed the chase for the imposter inside the gates. He'd even banged his hands on the steering wheel.

Neil thought the steering wheel looked a bit bent, but Jones seemed to have little trouble using it to guide the vehicle through the streets of London. Not that they had any idea where they were going.

"*Othello? Othello?* It makes no sense!" Neil said. "There's no food, no nothing, no misdirection. This is stupid."

"Isn't that your particular area of expertise?" Jones grumbled.

"Do you want to find Rose or not?" Neil said, and immediately regretted it. Jones gripped the steering wheel so hard it seemed to bend even more.

"I thought I made it clear earlier that I am tiring of your act."

Neil considered how he and Jones had been fighting a battle for the past couple of days. He knew Jones had hurt him, but he also knew Jones cared about people, people such as Isabella and Rose. Neil was finding out that this was something that mattered to him more and more.

He uttered two words he'd rarely uttered in his life: "I'm sorry." It was said in barely a whisper, but it stunned everyone in the van. Neil took a deep breath. "Look, I know I'm not always the easiest person to, well, get along with. I don't mean to put us in danger. Jones . . . I'm doing my best to help find Rose."

Jones actually turned around to look at Neil, a confused look on his face. "I—I . . . okay" was all he could sputter before the honking of an oncoming cabbie yanked his attention back to the road.

Isabella gave Neil's hand a tight squeeze. "*Grazie.* Neil, it means a lot," was all she said. Neil thought he saw tears in her eyes.

Neil hadn't known saying sorry—and actually meaning it—could have such an effect. "I still think beating everyone to the jewel is the best way to solve this whole mess and get Rose back safely."

Jones didn't say anything. But he hit the gas, and they sped on faster through the traffic and over the bridge.

Neil's phone started ringing. This time it was the theme from *Batman*, which meant Sean Nakamura had finally gotten around to doing some police work.

"I see you finally got around to doing some police work," Neil said.

"You have a way about you, Nose," Nakamura said. "It's not endearing."

"Sorry," Neil said, trying out his new word.

"You feeling okay?" Nakamura said. "Or is this an imposter?"

Neil ignored that. "The Queen already assured me it wasn't her police force shooting at us."

"Thanks for passing that on to me," Nakamura said, now annoyed. "Anything else I wasted time finding out about?"

"She said Lord Lane was in financial trouble."

"Okay, so that's strike two. Did she mention that the police also think he might be dead?"

"Um, no . . . no, she didn't say that."

"The blood on the clothes was definitely his."

"Why didn't the Queen mention that?" Neil wondered.

"Can't say. I would suggest the Queen has a lot at stake here and perhaps is only willing to share information on a need-to-know basis."

Neil already knew that was true. "Thanks, Nakamura," he said.

"Thanks? Nose, seriously, go see a doctor. There's something wrong with that head of yours."

"Ha-ha. Actually, can you do one last thing for me?"

"I do have a job, you know."

"The Crayfish brothers. They have Rose. Do you know anything about them?"

"*The* Crayfish brothers? I don't even have to make a call for that info. They are notorious for loan-sharking, blackmail, murder, and way worse stuff than that."

"Worse?"

"They are dangerous. Be careful."

"Too late. Hey, since that was so easy, can you do one last *last* thing for me?"

Nakamura sighed.

"Can you check in on Angel and see how the restaurant is doing?"

"I ate there last night. Everything was fine, absolutely fine. Gary has a way with salmon!"

"Nobody suspicious hanging around?"

"Not when I was there."

Neil let out a sigh of relief.

"Although Gary said he did see a guy taking pictures outside."

Neil sat bolt upright.

"Pictures?"

"Gary said he was probably a tourist or something. Hey, sorry, Neil. I have another call coming in. Gotta run. See you later."

"Wait!" Neil said, but Nakamura was gone.

"Everything cool?" Larry said.

"Um, yeah," Neil said, but the phone call left him rattled a bit. Who was the man with the camera? He'd have to call Gary or Angel later. "He says everything's cool at home. But the police feel that Lane is possibly dead."

"Well, that probably explains why the Crayfish have decided to take a more proactive role in the search for the jewel. They can't rely on Lane to hand it over to cover his debts."

"Let's find it first and end this thing," Neil said.

Larry was poring over the script for *Othello*, trying to make some sense of the final clue.

"There's only the one raven reference in the play. Othello and Iago are talking about cheating. Iago mentions a handkerchief. It's a bit of fore-shadowing in the play."

"Foreshadowing?" Isabella said.

"It means that he's hinting at stuff that's com-ing later. Later on Othello accuses his wife of cheating on him, and the proof is a handkerchief she left behind. Except she was set up. Othello still kills her."

"This isn't a comedy, I take it?" Neil said.

"One of the bleakest tragedies, actually, even more so than *Richard the Third*. In that one you want Richard to get his butt kicked, but in this one you're hoping things won't be horrible. It's a shift in Shakespeare's plays. You see, he uses the same kinds of situations in his comedies. But things work out well in the end in those."

"*All's Well That Ends Well*," Jones said, naming one of Shakespeare's funniest plays.

Larry smiled. "Jones, you *can* read! That does pretty much sum up his comedies. But in the tragedies, the exact same misunderstandings, mistaken identity, and articles of clothing lead to horrible results. There's not much difference between comedy and tragedy."

Neil thought about this. The last clue was meant to sting, to make Shakespeare stop thinking of comedy and start thinking of tragedy.

"Kemp was a clown, right?"

"That's what Rose said. Kemp acted the goofy roles in Shakespeare's plays, and then Shakespeare stopped writing those roles after they had their falling-out," Larry said.

"So what if that's Kemp's final point? He's saying to Shakespeare, 'Comedy is over for you, now that I'm gone from the troupe.'"

Larry considered this. "And just like Othello's wife—Desdemona was her name, by the way—he's suggesting that he's been set up."

"He's defending his innocence by making this the final clue about a mistake—a horrible, horrible mistake."

"If only Kemp, or Shakespeare, had said 'I'm sorry,' perhaps things would have turned out differently," Isabella wondered.

Neil nodded. "Let's put aside the question of how Kemp knew about *Othello* and just assume he did somehow. The reason Othello accuses his wife is a handkerchief. Maybe Kemp is making some fashion-related hint?"

"After all the food clues?" Isabella said.

"Well, let me look at the play again." Larry searched for the word "handkerchief." "It comes up like thirty times in the play. But, whoa . . ."

"What?" Neil said.

"A few scenes later, as they get closer and closer to the tragedy, Iago is describing the handkerchief to Othello, and Othello knows it's the right one because it has stains on it from strawberries."

"The same food Richard the Third was eating in the last clue?" Neil said.

"Exactly. But here the red stain of the strawberries is foreshadowing the red of the blood that will be spilled over this tragic handkerchief."

Neil tapped his fingers on the car seat. What was Kemp getting at with this clue? Thinking as someone walking around five hundred years ago had helped him see the tower in a different light. "Maybe we need to stop thinking like modern people and put ourselves into their brains."

Larry snapped his fingers. "What if Kemp and Shakespeare didn't fall out over any of the stuff we think of as normal today?"

"Like?"

"Well, we assume they argued and broke up over money or power, or some battle for control of the Globe Theatre."

"But Shakespeare is all about those problems. They aren't just modern," Isabella said.

"Yeah, but this last quote is about infected houses and the plague and tragic misunderstandings, not power or money or that other stuff."

"So?"

Larry moved to the edge of his seat in excitement.

188

"It might be crazy, but what about this? Kemp is sick. He's coughing blood into a handkerchief or something. Shakespeare sees this, and like anyone else from that time period, he panics. Illness, the plague—this is *the worst* thing that can happen, right?"

"Understandable," Isabella said. "It sounds awful."

"Exactly, so Shakespeare exiles Kemp. He maybe even rats him out to the health authorities. Kemp gets banned from public spaces. He's not allowed to work for weeks or maybe months. That essentially finishes Kemp's career."

"Which might explain why he was living in a seedy part of town," Neil said.

"As a possible plague victim, he's refused food and medical treatment and thrown out of the high society of the theater. Maybe he's even locked up in a house."

Neil nodded. "But this first time, Kemp doesn't die. They only thought he had the plague."

Larry clapped his hands, his mind racing. "And he's so cheesed at Shakespeare that after he gets out of the 'infected house,' he sets out to ruin him. He steals one of his jewels and hides it as a kind of revenge. But then he does actually get the plague, and dies before he can deliver his poem."

They sat in silence for a few minutes, considering Larry's idea. "It's not actually that crazy," Neil said at last.

"High praise, golly, thanks," Larry said. "It's the best I can do in a tea-drinking country."

"It does tie in a lot of the references. It might even explain his fixation on food, something that had become a luxury for him."

Isabella joined in. "And why he goes on this *pazzo*—crazy—dancing journey. He's desperate for fame, attention, a way to get back into that world."

Jones slowed down the car and pulled into a side street and parked.

"Why are you stopping?" Neil said.

"Did you see something? Are we being followed?" Isabella asked.

"No," Jones said. "I actually think Larry's theory might be right."

"Great!" Larry said. "So let's get moving!"

Jones leaned back in his seat and turned off the ignition. "Think just a tiny bit more."

"I might actually need a coffee for that," Larry said. "I'm exhausted."

Isabella slumped in her seat as well, clearly more used to Jones's body language. "*Sì*, I understand. There's just one last problem. We have absolutely no idea where this last clue is telling us to go!"

CHAPTER TWENTY-TWO

BAKING

Neil and Larry stood on a windy corner in North London. Neil looked up and saw the nearby tube station was Baker Street. Home of Sherlock Holmes and Dr. Watson.

"Well, that's ironic," Neil said, as he watched the dark SUV drive off into the distance. "Since we're stuck with a mystery we can't unravel."

Jones had suggested a solution to their impasse. He and Isabella were done with the search for the jewel. They were off to look for Rose, and Rose alone. It was now up to Neil and Larry to figure out what Kemp had stolen and where he'd hidden it. If that led them to Rose, then all the better. But chasing a clue with no obvious meaning was just a waste of time right now.

It began to rain.

"I wish we'd asked Jones for an umbrella," Larry said.

"I wish we'd asked for a vote," Neil said.

Larry shook his head. "It would have been two-two. Tie goes to the enormous scary guy with the keys to the car and the leg wound that makes him even more ornery."

"Two-two? You think Isabella would have voted for the split?" Neil said.

"She went with Jones, you'll notice," Larry said.

Neil said nothing. The SUV turned a corner and disappeared.

"Are you getting the feeling there's more to Isabella's job than she's letting on?" Isabella's mysterious nature was one of the things Neil found so interesting about her. But he was finding himself wondering what she might be up to when they weren't together.

Larry gave Neil a condescending look. "Haven't you ever wondered why a perfume maker has a full-time bodyguard?"

"She always says he's a friend of her mother's," Neil said, knowing as soon as he said this how odd it really did sound.

"Let's talk about that over some dinner. Put that nose to some good use, cuz."

Neil sniffed the air, and was happy to discover the smell of some seriously good pork sausages being carried on the wind.

"Good boy," Larry said, patting him on the head. "Which restaurant? Fetch!"

Neil growled like a dog. "It's actually coming from inside that park over there." He pointed to a large field that seemed to have about a hundred soccer fields and a small collection of trees in the middle.

A wisp of smoke rose from the tiny collection of trees and bushes.

"Let's go!" Larry said. A few minutes later they were standing on a pebbled path outside a stone lodge with THE HONEST SAUSAGE written on a sign over the door.

"It looks like it was built by elves," Larry said.

"Don't eat the candy-cane doorway," Neil said, walking past Larry. He opened the door and was met by a rush of incredibly aromatic food and the unmistakable sound of a barista steaming milk.

Larry heard it too and sprinted past Neil.

A few minutes later Neil was sitting with a full tasting platter in front of him and had placed an order for a hundred sausages for the command performance at the palace. Larry was on his fourth cappuccino and wore the most contented grin Neil had seen in days.

Their satisfaction soon faded as they got back down to business.

Neil put down his napkin. "I do think Jones is right that splitting up might give us a better chance to find Rose."

"So let's see where *we* are at." Larry pulled out a map of London. He'd marked the location of the previous clues on the map. "The tower is on the right of the map.

The tavern where Kemp hid the honey is at the bottom. Westminster is on the lower left. Clement's Inn is this bit on the upper left in between them."

"A pattern?"

"Possibly. I was kind of hoping that the places would be on the edges of a circle."

"'Merry Drake goes round the globe,'" Neil quoted.

Larry nodded. "I like circles."

"I remember," Neil said. Larry's knowledge of Japanese *wasan* math—based on circles—had helped them crack their last case.

"And the great thing about circles is that when we don't have all the coordinates, we can still figure out the center with as few as two, and that would help us narrow down our search for the actual final location."

"Really?"

Larry gently tapped Neil's head. "Repeat after me. Geometry. It's a good word. You may have heard it in school once or twice. You sometimes only need to know two points on a circle to figure out the rest of the circle."

It was like Larry was speaking a foreign language, so Neil just nodded.

"So, class, we have all these places so far," Larry said, pointing at all the Xs on his map, "but they are clearly not points on a circle. They might form a square or some pattern we haven't guessed at yet."

"But there's only one more place we need to plot in, right?"

"Yes, but until we know that place, there are millions of possibilities. Triangles, boxes, rectangles, lizards."

"Lizards?"

"Sure. Maybe he drew a lizard on a map and then figured out what places fit."

"Sounds a little weird."

"Look at how his life was falling apart."

"I was talking about you."

"Ha-ha."

"There's got to be some way to figure out this pattern. Rose used all her biographical knowledge of Kemp and Shakespeare to find patterns and crossovers in the text." Neil looked at the map. "Maybe we should go see some Shakespeare."

"What do you mean?"

"Well, remember the theater where you found Lane's clothes?"

"Yes."

"They were putting on *Macbeth*. It's one of Shakespeare's greatest plays. There's even a scene with witches making soup with eyes of newt and stuff. We should head back there. Maybe we'll see some other clues, or at the very least it will get us thinking about Shakespeare."

"If they are still doing the play," Neil said.

"As they say in theater, 'the show must go on.' Heck, they even continued to put on plays when the Germans were bombing London during World War Three."

Neil blinked. "I thought there were only two world wars."

Larry smiled. "It was a test. Glad to see some useful knowledge is sinking through that thick skull of yours."

The theater was, in fact, open for business, but Neil and Larry seemed to be the only ones there. Larry paid for their tickets—from a young and very cute woman in the box office—and they walked into the theater.

"Her name is Cordelia," Larry said.

"She seemed pretty talkative."

"I think she's bored. She said we're the only two people to buy tickets so far."

"I thought you only had eyes for Rose right now," Neil joked.

"'Let every eye negotiate for itself and trust no agent; for beauty is a witch against whose charms faith melteth into blood.'"

"I have no idea what that means."

"It just means that the world is an interesting place, and don't ever limit your horizons."

"I'll bet it does. I'll ask Isabella for a translation later."

Larry gulped and quickly changed the subject. "I wonder if they sell coffee?" Larry said, climbing the stairs in the foyer in search of a concession stand. "Maybe some Yorkie bars and treacle tarts as well!"

"So who is this Macbeth guy anyway?" Neil said as they reached the first floor.

Larry smacked Neil on the head with the program.

"*Ouch!* What was that for?"

"You goofball. You never say that name in a theater."

"What name, Macbeth?" Neil said. Larry smacked him again.

"It's considered bad luck. Inside a theater you refer to it as 'the Scottish play.'"

"That's the stupidest thing I've ever heard. What do the actors call Macbeth in the play? The Scottish guy?"

Larry responded by smacking Neil again.

"Stop that!" Neil said, defending himself from another swing of the program.

"Fine. Actually, you're right. It is a bit of a silly tradition."

"Was that the play they were putting on at the Globe when it burned or something?"

Larry shook his head. "Nope. That was *Henry the Eighth*. Remember, Rose told us about the cannons. No, there was a staging of the Scottish play about fifty years ago or so where the lead actor died during rehearsal, there was something else like an electrical fire, and I can't remember what else. Voilà, a curse. Actors are a superstitious lot."

Neil stopped for a second and looked around. "Speaking of actors, and audiences, where is everybody? This is the emptiest theater I've ever been in. It's weird, though, because I do smell food."

"Popcorn? Coffee? Popcorn with coffee?"

"No, weirder than that, as appetizing as it sounds. It smells like roast chicken, some potatoes, and maybe even some fruit—berries."

"Sounds delicious. I'll tell you what. The play doesn't start for another fifteen minutes. I'm going to run back outside and grab a coffee or, gag, yet another tea. I'll be right back."

"Okay," Neil said. "Make sure you have your cell phone. I'll go find us some seats."

Larry was off like a shot. Neil heard him bounding down the stairs, hollering a loud "huzzah" as he passed Cordelia again, and then the doors closed.

Neil turned his attention back to the smells coming from inside the theater. A heavy red curtain separated the corridor from the seating section. It was closed. Neil assumed an usher would come out just before showtime.

Where was everybody? Neil was starting to feel uncomfortable. Perhaps the ushers had already seated the other guests and then closed the curtains. Maybe Larry and Neil were late, not early. Neil wasn't a big theatergoer, so he wasn't completely certain of the protocol.

He took out his phone and dialed Larry to tell him to hurry back; then he snuck his head around the curtain. It was pitch-black inside.

Larry answered the call. "Neil. Hold on—I'm just paying the lovely Juliet for the coffee; I've got to put the phone down for a second."

At that precise moment, Neil felt a hand over his mouth and smelled the unmistakable odor of chloroform. The last thing he heard before losing consciousness was the click of a lock, and the sound of Larry calling his name from somewhere in the distance, followed by a heavy foot crushing his cell phone.

CHAPTER TWENTY-THREE

MENACING MENU

Neil awoke, his head lurching from side to side. He could make out faint lights in the gloom, but they were spinning around in circles. He closed his eyes and fought the urge to throw up.

He lost the fight.

Instead of leaning over far enough to throw up away from his lap, he found he could only lean forward a few inches. Ropes held his arms tightly to his chest, and the ropes kept his body bound to an uncomfortable chair.

A familiar voice came at him from the swirling lights. "Ah, Chef Flambé. I see that you are awake. A pity you've ruined your trousers, but far better than throwing up on the wonderful banquet I have prepared for your funeral."

Neil could smell food, but it was coming faintly from somewhere in the room, not from a table in front of him.

"Lord Lane!" Neil spat. "I thought you were dead."

The man gave a high, long laugh. "Lord Lane *is* dead! You fool!"

Neil could hear footsteps as the man circled around him, but he was still too sick to open his eyes.

"I can smell honey in your hair," Neil said. "Your voice is the same!"

"Tsk, tsk. Young boy. Lord Lane was long dead before we ever met at your charming little dump of a restaurant. How would you know what the real Lord Lane even looked like?"

Neil tried again to open his eyes to see the man's face, but a rush of nausea forced him to shut them again.

"Who are you, then?" Neil croaked.

"The name is Cullen Skink."

"The actor on the poster?" Neil said.

"The very same. You see, Neil, Lane was a very large backer of my career. He built theater after theater to try to hit the big time. But he had a penchant for picking bad theaters. They all needed millions in renovations; some were condemned before we could even put on a show."

"Sounds like all he did was pick a bad actor. You must stink for him to keep losing money on you," Neil said.

"Not at all. He needed me to help him with his master plan."

"His master plan? Building theaters?"

"It was never about the plays, or his love of theater, much as my patron loved Shakespeare."

"What was it, then?" Neil needed to stall for time. There was no way he could muster the energy to escape, but Larry must be on his way.

"Long ago, Lane bought a building, a dilapidated building, a dump. He wanted to make a theater for a special person in his life. But when they started digging the foundation, they discovered an even older theater underneath."

"Whoopee," Neil said.

"Whoopee indeed. It was a theater from the time of Shakespeare."

"That must have made headlines," Neil said, still too queasy to open his eyes and see for himself if this was the same man who'd visited his restaurant.

"Yes, but it stopped that project dead in its tracks. In the subsequent excavation Lane discovered something else. There was an iron box that had been buried for centuries in the stone foundation. Inside, Lane discovered a piece of very old metal."

Metal? Neil thought. *That's different from all the other clues.*

"But not just any metal. This had an inscription carved into it. 'Dearest Shakerags. If thou hast discovered this shield, you are not without guile and thine own precious jewel is now close to your right hand. The key is ready for the lock. Master Kemp bows to your propensity for wonder.' A precious jewel? Shakerags? Could that be Shakespeare?"

Neil felt a dawning realization. "Let me guess. It was the final clue."

"*Final* clue? Hmmm. Thanks for that tidbit of information. It makes the picture a bit clearer now."

Neil cursed himself for his stupidity. He struggled with the ropes. But even that little effort left him exhausted.

Skink continued. "Lane didn't go public with the find, as valuable as it would be. He knew from the inscription that it was just one part of a larger mystery."

"With an even bigger payday at the end of the rainbow," Neil said.

"He spent years looking for the other clues. He assumed that they were hidden in the same way. He bought buildings on top of, next to, a block away from all the Elizabethan theaters he could locate. He was obsessed."

"Sound familiar?"

Neil felt a slap across his face. "He lost all his money on this search, always looking for boxes, metal signs, some scrap of evidence left behind by this Kemp."

"But he never gave up the search," Neil said.

"He borrowed money from some incredibly disreputable characters. Perhaps you have met them. They also have a propensity for wonders, such as the oh-so-useful chloroform, and more . . . persuasive techniques."

"And now they are helping you search for the jewel?"

Skink merely chuckled, then stood up and walked

away from Neil. Neil heard him fiddling with some sort of bucket or canister.

"So let me guess, Skink, you're going to keep me tied up here until I tell you the solution to the rest of the code?"

"Tsk, tsk. So naive. My very close friend Rose has already filled me in on the code. She and I are very appreciative of your help."

"Nice try," Neil said. "Rose would never work for you."

"Such loyalty to someone you met only this week? Pathetic and, in keeping with Shakespeare, tragic." His voice seemed distracted, as if he were answering Neil but concentrating on something else. Neil heard him moving some chairs.

"You're lying!" Neil shouted, trying to rivet Skink's attention back onto him.

Skink didn't respond right away. "She does an incredibly realistic impression of the Queen. You should hear it. Oh wait, you have!"

"You're lying!" Neil said, but he wasn't sure. He had trusted the voice on the phone almost immediately. Her knowledge of the dinner with Lane had just clinched the deal. What if it had all been just an elaborate sting operation?

"What have you done with her?"

"I married her more than a year ago. Don't tell that lummox Jones. He'll be very angry, and I haven't had a chance to kill him yet. It'll be easier if he's not agitated."

Neil heard the telltale sound of a screw-top lid being removed. Skink was pouring a liquid over the stage. Neil didn't need a supersensitive nose to realize immediately that it was gasoline.

"Lane isn't just dead. You killed him!" Neil could hear the panic in his voice.

Skink chuckled. "I had no choice. Lane had become a liability. He had to go, so that I could take over the search for the jewel without his enemies at my heels." Skink was getting farther and farther away. Neil tried yet again to open his eyes. He could see Skink climbing quickly up the stairs toward the curtained entrance, unrolling some kind of string from a spool as he went. A fuse, Neil realized. Skink was now too far away for him to get a clear view.

"You won't get away with this!" Neil yelled, all the time straining against the ropes.

Skink gave an evil laugh and then was gone.

"Skink. Skink! *Skink!*" Neil yelled. Then he heard a low hissing noise from back up the stairs. Skink had lit the fuse. Neil could still smell the gasoline. In just seconds he was going to be burned alive.

Frantic, he struggled with the ropes, but it was no use.

"*Help!*" he yelled, certain no one could hear him. He gritted his teeth and tried standing up. His legs felt like jelly, but the hissing was growing nearer and nearer by the second.

His legs gave way, and he and the chair fell to the surface of the stage. He could see the flickering light of the burning fuse making its way down the steps. In a few seconds it would hit the stage. Neil kicked and kicked.

Then he felt a cool breeze next to his face, followed by a loud *thwack!*

He braced himself for the inevitable explosion and flames. But the hissing had stopped. Neil opened his eyes and waited for the room to stop spinning. He looked down at his feet. A large knife was sticking out of the front of the stage, just a few feet away. It had cut the fuse, just before it would have reached the gasoline.

"Larry!" Neil called. "Larry!"

"Neil!" It was Larry. Neil heard him running across the stage.

"I'm sorry it took me so long to get inside. Cordelia was gone when I came back with the coffee and all the doors were locked. I remembered the stage entrance we'd gone through the other day, but boy did it take me forever to jimmy the lock."

Larry cut the ropes and helped Neil sit up.

"The knife was lying on a table of props at the back," he explained. "Now, see what happens when you don't say 'the Scottish play' inside a theater? Think, you goof-ball." But Larry was beaming as he said this.

Neil felt tears of joy and relief streaming down his face.

Larry seemed shocked. "Hey, Neil. You're okay. I'm here. Man, when did you get so emotional?"

Neil couldn't answer. He just shrugged. "I don't know," he finally croaked. When *had* he become so emotional? He suddenly missed his younger self, the cocky, always-sure kid who could face anything.

But now Larry smiled at him. "It's cool, cuz. Truth is, it suits you."

"How?" Neil wiped his eyes.

"Look. You've seen a lot of weird stuff for a teenager, okay? I've been waiting for a little emotion to creep through that gruff cheffy exterior. There've been glimpses before, but this is good. Don't hold back anymore."

Neil nodded and let the tears flow again.

"Okay, hold back now, Neil. We gotta move," Larry said.

Neil laughed and took a deep breath, filling his lungs with air. "But if you tell Amber and Zoe, I'll kill you. The last thing I need is two employees who think their boss is a human being. I can't afford it."

"Nice to see the old Neil isn't totally gone," Larry said, laughing and helping Neil to his feet.

Neil steadied himself on Larry's shoulder as they walked toward the back entrance. "We need to get back in touch with Jones and Isabella."

"Okay. But first, can we buy you some new pants?"

CHAPTER TWENTY-FOUR

EGG ON HIS
FACE MAN

L ane *is* dead. Rose is working with this crazy actor
named Cullen Skink. Apparently she has been this
whole time." Neil prepared for a crashing punch or at least
a devastating glare from Jones.

Jones just closed his fingers into a tight fist, released
them, and repeated the motion over and over. "Well, I'd
like to say I'm surprised." He stood up and stormed away
through the front doors of the hotel.

Neil, Larry, and Isabella were left standing in the
lobby.

"This is insane," Isabella said, clearly furious.
"Insane!"

"I'm sorry, Isabella; I know she was a friend of yours.
But I've been going over what Skink told me, and it
does make sense. The Queen's call right after Rose got
kidnapped, telling me not to go to the police. That was
Rose."

"No." Isabella shook her head.

"The cops were actually after her, not the Crayfish. She staged her own kidnapping."

"No," Isabella said again.

"She was using us to help her figure out the code. Once we'd discovered it had to do with food, she needed to keep us around. Now she and Skink are going to piece the final clues together, and we've lost."

"I said *no*! *Impossible*."

"Jones seems to think it's possible," Larry said.

Isabella let out a long sigh. "That is because Jones wants to believe the worst about Rose, always. After her brother died, she did some awful things. Illegal things. She was a very wild person when she was younger."

"How I wish I'd known her then!" Larry said, which got him a step on the foot from Isabella.

"This Skink was lying to you," Isabella said firmly.

"Skink told me this as he got ready to kill me. It was information he thought I'd take to my grave! If it hadn't been for Larry, he'd have been right."

"Hmph! And Jones said he *wished* he were surprised. That is not the same thing as saying he believes it."

"I didn't know Jones was so grammatically precise," Larry said, getting another

jab on the foot from Isabella. "Luckily, I bought these great steel-toed Docs when we got Neil his new pants!"

She gave him a swift jab in the ribs with her finger. "Next time get the steel-toed shirt as well."

"Well, I'd better get some sleep," Neil said. "I'm exhausted."

Isabella yawned. "It has been a very rough few days." Neil hadn't mentioned the crying to Isabella, but she gave him a softer kiss than usual on the cheek. He was a bit taken aback by her tenderness, and how warm it made him feel. He kissed her cheek, then stepped back to gaze into her eyes.

She was so beautiful.

"Okay, any more of that and I'll be puking on my pants!" Larry said. "C'mon, chef boy. Time for some shut-eye."

Neil awoke the next morning feeling unexpectedly refreshed. The jet lag had finally gone away, or maybe it was the lingering effects of the chloroform, but he'd slept straight through, untroubled. Maybe it had been the kiss from Isabella. It had certainly been his last thought before falling asleep.

"Time for breakfast!" Larry said, jumping out of bed and practically leaping into his rumpled clothes. He ended with a blue baseball cap and a loud "tada!"

"If there were a medal for quick dressing, you'd win the gold," Neil said.

"A chef complimenting my dressing!" Larry said, bowing.

Neil took a little longer to shower, and then finally got dressed.

They made their way down the stairs to the smell of a traditional English breakfast of blood sausage and eggs, with rashers of bacon and good strong tea to wash it down.

Neil sniffed the air and felt an immediate declension in his spirits. "Frozen sausage? Canned milk? Sliced bread? They lied on the check-in form. This was supposed to be a foodie hotel. And the coffee isn't that fresh either."

"Coffee?" Larry yelled, and was off like a shot. Neil's mood worsened with each step. It wasn't just the greasy food that awaited him at the bottom of the steps. He ran

back the conversation with Skink in his head and the mounting evidence that Rose had played him like a stooge.

Breakfast was as lackluster as he'd expected, but at least it was served outside in a little courtyard, and the rain had stopped. The tea was warm, and Neil used it to soften the bricklike biscuits he'd decided he could safely consume.

Isabella soon joined them. She looked worried. "I haven't seen Jones all night. Usually he checks in to make sure everything is okay. All I got was one text."

She held up her phone.

Walking. Thinking. Go sleep.

Larry chuckled. "Wow! Four words! That's practically a novel coming from Jones. Maybe it's the land of Shakespeare that's got him being so eloquent."

Isabella sat down, frowning. "Why are you always joking?" She took some tea and added a little milk, eating a biscuit before throwing it away to a waiting sparrow.

Larry smiled and gave a small shrug. "With you two usually walking advertisements for stress and woe, I figure one of us has to look on the goofy side."

"Even when we were on top of that tower in Paris, you were joking," Neil said, remembering one of their most recent brushes with death.

"And even your funeral was funny," Isabella said, smiling despite herself.

Neil gazed at her smile. Maybe Larry had a point about being in a good mood even when things looked bleak.

Larry gulped his coffee and signaled the waiter for a refill. "Look, it doesn't mean I'm not worried. But getting in a low, dark place is, in my humble experience, the worst way to deal with a problem. Your mood becomes just one more problem you have to overcome."

They sipped their drinks in silence for a few moments. Neil could see that he and Isabella were still on the low side of things rather than the goofy.

"Much Ado About Pudding," Larry said suddenly, for no apparent reason.

"What?" Neil and Isabella said together.

"Oh, it was just something that went through my brain. I play word games when things get a little quiet. It keeps the old noggin working." Larry tapped his forehead. "So since food and Shakespeare are the themes of the day right now, I wondered what Shakespeare would call his plays if he were also a chef!" Larry held out his hands as if to suggest this should have been obvious.

Neil turned his attention back to the bird Isabella had given the biscuit to. It was busily nibbling away. Neil thought of the cats that loitered outside his restaurant and felt homesick. He should call Angel. At the very least he should ask about the photographer. He reached for his phone, then remembered it had been destroyed by Skink.

"*Julius Caesar Salad,*" Larry said, chuckling to himself.

Neil looked at Larry for a few seconds and then said, "*Macbroth?*"

"You're supposed to say 'the Scottish plate'!" Larry almost doubled over laughing. "Way to go, Neil! Give us another one!"

Neil racked his brain. "Um. Sadly, that about uses up my knowledge of Shakespeare's plays."

"Really? Nothing else has snuck into your brain during this whole trip?"

Isabella put down her tea. "*Green Eggs and Hamlet,*" she said, laughing.

Larry and Isabella started a pitched pun battle, rattling off titles, laughing, and pointing at each other for particularly good and horrible puns.

"*Measuring Spoon for Measuring Spoon!*"

"*The Taming of the Stew!*"

"*Romeo and Omelet!*"

"*Twelfth Bite!*"

"*A Midsummer's Light Cream!*"

"*The Merchant of Venison!*"

Neil watched, amazed at how much lighter they all felt. Larry might be a goofball, but Neil was glad he was his goofball.

They were so distracted they didn't hear the patio doors opening. But there was no missing the heavy footsteps that marched toward them on the stone tiles.

Neil swung his head around, ready to bolt, in case the Crayfish had found them again and were coming, with Rose and Skink, to finish him off. But it wasn't them; it was Jones, unshaven and with bags under his eyes, coming at them like a demented tank.

"*King Steer!*" Larry said, spying Jones. "Hey, Julius, you look pretty rough. Did you get any sleep?"

Isabella got up and rushed over to hug him, but Jones held up his hands to stop her.

"I think that's his way of saying he needs a shower," Larry joked.

Jones leaned down to meet Neil face-to-face. He frowned, or at least frowned more than he usually did when he looked at Neil.

He slowly shook his head and said, in almost a whisper, "No."

Then he stood up straight and looked at Isabella. "Sorry." Isabella hugged him, shower or not, and smiled.

Jones looked at his watch. "Two minutes," he said, and marched off.

CHAPTER TWENTY-FIVE

SHIELD AND SWORD

Neil wasn't sure what had convinced Jones that Rose was innocent, but Neil was still pretty convinced of the opposite. He'd tried to suggest they were heading for a trap, but Jones shook his head angrily.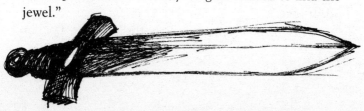

"While we drive to the theater so I can have a look around," Jones said, "you figure out what all the clues mean when you put them together."

Neil tried to remember all the details Skink had told him. Larry drew a picture.

"So this shield, or whatever it was, seemed to suggest Shakespeare now had everything he needed to find the jewel."

"It might have had numbers, but Skink didn't mention them. He just said the jewel was now close at hand, and that the key was ready for the lock."

"I don't get it. We should have all the pieces now. We have all the clues that Kemp refers to in the key code." Larry rubbed his scraggly beard and leaned back in his seat.

"Maybe this was just a cruel trick all along," Isabella said.

Neil looked out the window and saw the marquee for the theater. The posters were still up for *Macbeth*, as if nothing had happened. Maybe Cordelia was in the ticket booth. Maybe she could answer some questions?

Jones didn't stop.

"Hey, Jones, we're passing the theater!" Neil said. He tapped on the driver's seat. "Jones, that's the theater back there!"

Jones said nothing, but drove on.

Neil slumped in his seat and watched the theater disappear. "Why aren't you stopping?" Neil said again to the silent back of Jones's head.

Had Jones seen someone milling around? Were the police back there, cordoning it off? Neil had wanted to call them to let them know what had happened, but Jones had said no to that plan. "If Rose isn't working with them, then it was the real Queen who called you, not Rose, which means involving the local constabulary will only complicate things."

Jones was getting more loquacious the longer they spent here.

They kept driving through the winding London

streets. Finally Jones made a quick right turn and then stopped.

"That's why you didn't stop; we're being followed." Neil turned to look out the back window and finally heard Jones's voice: "Don't let them see you. If we are being followed, we don't want to tip them off that we know."

"Don't we?" Neil said.

"No. We want to trap them and then jump them," Jones said, stealing a quick glance in the rearview mirror.

"Are you sure we want to do that?" Neil said, imagining the guns and knives that might actually be in the pockets of whoever Jones was planning to "jump."

Jones said nothing, but Neil thought he saw his shoulders relax. "False alarm," Jones said. He gunned the engine, then drove a few more blocks.

"So now we can go back to the theater?" Neil said.

Jones shook his head. "No need. Wrong theater."

"What do you mean, 'wrong theater'?" Neil said. "Skink was there. He attacked me. He probably has the shield with him."

"I did a little research last night while you were having your beauty sleep," Jones said. "That wasn't the theater where they found the shield. Think about it for a second."

Neil could have kicked himself. Of course! Skink had said that they'd found the shield in the foundation of Lane's original theater. The theater where they were staging *Macbeth* had been bought later.

"But Skink never told me where the original theater was," Neil said.

Jones didn't say anything, but he did pass a sheet of paper over the seat to Isabella. It was a photocopy of a newspaper article from about twenty years before.

SHAKESPEARE'S FOUNDATIONS UNCOVERED screamed the giant headline.

Then there was a half-page picture of a giant hole with what appeared to be the ruins of numerous brick and stone walls. A caption underneath read, *The remains of an Elizabethan theatre, discovered this week near the Thames.*

Isabella read the first few paragraphs.

"'Lord Aloysius Lane thought he was building a theater to stage Shakespeare; instead he found a theater where Shakespeare staged himself. Lord Lane's company had just completed demolition of a Victorian-era factory.

Local legend always held that an old theater—the Raven—had once stood on the spot. However, there was no physical evidence to support the claim.'"

"It fits with Skink's story so far," Neil said.

Larry beamed. "And it was called the Raven!"

Isabella continued. "'But now that crews have uncovered

the remains, there seems little doubt that the Raven *was* here. Scholars are already flocking to the scene. "It's an amazing discovery," said Lord Lane, looking over the site. "We also found an old iron box, but the contents had rotted with the damp." Scholars such as Oxford's Arthur Gawain say the planned development must stop at once. "This site must be preserved for future generations," said Mr. Gawain.'

"It says the story is continued on page twelve, but this is just a copy of the cover page," Isabella said.

"What's this story down here?" asked Larry. He pointed to a box on the lower left of the front page. The headline read SHAKESPEARE'S IDENTITY QUESTIONED.

Isabella had to hold the paper up close to read the small print. "It's a little smudged from the photocopier, but it quotes some scholar suggesting the Raven shows Shakespeare couldn't have written his plays."

"Why not?" Neil said.

Isabella read the bits she could make out.

"'The Raven was in a wealthy part of town, built before Shakespeare became famous. It's more proof that a commoner such as this Shakespeare could not have written the plays himself. Where would he have found the money to build a theater? No, it's evidence that the real Shakespeare must have been a member of the aristocracy. Too ashamed to admit to the lowly art of theater, he hid his true identity," Lord Lane agrees. "It is obvious!" he told the *Daily Moon*.'"

"That seems a bit snobby," Larry said.

"Exactly," Jones said from the front seat. "That's why Rose has always been such a Shakespeare nut. She detests the so-called deniers."

Isabella nodded. "She doesn't come from what you would call the upper class. She wants to prove that Shakespeare wrote his plays himself, that even people from the so-called lower classes could make it to the top. Perfume is her genius, but proving Shakespeare wrote the plays is her passion."

"That's why the whole story rang a bell last night," Jones said. "I remember Rose mentioning this Raven Theatre. It's also why I know she would never work for someone who thought Shakespeare was too 'lowbrow' to be great."

"So what does the rest of the article say about the Raven?" Larry asked.

"Later," Jones said, pulling the car into a parking lot. "We're here."

"Here" turned out to be a giant hole in the ground. Neil thought it looked like the hole they'd seen in South London, where Kemp had buried the honey. In short, a construction site.

But there didn't seem to have been any construction

on this site since the photo in the paper twenty years before, excluding a chain-link fence that the city had erected around the perimeter.

Jones gave a sharp laugh. "Lane lost a bundle when the protestors and scholars stopped the development. The government refused to compensate him. Told him he should have done more research."

"Couldn't he sell tickets or something?"

"To see what? Old rubble? You trip over this stuff all the time in England. Unless you can come up with a plan to rebuild the theater, like they did with the Globe, you won't make much money."

"Did he try that?"

"They wouldn't let him cover up the foundations."

"And they wouldn't let him use them to rebuild the theater," Larry said. "I believe they call that between a rock and a hard place."

They walked around the entire site. Neil looked over his shoulders nervously, hoping they weren't being watched.

"What are you looking for, Neil?" Isabella said, watching him fidget.

"Skink. Or Rose. Or . . . both." Neil was still reserving his judgment.

"Why would Skink come back here?" Larry said. "Doesn't he already have the shield from this place?"

Neil nodded. "But Skink has been following us this entire trip. I've been smelling my food—faintly, but there—for days. Also, traces of the honey and even the pee from those tweed jackets. Skink was with us at Clement's Inn. He was with us at Westminster and at the tower."

"He was the fake yeoman!" Isabella said. "Of course. The uniform was a theater costume from some play he'd been in."

"I should have trusted my nose more," Neil said.

Jones walked over. "And if Rose were working for him, why would he need to be at any of those places at all? Let's go."

"Go? Aren't we here to look for something?" Larry said.

Jones stared from Larry to the gaping hole. "Good luck," he said. "I only came here to show you the actual location of the last clue, in case it triggered something."

As they walked back to the car, Neil had an idea. He snapped his fingers. "Larry, give me the map." They spread it out on the hood of the SUV.

"So where are we now?" Neil asked.

Jones scanned the map, and then pointed to a spot in South London, near Waterloo tube station. "We are here."

"But if we know that, then we know all the points Kemp wanted Shakespeare to find, right?" Neil said.

"Let see if there's any shape there." Larry pulled out a pencil and drew a line between all the places where Kemp had hidden clues. Then he stood back and looked.

"It looks like a, well, it looks like a snake," Larry said, confused. "Was there ever a theater called the Snake?"

"I doubt it," Jones said.

Isabella looked at the map and then the area around them. "And the last clue was about *Othello* and a handkerchief. How does this place tie in to that?"

Larry and Neil looked at each other.

"Dunno."

"Stumped."

"Maybe the final clue was a really personal one . . . one only Kemp and Shakespeare would understand."

"Maybe this was where they had a fight, or first met, or . . . I have no idea," Neil said. "Or maybe we were wrong about the whole *Othello* thing."

"The snake might seem weird, but is it a pattern?" Isabella said, looking back at the map.

"Yes, but a pretty useless one," Neil said.

Jones honked the horn and they all jumped.

"We can take a hint!" Larry said, folding up the map and sticking it back in his pocket.

Jones honked again.

They tumbled into the car and Jones pulled away. "So, Holmes and Watson, where to now?"

"Either a snake emporium or the zoo," Larry said. "But I think a café first."

Neil felt frustrated, a feeling he was growing sick of. His eye fell on the photocopy of the front page of the *Daily Moon*. He picked it up as a soft drizzle began to fall outside. Something in the upper left of the picture caught his attention. A man, wearing tweed, was posing to the side of the rubble, his blinking face caught in the light of the photographer's flash.

Neil didn't know what Cullen Skink looked like, but the man who stared back at him now was definitely the man he knew as Lord Lane.

CHAPTER TWENTY-SIX

PUDDING IT ALL TOGETHER

They stopped for lunch at a remote bistro. Jones sat keeping his eyes on the door and his hand near a mysterious bulge in his coat pocket.

Neil had brought in the photocopy of the newspaper story, and Larry had the map spread out on the table. "That's Lane," Neil said, pointing out the picture to Larry and Isabella. Isabella had never met Lane, but Larry had to admit the resemblance to the man who'd eaten at Chez Flambé.

"But it's a pretty fuzzy picture. Maybe they look similar."

"Skink said Lane was his patron. He didn't say he was his twin brother. This is the man we met. If Skink was impersonating him at the restaurant, there's no way he'd have looked so exactly like him."

Larry shrugged. "He is an actor, so maybe he was made up really well?"

Neil considered this. "Are there any pictures of Skink online?"

Isabella did a search on her phone. There were only a handful of hits, and most were for posters advertising plays he was in, followed quickly by horrible reviews and notices of cancellation.

"Apparently he's not successful enough to warrant anything other than a few action shots, in incredibly elaborate costumes," she said.

"Made up as an old man?" Neil asked.

"Not really. He's dressed in a donkey's head in this one," Larry said, pointing to a still from an outdoor performance of *A Midsummer Night's Dream*.

Isabella scrolled down the page. "He's here as well, in *Much Ado About Nothing*, but he's in a huge false beard and wig. You can't even see his eyes through all the makeup."

"Both shows closed after one night," Larry said. "Then, and this is interesting, the theater for *Much Ado* burned down."

"Well, he's consistent, anyway," Neil said. "Consistently bad. Maybe Skink lied. Maybe it was Lane who came to the restaurant, but Skink killed him when he got back. Maybe Lane told Skink about the key code or something, but then Skink killed him after we got here?"

"That blood you found on the coat did look pretty fresh," Larry said.

"And then he was going

to burn down the theater to get rid of the evidence, but we found it first and alerted the police."

"But then where was Lane's body?" Isabella said.

"Maybe he was there when we saw the clothes and got the body out before the police arrived?"

"Or he called the Crayfish to come and shoot us before we could call the police," Neil said.

"It's a possibility," Larry said.

"But why lie to me?" Neil said.

"When I find him, I'll ask him," Jones said in an even voice that sent shivers down Neil's spine.

Isabella poured some tea for everyone. "Well, there's some good news, I suppose. If *we* can't find a pattern to lead us to the jewel, then Skink is probably having the same problem."

"Yeah, that's some really good news," Larry said. "I'd hate to hear what the bad news is this time." He chugged the tea, shuddered, and turned his attention back to the map. "There has to be a clue hidden in here, but I can't figure out what it is."

Neil thought back to the inscription Skink had described on the shield. "It says there's a key that is ready to go into the lock. It doesn't say that the mystery has been unlocked already."

"So there's still more to figure out." Larry nodded. "No wonder Shakespeare hated this guy. I even wish I could go back in time just to kick his butt."

"Every single thing we've encountered has been a misdirection, leading to something else. So what could this pattern lead to?" Neil asked.

Larry shrugged.

Neil reread the original key note. "We figured out that the clock and robes and stuff all linked to different places in the plays."

"Tasteless gruel is a reference to the plays themselves," Isabella said.

"So maybe the Drake thing is a reference. The globe is important, maybe?" Neil asked.

"Yeah, but all the points on the map don't make a circle, or an oval, or any globe-shaped thing!" Larry said.

"Well, how about the Globe Theatre? We keep dismissing that, but maybe that is the key."

"Rose was positive that it wasn't there," Isabella said.

Neil thought that was exactly the sort of thing she would say if she were working against them, but he kept his suspicion to himself.

Larry held his hands up. "Anyway, the original Globe is gone. The replica is on a different spot. If the jewel was hidden there, this has been a long and incredibly dangerous hunt for something that's been gone for four hundred years."

"Cheerful," Isabella said.

Neil rubbed his temples. "Well, maybe Drake is the key. Who was the guy again?"

Larry shook his head disapprovingly. "Well, he's famous, world famous, super famous. But of course you remember that from the *Great Explorers* textbook you picked up from school."

"I have a *Great Explorers* textbook?"

"You've been using it to prop up the dishwasher."

Neil smiled. "Oh yeah. It's a great book."

"Anyway, Drake was an explorer. He was one of the

first captains to circumnavigate the globe. He did it in 1580 and became gigungously famous."

"Gigungously? Is this a real word?" Isabella said.

Larry beamed. "It should be. I made it up. Shakespeare used to do that all the time. He invented 'majestic,' 'mountaineer,' and, get this, 'skim milk'!"

"You're kidding," Neil said.

"Nope. I read it in that English slang book. There's also 'luggage,' 'frugal,' 'lackluster,' 'dauntless' . . ."

"Okay, okay. Got it. I'm more confused by 'circumnavigate.' Did you make that one up as well?"

Even Isabella groaned this time.

"It means to go around things, in a circle . . . like the earth?" Larry said, making a fist with his left hand and then using his right pointer finger to go around in a circle. "See, my hand is the earth, and my finger is a ship, going around and around."

A vague shadow image of an actual globe somehow presented itself to Neil's imagination. "Wait. If he tried to sail around the middle like your finger, wouldn't he eventually crash into something?"

Larry threw up his hands. "Well, of course he didn't go in a real circle."

"But you said circumnavigate meant he went in a circle."

"Not a literal circle. Drake went all over the place. He started from England, then went around, I don't remember exactly, South America and then . . ." Larry stopped. He looked down at the map. "Neil. You're a genius."

"I've been trying to tell you that for years," Neil

said. He expected a snarky comeback, but Larry had his phone out next to the map and was frantically looking from the screen to the map and back again. He smiled and started patting his pockets. "Shoot," he said.

"What is it?" Isabella said.

"Does anyone have a pen or a pencil? I can't find mine."

Jones reached across and handed Larry a silver pen, not for a second taking his eyes off the front door.

"Jones, you have good taste! I'll make you and the pen proud!"

Larry took off the lid and started carefully drawing small dotted lines across the map. After a few minutes he leaned back in his chair. His arms fell to his sides and he shook his head, still smiling. "Kemp, you evil, evil *snake*," he said.

"It *is* a snake pattern?" Isabella said.

"Nope. Just written by one. Look."

Neil and Isabella looked at the map. Larry had changed the dotted line that connected the places they'd found clues. He had added an arched dotted line that connected the Raven and the tavern where Kemp had died. It rose to a point between them, like a mountaintop. The peak was just north of the Thames, between the Southwark and Blackfriars Bridges.

"I know why you drew the lines from the snake pattern. They link all the places we found clues. But why does Mount Everest rise up suddenly?" Neil asked.

"Remember when I said you were a genius?"

"I'll be ordering the quote on a me-shirt as soon as we get back home."

"You were right about Drake. He's the key, but the globe was a misdirection, of sorts."

"Meaning?"

"He *didn't* go around the globe in a circle. He went down to the bottom of South America first; then he rose back up again and headed toward Asia." Larry took the pen and drew tiny arrows on the dotted line to show the direction of Drake's journey.

"He started at the peak of the mountain, England, and then down and then back up again and then down again below Africa . . ." He drew more arrows.

Neil got it. "And then back up to England to finish the trip!"

"It took Drake three years, and the route was put on all the English maps, on posters, even on special medals celebrating the achievement. It was the Elizabethan version of putting an astronaut in space."

"And Kemp superimposed the route onto the map of London," Isabella said.

Larry nodded. "And then he hid the clues at the key points where Drake made a major shift in his route."

Neil looked at the map. It was making sense. "If he'd done a globe or circle, Shakespeare could have figured it out without having to search for all the clues."

"Exactly, but with this pattern, even if he guessed that Drake's route was the template, he needed to know the exact location of all the points to figure out where the pattern started and ended."

"Which was England," Neil said, smiling. "The peak of the line."

"So where does it end when you put everything on top of the map of London?" Isabella asked.

"Somewhere around here," Larry said, circling the top of the mountain. "This is where we will find our virtual England and Shakespeare's jewel!"

CHAPTER TWENTY-SEVEN

OLDE ENGLANDE

Jones drove around and around the area Larry had highlighted on the map. Almost all the buildings were modern, including the stock exchange, numerous condos and office towers, and, at the shore of the Thames, the Millennium Bridge, a combination of shiny metal and twisted steel cords.

The only really old thing they saw was Saint Paul's Cathedral, and they saw it a lot. It dominated the skyline for blocks around.

Neil pointed at it as they drove past for the thirtieth time. "Is that the place we're supposed to be looking for? It's certainly old, and big!"

Larry seemed skeptical. "Old, but not Kemp and Shakespeare old. Saint Paul's was rebuilt after the great fire. Christopher Wren was the architect."

"He was named after a bird?" Neil said.

"People get named after all sorts of stuff."

Neil nodded. "Food is like that too. Peach melba was named after a famous opera singer named Nellie Melba. Margherita pizza is named after a famous royal. Names go both ways a lot."

"Wren was a genius, actually. He redesigned and rebuilt most of London after the fire. Under the dome of Saint Paul's there's a whispering gallery. You can sit all the way across from someone, but if they turn their head sideways to speak, even to whisper, you hear it!"

"Whispering Wren. That has a nice *musicale* feel." Isabella took out a notebook and jotted down some notes.

Neil was still looking at the dome. "But Kemp could have hidden the jewel in the original Saint Paul's, right? It was around when they were both here?"

"Sure, but apart from the fact that the church is in the general vicinity of our 'virtual starting point,' there's nothing else to suggest Kemp wanted Shakespeare to look there."

Jones pulled to the side of the road. "I'm done wasting gas. If nothing here is obvious, then let's stop and figure out what we should be looking for." Jones turned his attention back to checking all the mirrors repeatedly.

Larry put a hand on Jones's shoulder. "You know, if you rented a smaller car, or even a *normal* car, we might be a lot less conspicuous."

Jones frowned. "This time I want to be followed. If they do follow us, I can spot them." Then he went back to watching the mirrors.

Larry made a low "cuckoo" noise, and turned back to the conversation. "So, what are we looking for?"

Neil ran all the clues through his head again. "Why did Kemp put the last clue on a shield instead of paper?"

"I assume it was a prop of some kind. Maybe it's a reference to a play?"

"Too bad you never actually saw the shield," Isabella said.

"Maybe Skink was lying about it, trying to coax even more information from you," Jones said.

"All right, I'm fully aware I wasn't very tactful. But I do think he was telling me the truth. He gave up some information too, remember! The shield? What it said? If I hadn't almost died, I wouldn't know any of that."

Neil only saw Jones from behind, but he was pretty certain he rolled his eyes.

Larry got the conversation back on track. "Well, there are lots of references to shields in Shakespeare. The guy liked battle scenes. Swords, maces, axes, pistols, cannons . . . I'm surprised they let kids read the stuff!"

"Maybe the clue is hidden in what the shield actually says?" Neil tried to remember exactly what Skink had told him. He grabbed a pen and wrote on the back of Larry's map.

"Skink said something like, 'Shakerags . . . you discovered this shield,' and then there was one weird bit I remember. It was something about him being 'not without geese' or something."

"Seriously?" Larry said. "That can't be right."

"Then there was something about 'the jewel is now close to your right hand.'" Neil racked his brain. "Then he said the key was ready for the lock and then 'Kemp bows to your propensity for wonder.' That's about what I remember."

"That's even worse poetry than the key code. Well, we can be pretty sure that if someone else wrote Shakespeare's plays, it wasn't Kemp."

"But the original code wasn't that bad. Maybe they go together? You have to think of them together?" Isabella asked.

"I remembered that one sentence because it was so clunky," Neil said. "What do 'you are not without geese' and the bit about the right hand mean?"

They were stumped and sat in silence, while Jones continued his vigilant watch over the mirrors.

Larry continued to scroll through various web pages, looking for some shield reference from a play before 1603. "Hey! This is interesting."

He held up his phone and showed them a crude drawing of what seemed to be a shield with a bird on top of it, and a stripe across it with a sword inside.

"Did you draw that yourself?" Neil said, unimpressed.

"No. Some guy named Ralph Brooke drew it way back in 1602."

Neil was still unimpressed. "Did they have crayons back then?"

"Not that I know of. The reason I'm showing this to you is that this is Shakespeare's coat of arms."

"He had a coat of arms?"

Larry read more of the page. "Yeah. Apparently he applied for it a few years before 1602."

"That's his handwriting next to the picture?"

Larry clicked on a description. "No. It was all written down by the head of the College of Arms."

"Shakespeare went to military school?" Neil asked.

Larry slapped him on the head with the phone. "Not that kind of College of Arms. This one decided if your family was 'up to snuff' and could get a coat of arms, and don't ask if it's a real coat. It's a symbol."

"My family's coat of arms, in Italia, is an eagle rising above a field of flowers," Isabella said, smiling wistfully. "It goes back generations."

"Oh! I didn't know you were so upper class!" Larry said, making a low bow in his seat.

She raised her nose high in mock disdain. "I do not normally associate with such common people . . . but the redheaded one knows how to please our taste buds, so we will make an exception!"

Neil blushed.

Jones snorted.

Larry laughed and bowed again.

"So was Shakespeare as upper class as a Tortellini?" Isabella asked.

"Well, in a way. The website says that he was awarded the coat of arms for the Shakespeare family's support of Henry the Seventh."

Neil looked at the picture of the document. "What's that bit on the top?" Most of the writing was small and scratchy, but three large words were written across the top of the page.

Non Sanz Droict

"Shakespeare apparently requested a motto to go with the falcon and shield."

Isabella looked at the image. "It's an old form of French, I think. It means 'not without right.'"

"Not . . . without . . . right," Neil repeated. He grabbed the map quickly and looked at his version of the last clue. "Wait, *that* was the thing Kemp wrote on the shield. It wasn't 'not without geese.' It was 'not without guile.' That's the phrase Kemp put in that sentence to make it so clunky." He passed the poem over to Larry.

"I bet he wanted Shakespeare to notice how bad the poetry was. Shakespeare would know right away which words were killing the meter and the rhyme. Clever."

Isabella looked too. "I bet he's also using it to take another dig at Shakespeare. I took your jewel, but I was 'not without right.'"

Larry nodded. "It echoes the bit from *Othello* that we tied into the clue about the tower."

"So where is Kemp telling Shakespeare to go with this clue?"

Larry considered. "He knew Shakespeare would get the reference. And, adopting your newfound method of looking at the world through the Elizabethan lens, not a lot of other people would get it."

"Everybody knows Shakespeare now, but back then only he and his closest friends—"

"Or former friends," Isabella said.

Neil continued, "Only they would know what the

reference meant. That's why the clue is less tricky than the others."

Larry tapped his fingers to his chin, thinking. "And there are no references to any play this time, so he's pointing to some place more directly."

"But where?" Isabella said.

Neil hesitated before suggesting his idea. "You said this college wasn't like a school type of college, but was there actually a building or something?"

Larry patted him on the back. "Smart thinking! If the muses are with us on this one, then it will be close." Larry started frantically tapping into his phone. "Bingo! The College of Arms was located at Derby Place, which was about three blocks from here. The original building was destroyed in the great fire in 1666."

"Argh!" Neil said. "We were so close!"

"Chill, cuz. Believe it or not, the records were saved! They were housed in Westminster for a few years and then moved back to the same location, different building, where you can find them today! *Awesome!*"

"Well, what are we waiting for?" Neil said. "We've got the address, and I would love to get this whole mess over with."

"First things first," Jones said, carefully opening his door a crack. "We got company."

CHAPTER TWENTY-EIGHT

STAGED DIRECTIONS

The Crayfish brothers were not known for their subtlety, and they lived up to their reputation as they slammed their car into the back of the van. Neil lurched forward and his head quickly snapped back. He felt dizzy.

Jones turned off the car and practically flew out of his door. Neil watched as he passed the window, a perfect picture of rage and danger. Neil felt sorry for the Crayfish, if they didn't come up with a way to mollify Jones quickly.

Neil turned around and was a little surprised to see both brothers emerge from their car with smiles on their faces and their hands in the air in front of them, clearly suggesting they had no intention of fighting.

Neil rolled down his window a crack, listening. He also noticed the twins still smelled like cheese.

"Now, mate, let's not get too hasty. We would like to make a deal," Reggie said.

Jones said nothing but stopped walking and clenched his fingers into fists.

"You know we've got Rose. She's been very helpful . . . up to a point," Ronnie said. "But she don't know as much as what we hoped."

Jones gritted his teeth. "If you so much as laid a finger on her . . ." He didn't finish the sentence, but his threatening stance sufficed.

Reggie smirked. "She's okay, for now."

"What do you want?"

"A trade. We know Lord Lane was onto something, something big."

Reggie nodded. "He told us so. He kept promising he'd pay us back as soon as he 'discovered the Bard's jewel.' We assumed the Bard was some other richy friend of his."

"Morons," Jones said.

"But then he kept asking for more and more money to help him. More and more and more."

"That's when we got a little tired of being the personal bankers to the esteemed gentleman." Reggie cracked his knuckles.

Neil shuddered. Had that been when they'd decided to kill him? Had they made a deal with Skink to get the treasure and get Lord Lane out of the way?

"So here's our offer to you and your little group of precocious children. You get us the jewel, and we'll let Rose walk free."

Jones was silent. Neil looked out the window and could see the blood vessels of Jones's forehead bulging. He was taking deep breaths, but never took his piercing eyes off the twins.

"Just a simple exchange." Ronnie smiled. Neil thought it looked like the smile on a crocodile.

Jones finally nodded. "Okay."

A horrible thought occurred to Neil. Jones was so sure Rose wasn't working for the bad guys, but what if she was and this was another trap? What if she knew that Neil was closer to finding the jewel and was trying to trick Jones into giving the Crayfish the last bit of information she needed?

Jones, convinced of her innocence, would give that information up to save his friend. It might be noble, but it might also mean that the brothers would lose any barrier to killing them all.

Neil got out of the car. A stiff breeze had come up and shook his jacket.

"Jones. This could be a trap." He turned to the twins. "Not that it matters. We have no idea where the jewel is. Rose is the one who knows Shakespeare."

"Shut up," Jones hissed.

Neil ignored him. "She's everyone's best chance to find the treasure. Give her back to us now and we promise we'll work together. We can split the reward, or treasure, or price or whatever . . ."

Reggie narrowed his eyes. "I should've taken care of you back at the cheese shop."

Ronnie nodded. "You little runt. You know more than you been letting on."

The twins took a step toward Neil and Jones.

This was not going as well as Neil had hoped.

Jones reached for his coat pocket, and the twins stopped, looking less like crocodiles now and more like rabid dogs.

"Don't be a couple of idiots," Jones said, keeping his hand clutched on whatever was in his pocket. "We're in the middle of a busy street."

As if on cue, a police officer turned the corner and saw them all poised for a fight. He walked over.

"What's all this, then?" he said.

Jones carefully pulled his hand out of his coat. He was holding not a gun but his wallet. "We had a bit of a fender bender, officer," Jones said. "I was just getting out my insurance papers so we could exchange information."

The officer cocked an eyebrow but seemed convinced. "Is that the way of things?" he asked Reggie.

Reggie smiled. "Just a bit of a ding. The American

bloke hit the brakes a little hard and we banged into the back. No biggie."

The officer rocked on his heels for a second, considering. He turned to Neil, seeming to notice him for the first time.

"Well, what have we here?"

Neil was desperate to blurt out the truth, to tell them that the Crayfish brothers had kidnapped Rose or were possibly working for her, or with her and the actor Cullen Skink, or maybe the Queen, or not, or . . . He was having trouble deciding where he could start and still have time to finish before the brothers decided a gun-filled escape was there only chance.

"Well, officer. I'm here because the Queen is expecting me to—"

But the officer cut him off. "The Queen?" His expression was one of bemused dismissal. "Now, now, my fine lad. This is no place for a juvenile, especially one with an overactive imagination. Please get back in the car while we grown-ups settle this affair."

"But officer!" Neil said, but the bobby held up his hand to stop Neil and then waved him back toward the car. A quick glare from Jones also convinced Neil that he should stop talking.

Neil frowned. The Crayfish brothers were laughing at him quietly. He walked back into the car, gritting his teeth.

"Neil, what is—" Isabella began to ask, but Neil shushed her. He carefully pointed to the window, which he'd kept open a crack to hear the rest of the conversation.

"Here's my insurance information," Jones said. Neil

stole a glance at the side mirror and saw Jones handing the brothers a piece of folded paper. The officer nodded his approval, but Reggie handed the paper back, the breeze making it flap.

"And maybe you could write down your telephone number, the one I was asking you for before the nice constable arrived, on the back."

Jones scribbled something down on the paper and then handed it back. It seemed to please Reggie, and he waved to Ronnie that they should leave.

"We'll be in touch after we speak to our solicitor," Ronnie called as they walked back to their car.

They waited until the officer had tipped his hat to Jones and walked away, back to their car.

They got in, started it up, and then pulled up alongside the van. "Glad you didn't try anything funny with the copper," Ronnie said. He held up the paper. "If we

find the jewel, we'll let you know where you can find Rose. If this is a trick, we'll let you know where you can find her body." Then Ronnie gunned the engine and they were off.

Jones climbed into the driver's seat and slammed the door behind him.

Neil kicked the back of the driver's seat. "Jones, you know they are lying—"

Jones cut him off. "Neil, we're done. I made a promise years ago to protect Rose, and that's what I'm going to do."

"But they are going to get to the college first and then they'll find the jewel first!" Neil said.

Jones turned the ignition and pulled into traffic. "How stupid do you think I am? Those two idiots are off to see a grave in Stratford-upon-Avon."

"Shakespeare's hometown," Larry said.

Jones drove along slowly, until they all saw the Crayfish brothers take a left turn a few blocks ahead; then he sped up and turned right quickly, down an alleyway.

"Two hours to drive there. An hour to dig. Two seconds to get furious. Then all bets are off."

Isabella took a deep intake of breath. "So we have about three hours to find the jewel and then find Rose."

Jones responded by gunning the engine. He looked back over his shoulder. "And Neil, call Nakamura."

CHAPTER TWENTY-NINE

LARCENY, RAGE, FELONY, AND CRIME

The entrance to the College of Arms was impressive. Huge iron gates, topped with gold leaf, opened onto a square courtyard. A huge stone staircase led up to a raised walkway. The doors were tiny by comparison and stood at either end of the walkway.

Neil gazed around at the simple but imposing brick building. He was hoping this was the right place, but now that they'd arrived, he wasn't sure what to look for.

"So, where do we start?"

Larry pointed at the college. "We know all this was built after the fire, so if there's any jewel hidden, it would have to be inside, with the stuff they saved from the old building."

"This is stupid," Neil said. "It's the same as the Globe Theatre. If there was a jewel, they'd have found it in the rubble."

Larry shook his head. "This is different. The Globe was a private building. So it was finders keepers in that case. This is government property and always has been. Anything found here would be property of the monarch. And we know this monarch doesn't have it."

"Tick, tock," said Jones, pointing at his watch and marching past them through the gates. Traffic had been brutal, and Jones had grown more and more angry as their precious minutes flew by. Isabella followed him quickly and waved to them to follow. They hurried up the steps and through the door on the left.

There was a large wooden counter at the end of the hallway. A woman with horn-rimmed glasses sat on a high chair behind the counter.

"We'd like to see any files you might have on Shakespeare," Neil said, walking up to her. "We have an appointment under the name Nakamura."

Nakamura had agreed to pull some strings with his friends in the international police to get them an appointment to see the Shakespeare records. He had promised to stress both the urgency and secrecy of their investigation. Neil hoped he'd been successful.

"Ah yes," said the woman. She took some keys from a drawer and stood up. "Follow me." Neil breathed a sigh of relief. The woman led them down a bright hallway toward a pair of oak doors. "All the records you will need are in here," she said, opening the door and then standing aside.

They walked in, and she closed the door behind them. There was a click as the lock reengaged. Neil looked around the room.

It was small and square and had only one window, which seemed to be sealed shut.

An oak desk sat in the middle with a number of boxes and files laid out on top. A pile of white gloves sat next to a leather-bound book. There was an electronic buzz and then the woman's voice came through an intercom that was next to the door. "You are being monitored at all times. You have fifteen minutes. Then we will close for the day."

"There's a hundred documents here at least!" Neil said.

"There *are* a hundred here at least," Larry corrected him. "So let's get to work!"

Neil put on a pair of white gloves and carefully opened one of the boxes. Inside were a number of stiff papers. "They all look like property deeds, some notices of funerals, and lots of pages of drawings." Neil scanned through the pages. He didn't see anything that resembled a jewel or any of the other clues. "There's definitely no treasure hidden in here." He lifted the papers out of the box and shook it, in case there was a secret drawer or compartment.

The others weren't having any better luck.

Jones had the actual Shakespeare application in his hand and was alternately reading it and holding it up to the light. "Lemons are often used to write invisible messages. Maybe Kemp hid something in the documents."

Neil suspected he'd be able to pick up whatever trace of lemon remained on the pages with his nose, but he wasn't sure, so he let Jones continue.

Isabella was searching through a list of deeds for land that was owned in and around Stratford. "These seem pretty straightforward. They list all sorts of people, but there's no marginalia or added notes that might be from Kemp."

Larry was looking through a number of books, but was also quietly taking pictures with his phone. "In case we think of something later that might tweak our brains." Neil had to admit this was a smart idea, but he also knew the Crayfish brothers were only an hour and a bit from figuring out they'd been duped.

Ten minutes later they had gone through all the documents as quickly as they could. They'd set aside about twenty documents that they thought might be worth looking at, including the application for the Shakespeare coat of arms.

"Some potential clues, but no jewel," Neil said sadly.

Neil looked at the Shakespeare coat of arms again, and again and again. Had Kemp hidden something on the document? How would he have done that anyway? It wasn't like it was *his* family's document, so why would they even have let him loo . . .

Neil ran to the door and hit the button on the intercom. "Hello, hello?" he said.

"Neil, what is it?" Isabella said.

"An idea, that's all," Neil said.

It seemed to take forever, but the woman's voice finally crackled through the speaker. "May I be of assistance?" she asked.

"I'm wondering if there are any files for the Kemp family. Does the Kemp family have a coat of arms registered here?"

There was a pause and the sound of paper being moved. The woman seemed to be shuffling through something on her desk. "Well, yes there is, but it is from well before the dates you requested."

"That's okay. Can we see the application?"

"I'm sorry, but you only have one minute left before—"

"Please," Neil said, fighting a rising sense of panic and the excitement of feeling he was on the right track. "It's—it's my grandfather's family name, and I came all the way from Canada to see it. Please?"

"I've never heard Neil sound so humble!" Larry whispered to Isabella, just loud enough for Neil to hear.

The intercom crackled again. "Fine. I will bring some files to you, but I cannot stress again that you will only have a short time before we close."

"Thank you!" Neil was grinning, but there was no guarantee that this was right. What if he was just wasting more time?

"I think it's the final misdirection," Neil said as they waited. "Kemp sends Shakespeare here looking for the jewel."

Larry swirled his chair. "But it's not hidden in the Shakespeare family papers . . . it's in the Kemp family papers!"

"It's the last reference from the key code. '"Point

thee to a finer robe' also refers to Kemp's family. He's saying his family is better than Shakespeare's."

Larry and Jones said, almost at the same time, "Let's just hope you're right.'"

The door clicked and the woman entered with a dusty old leather-and-iron box. Neil couldn't be sure, but it looked eerily similar to the picture of the box Lane had found buried in the ruins of the Raven Theatre.

She laid it down on the desk and unlocked the clasp that held it shut. The old lock creaked and groaned but, with a click, opened.

"I will give you two minutes," the woman said as she walked back outside and locked the doors again.

Neil sat down quickly in the chair. "That's all this should take." He took a deep breath and then opened the box as carefully and quickly as he could with shaking fingers. The hinges were as tight as the claws of a live lobster. This box hadn't been opened in ages, maybe centuries. He was sure of it. The jewel that had been waiting for Shakespeare, and that had then waited for centuries, was now about to be revealed.

Jones, Isabella, and Larry leaned over Neil's shoulders in anticipation.

The hinges creaked and the lid reluctantly gave way. A musty odor reached Neil's nose, and he had to turn his face away as the light from the windows reached inside the box.

Isabella gasped.

Larry made a sound like a falling bomb.

Jones gave a heavy sigh.

Neil looked back at the box. It was . . . "Empty?" The

inside of the box was lined with a kind of purple silk, but that was it.

"Empty," Jones said. He slammed his fist down on the table, sending the other papers jumping and then landing in a whiff of dust.

Neil shook the box. This couldn't be. Was Shakespeare supposed to have felt the same anguish when he opened the box?

"Maybe Kemp laughed into the box and then closed it," Larry said, banging his head lightly on the table.

"Or had second thoughts and took the jewel away?" Isabella suggested.

"Or someone got here first!" Jones waved his hand with such force it created a small breeze that passed over the empty box and carried with it just the faintest odor of . . .

"Honey?" Neil said. He sniffed again to be sure, jamming his face right into the box. Definitely honey! "There's something else in here!" He began to run his fingers all around the inside of the box. Corner to corner and then up the seams. There was nothing. He smelled again. Was the smell coming from the lid?

Neil turned the box upside down and started to search the inside of the lid. A small knock revealed that there was a false lid with a compartment behind. "Yes! But where's the latch?" Neil ran his fingers around and felt the smallest bump in the fabric.

There was a click, and the lid came apart.

"Is there a jewel?" Isabella asked.

"It's another piece of paper," Neil said, confused. "It looks like more poetry."

Larry came over and looked. "Oh my . . . that's not poetry. It's a list of plays. And look at the bottom of the page."

Neil and Isabella followed Larry's finger to a scribbled signature.

Will Shaftsbpear

Larry just let out a low whistle. "The jewel isn't a real jewel after all!"

Neil felt his hand shake. He was holding one of the most valuable pieces of paper in the world. A true Shakespeare signature was worth millions. He'd picked up enough of Rose's conversation to figure that out.

"Now let's find Rose," Jones said.

Suddenly, the intercom crackled. "Mr. Kemp, I'm afraid that time has—wait, who are you? What?" There was a loud noise from somewhere in the background, followed by a scream and shouts and a very clear and loud "Run!" Then the intercom squawked and died.

Jones immediately took in the dimensions of the room and started to bark out orders. "Neil, secure the signature. Larry, shove that desk against that window. Isabella, formation two."

"Formation two?" Neil said. In a panic he rolled up the precious jewel and stashed it in his coat pocket.

"You and Isabella need to have a serious talk," Larry

said, shoving the desk quickly against the wall.

Formation two seemed to consist of Jones standing on the table and then bending down to form a kind of human stepladder. Isabella climbed on his back and took what Neil thought was a tube of lipstick from her pocket. She flicked off the cap, then jammed the tip hard against the glass, shattering it into a thousand pieces.

"That's some lipstick! Now you know what to get her for Christmas!" Larry said.

Jones took Isabella's feet in his hands and then lifted her up. She gripped one edge of the sill and then pulled herself up and out.

There was a pounding on the door, followed by the rattling of keys.

"Hurry!" Jones said.

Larry ran over and Jones lifted him the same way.

There was a click in the door as whoever it was found the right key. Neil ran over to Jones. "Put your feet in my hands." Jones said, lifting him up almost effortlessly. Neil grabbed one of the iron supports of the window.

"Jones, c'mon, take my hand."

Jones waved him off. "First of all, you couldn't lift my pinky finger. Second of all, you are going to need some time to escape." Jones rolled up his sleeves. "I'm going to buy you that time with a few teeth, and they won't be mine."

The door slammed open and Neil saw two figures silhouetted in the entrance.

It was Cullen Skink, or Lord Lane, or whoever he really was. Behind him, partly in the shadows, was a woman. Was it Rose? Was it the woman from the front desk? Was it someone else?

"Get out of here!" Jones yelled before sprinting over to the figures. Neil took one look back and then jumped. He hit the ground and fell over, rolling on the hard stone. The impact sent the jewel flying. Neil grabbed it before the wind could take it and shoved it back into his pocket.

"Not very respectful of history," Larry joked as he reached down and helped him up. "There's a gate over there. Let's go." There was a low brick wall a short distance away, with scary-looking iron points on top.

"What about Jones?" Neil said. "He could get killed back in there."

Isabella didn't slow down. "Formation two. No questions," she said. They sprinted over to the gate, and Isabella bent down to act as the stepladder this time. Neil and Larry jumped over, and then Isabella jumped up, grabbing an iron bar. Neil stood on top of Larry on their side and helped pull her over.

They landed in a heap, with Isabella smack on top of Neil.

"Ouch!" Isabella said, her chin banging into Neil's forehead.

"I think I broke a rib!" Neil said, gasping for breath and grabbing his side.

"That move always looks more romantic in the movies," Larry said.

"Never believe what you see in a movie," Isabella said.

"No kidding," Neil said, getting to his feet with a grimace. They ran off down the street.

"Where to now?"

"I think it's time we had a meeting with the Queen," Neil said. "To go over the menu."

CHAPTER THIRTY

BUCKING HAM

The guard at the door of Buckingham Palace clearly had no intention of letting two teenagers and what appeared to be a talking shaggy dog in a sweatshirt into the seat of royal power in all the British Empire.

"I tell you, she's expecting me," Neil pleaded.

"That is clearly an impossibility," the woman said. "Now, please, go away or I will have no choice but to have you arrested."

Neil felt a tap on his shoulder. He turned and saw Isabella pointing to a video camera over the guard's shoulder. Neil began jumping up and down and waving in front of the guard, making sure whoever was watching could clearly see his face.

"'Ere, what are you on about? Stop that!" The guard shooed Neil away.

They walked to a spot along the great iron front gates and sat down.

"Now we wait until they tell the Queen," Isabella said.

Larry looked sad for a minute. "So I guess we can't go try to spring Rose?"

"Formation two. That's not just an escape plan. It's also Jones code for 'do what we know we can do right now,' which is get this 'jewel' into the right hands. If we can get the Queen the jewel, maybe we can convince her to send out help."

"How do we know if the Queen is even home?" Neil said.

Isabella pointed to the top of the palace. Neil looked up and saw a flag. It was made up of four squares in red, blue, and yellow, with lions and even a harp.

"It's the royal standard," Larry said. "When the Queen is here, they fly that flag. When she's not here, they fly the Union Jack, the one we think of as the British flag."

"How do you know all this stuff? And don't say homework."

"Homework."

The guard approached.

Neil stood up. "Do we get to go see the Queen now?"

The guard didn't answer. Instead she beckoned for Neil to follow her. Isabella and Larry started to as well, but the guard held up a hand, stopping them.

Once they stepped inside the gates, the guard handed Neil a deep blue cell phone.

"Hello, why does this boy always take so long to answer?" said a familiar voice. Neil felt a sudden rush of excitement and relief. This was certainly the real deal, and not Rose.

"Hello, Your Majesty," Neil said.

"I have been trying to reach you! Why do you not answer your phone? My grandchildren practically have them glued to their heads!"

"My phone got a little . . . smashed. I'm sorry."

"You should take better care of your things. We do."

"Yeah. I'll have to get a butler to help me," Neil said quietly.

"Young man, that is enough of your cheek! But we shall let it pass. Have you found Lord Lane?"

"I'm afraid not. We think he may be dead."

"Dead?"

"Well, yes. Didn't your police tell you we found his bloody clothes?"

The Queen seemed to muffle the receiver to talk to somebody else. Then she came back on the line. "They said there were clothes, and some blood, but they never said anything about a body."

"There was a lot of blood."

"After more tests it was determined that some of his blood had been mixed with pig's blood. This was one of the things we tried to call you about."

Neil took a second to process this new information. So Lane was possibly not dead? Why go through all the trouble to make it look like he was?

"Hello. Are you still there?"

The Queen's voice shocked Neil back to the present.

"Yes, I'm here. There is good news. We found the jewel . . . or maybe the jewel." Neil wasn't sure. He'd been expecting some kind of actual jewel, not just a page with Shakespeare's signature on it—as valuable as that was.

"Then by all means, let us have it!"

Something made Neil hesitate. The Queen had invited him to England—no, ordered him to England to find Lane. But she seemed a thousand times more interested in the jewel.

"It's not here," he lied.

The Queen seemed angry. "Then where is it? You said you had it!"

Neil took a deep breath. He was treading on some very dangerous territory here. "Here's the thing. As valuable as this jewel is, there's something more valuable we need to find before I can give it up."

"What could possibly be more valuable than a jewel belonging to Shakespeare?"

"Lord Lane?"

The Queen hesitated. "Yes, yes of course. We will continue the search for our royal subject. But the jewel is a separate issue altogether."

"And we need to find my friend Rose," Neil said. "I think I need to hold on to the jewel until we get her back. If the kidnappers want it, then I'll need to use it as bait."

"This is unforgivable! Give us the jewel or else—"

Neil hung up. There were now only two options. One, the Queen agreed with Neil, and she'd let him keep looking for Lane, and for Rose.

Two, the Queen was going to be seriously cheesed.

"Cheesed!" Neil said as he tossed the phone back to the guard.

Neil ran back to Larry and Isabella, waving them forward toward a row of black cabs.

"Where you headed?" the cabbie asked.

"We're going shopping for cheese," Neil said.

Larry, Neil, and Isabella hid in the alleyway across from the Wensleydale's cheese shop. The windows were dark. It appeared to be closed, but Neil suspected there was at least one person inside: Rose.

"Tell me again why we are shopping for cheese?" Larry whispered.

"I already knew why I smelled cheese on Reggie."

"You smudged it all over his face," Isabella said.

Neil nodded. "But when the twins attacked us on the way to the college, I also smelled cheese on Ronnie. It didn't strike me at the time—"

"Although Reggie did." Larry chuckled.

"Ha-ha. I'd never met Ronnie before. But I smelled cheese on *both* their clothes, and not just the one I'd smudged all over him, but even some Camembert and Gouda."

"Gouda thing you have such a gooda nose." Larry smiled.

Isabella gave him a jab in the ribs.

"You Muenster," Larry joked.

"Go on, Neil," Isabella said.

"Well, the cheese had a pretty specific aroma, and I knew I'd smelled it before. It was from this shop."

"You think it was more than a coincidence that you were knocked out here."

"I'd assumed Reggie had followed me to the cheese shop, but maybe he was already there. Then, when I walked in, he recognized me as Rose's friend and attacked."

"They wanted you to take the message to her," Isabella said.

"Even worse. I think this is where they have their headquarters. I also bet if we look at the cheese they gave me as a 'gift'—the one Jones put in the van's fridge— we'll find a homing device. How could I have been so stupid?"

"It comes naturally to the younger Flambés," Larry joked.

"So you think they have Rose hidden inside?" Isabella said.

Neil nodded. "As Rose would say, it's a good working theory."

Isabella looked at her watch. "The brothers must have discovered that they've been duped by now. If Rose was in danger before, she is in mortal danger now. I wish Jones were here." She sighed.

"Call him again before we try to break in," Neil suggested.

She pulled out her cell phone and dialed, but there was no response. They'd tried Jones a few times, with no answer. They had checked the news on Larry's phone on the way to the shop, and there had been reports of an attack at the College of Arms, but police said no one had been found inside.

"So everyone we need to either find or talk to is, as Nakamura would say, 'at large,'" Neil said.

"Actually, Jones is just large," Larry joked.

Isabella responded by jabbing him in the ribs again.

"Not so Havarti!" he said.

"Shhh!" Neil said. "I think I see a shadow in the doorway."

They watched as the door opened a crack and a young woman poked her head outside, taking a look down both sides of the street.

"Brie," Neil said.

"Penny!" Larry said, at exactly the same time.

They stared at each other with absolute confusion.

"That's Penny Lane?" Neil asked, incredulous.

"Yeah!"

"But Lord Lane said she was on some backwoods field trip."

"Well, I've only met her a couple of times, but that's her. Maybe she just got back. Did you notice the tattoo of the Queen she has on her shoulder?"

Isabella raised an eyebrow and glared at Neil.

"No!" he said quickly. "We talked about cheese!"

Brie/Penny went back inside and closed the door.

"Why would Lane's daughter be working with the Crayfish?" Isabella asked.

Larry stood up. "Let's go and ask her!"

Before Neil could say anything, Larry had marched

across the street and begun to knock loudly on the door of the cheese shop.

Neil and Isabella hurried to catch up. They stood with their backs against the wall, keeping an eye on the street.

There was no answer. Larry tried turning the handle, but it didn't budge. He got down on his hands and knees and ran his fingers around the trim. "This is a solid door. Metal braces, and I'll bet multiple locks. I can't pick our way in."

All of a sudden, Neil caught a faint odor of cheese on the breeze. It wasn't ripe cheese, ready to be eaten or sold. This was cheese that was being left to ripen in a cool, dark place. Gourmet cheese.

"There's a cheese cellar," he said. "Incredible. This might be the Crayfish hideout, but it's also a real cheese shop."

"So?" Larry asked.

But Isabella and Neil were off, looking for the source of the smell, Neil with his nose high in the air.

They sidled along to the alleyway on the far side of the shop and peeked around the corner.

Neil jerked his head back. A woman on a motorbike was speeding toward them. She flew out of the alleyway. "Penny!" Neil said, catching a glimpse of her face. "Hurry! She must have come out of a back door." He headed to the rear side of the building.

Larry quickly sprinted ahead. "Which means there's another way inside for three intrepid sleuths!"

Neil followed his nose around the back of the cheese shop. He stopped. He expected to see a loading dock, or possibly a large door or something, anything. Instead they found themselves staring at a solid wall.

"There has to be a door," Neil said, running his fingers along the seams between the bricks.

"Don't touch them, you bonehead. Sniff them," Larry said.

Neil stuck his nose against the bricks. He could definitely smell ripening cheese. Where was it coming from? He sniffed along the bricks and down the length of the wall. Finally he smelled a faint breeze from a barely perceptible crack in the bricks.

"Larry, can you pick your way in here?"

Larry rushed over, tripped, and then fell against one of the garbage cans, knocking it into the wall. It dislodged a brick. There was a crack, and a portion of the wall slid back and then to the side.

"Apparently, the answer is 'yes I can,'" Larry said, standing up and brushing himself off. They rushed inside.

They were standing on an oil-stained concrete pad, big enough to fit a couple of large cars. On the right was the back door to the cheese shop. Isabella pointed to the numerous locks. "I guess they don't want anybody getting into this part of the building by accident."

Larry was examining the inside wall. "You two go check out the cellar. I'll figure out how to close this baby."

To their left, a set of stairs led down to the basement. Neil and Isabella rushed down the steps, where another door was locked. It was solid oak.

Neil could smell the cheese coming from the other side mixed with other smells, including rose-scented perfume. "There are no keys here," Isabella said, scanning the wall for a hook or chain.

"Larry! Is there anything up there we can use to knock down a door?"

Larry ran downstairs holding what

266

appeared to be a rusty old fire ax. "This is for Rose!" he said, immediately smashing at the door again and again.

Neil looked nervously up the stairs, expecting to see Reggie or Ronnie, or Brie, bearing down on them.

Finally Larry was able to smash a hole through the door near the lock. "Now, on the count of three, we all kick. One, two, three!"

Neil, Larry, and Isabella kicked the door, which creaked on its hinges and swung heavily open.

They rushed inside.

There, lying on the cold floor, and not moving, was Rose Patil.

"We're too late!" Isabella said.

CHAPTER THIRTY-ONE

SOUNDS AND FURY

Everything around them erupted at once. They heard the front door open on the main floor above them, followed by two sets of heavy footsteps in the cheese shop.

Isabella ran across the cellar to Rose, triggering a laser alarm that began to sound throughout the building. The footsteps above them grew faster. Isabella gathered Rose in her arms. Larry rushed over to help, triggering even more alarms. Neil had to cover his ears to stop the pain.

Isabella waved him over. Was Rose still alive? He stumbled over to help his friends, who were lifting her off the floor. He grabbed her legs. She seemed cold to the touch.

Isabella pointed at the stairs. They rushed to get to the top before whoever was upstairs could reach them. Neil remembered all the locks that had to be undone on the door. He hoped that bought them some time. They struggled to keep Rose steady as they stumbled up the steps.

But they were too late. As soon as they reached the

top step, they saw the Crayfish brothers come barreling through the back door. Reggie and Ronnie stopped and cracked their knuckles. Neil couldn't believe it, but he was sure that he could hear the sound over the screaming in his ears.

Reggie stood guard at the top of the steps while Ronnie walked over and flipped a switch to shut off the alarm.

Neil, Larry, and Isabella stood frozen on the steps. There was nowhere to go.

"Well, lookie what we have here, Ronnie. Three rats trying to steal our precious cheese!"

"Tsk, tsk. We can't have that vermin running around the streets of our city. I'll go get some more of our poison." Ronnie walked back over and pulled a large knife from out of his coat. He and Reggie took a step toward them.

"And we don't take kindly to being sent to the boonies in search of a jewel what wasn't there."

Neil realized with a gulp that he still had the signature in his coat. If they decided to search him, they'd have the jewel. And there'd be no reason left to leave them alive. In fact, there'd be even more reason to kill them all.

"Kill us and you lose all chance of finding the jewel!" Neil said.

"I'm so angry I'll just take that chance!" Reggie said, getting ready to strike.

Neil was about to let Rose drop and get ready to fight for his life, when Rose leaped out of his hands and spun in the air, landing on her feet.

The Crayfish were so shocked they stopped in their tracks.

"Bad move," Rose said, winking. With a high leg kick she cracked Reggie in the jaw, knocking him back into his brother.

"Hey!" Ronnie yelled, falling to the ground. Reggie was so big, and so unconscious, that Ronnie was pinned to the floor.

"C'mon, you three, follow me," Rose said.

Larry's smile grew so large Neil thought his eyes might explode.

Rose practically ran over the Crayfish twins, avoiding Ronnie's meaty hands, and leaped onto the concrete pad. "Darn it. I figured there'd be at least one car or motorcycle left here."

Just then the garage door, which Larry had closed, began to open.

"Penny must be coming back!" Larry said. He ran over to the door to the shop. "In here!"

Ronnie gave a final violent grunt and flung Reggie's bulk off his own. He got to his feet just as the four "rats" escaped through the back door of the cheese shop.

"Hurry!" Neil yelled as Ronnie tore the door off its hinges.

They sped through the curtain and around the front counter, spilling hundreds of dollars of gourmet cheese onto the floor. Larry was just reaching for the handle when the door swung open, the bell giving a tiny ring, completely inappropriate to the gravity of the situation.

A woman stood framed in the doorway, holding a set of keys in one hand and a helmet in the other.

"Penny?" Larry said.

Penny Lane stared back, wide-eyed. Then she narrowed her eyes and reached for something in her pocket. "Larry, I'm sorry to do this, but . . . actually, I'm not."

She was just about to say something else when Rose shoved Larry aside and then smashed Penny with another roundhouse kick.

Penny fell back against the door, out cold.

Rose stood over her. "That's for the chloroform."

Neil looked over at Larry, who looked both impressed at Rose's butt-kicking and confused over Penny's betrayal.

"Larry, you really have to start picking better friends," Isabella said. "This is the second time your buddies turned out to be evil."

"But she had a tattoo of the Queen. I thought she'd be more patriotic."

"Rose, we thought you were dead," Neil said as Rose walked back over to them.

"That's what she and the two idiots thought too. I knew if I stayed as still as possible, they'd think I was still drugged. I knew you lot were gonna blow the escape, so I kept the element of surprise in my back pocket."

Larry looked back toward the cheese counter. "Hey, shouldn't Ronnie the Rhino have caught us by now?"

Neil and Isabella also looked inside. The shop was eerily quiet.

"Careful, could be a trap," Larry said.

Rose marched past them. "Ha. Quiet isn't the Crayfish style. I think I know what happened. Jones! *Jones!*" she yelled.

As if on cue, Jones rose from behind the cheese counter, a rope in his hands. "Just finishing off Ronnie's legs. Reggie's tied up back there." Jones jerked his head toward the garage.

"Nice work!" Isabella and Neil said.

"Actually, I'm just cleaning up the mess." Jones nodded toward the floor, where a giant smudge of creamy cheese covered the entire surface. "He slipped and knocked himself out. Smart thinking."

"Yeah, that was a good plan," Neil said. "I wish it had been a plan," he whispered to Isabella.

"Better than banana peels for catching a gorilla like that!" Rose said, smiling. She leaped over the counter and gave Jones a huge hug.

Neil allowed himself a smile. "So, we are all here and accounted for. I guess it's time to deliver the jewel to the Queen."

"Well, I don't mean to burst your bubble, Neil, but we still haven't found Lane," Larry said.

"I think the Crayfish must have done him in when he couldn't pay them back, and then they decided to go after the jewel themselves. Penny must have been working with them all along."

"I guess we can ask her when she wakes up," Larry said.

"Okay, then one last *last* question," Isabella said. "Jones. What happened at the college? Where's Skink?"

"He escaped. His accomplice didn't." Jones was about to explain when a gunshot splintered the wooden beam above his head.

Neil swung around and saw a man silhouetted in the bright light of the doorway. Neil couldn't make out the man's features, but he could see the smoke rising from the gun he held in front of him.

"I can answer all of those questions in just one soliloquy from Hamlet.

> *Make mad the guilty, and appal the free,*
> *Confound the ignorant, and amaze indeed*
> *The very faculties of eyes and ears.*

CHAPTER THIRTY-TWO

SKINK THE SKUNK

Neil recognized the voice, even though he had no idea what he'd just said. "Skink! You're too late. I've already given the Queen the jewel," Neil lied.

"Oh, please," Skink said, closing the door behind him. "I've been trailing you for days. I know your every move. After I left poor Cordelia to battle with Jones, I followed you to Buckingham Palace. I know you left without leaving anything behind." There was a click as the man turned the key to relock the door.

"Poor Cordelia. So faithful. She thought helping me would give her a long career in theater. Now a long stay in the hospital is more likely."

Skink turned around, and Neil could clearly see his face. Neil recognized the man who had visited his restaurant and the man whose face had appeared in the newspaper photo about the Raven Theatre. "How? Wait. How can you be both Lane and Skink?" Neil said, confused.

The man smiled. "Only a thespian as gifted as myself could have pulled it off."

Lane stared down at his unconscious daughter. "'Ingratitude, thou marble-hearted fiend. More hideous when thou show'st thee in a child than the sea-monster!'"

"I'm not sure I'd pick King Lear as a model for parenting," Larry said. "What did you do to turn Penny against you?"

"We've never been close. Then, when she discovered that I'd used up her inheritance to find the jewel . . . well, she didn't take a future of poverty very well."

"She'd been working with the Crayfish all along," Jones said.

Lane shrugged. "As you can see, it is no great loss. I will have the jewel and make sure Penny never sees a penny." He chuckled. "A bad pun unworthy of me, but it does appear to match your level of intelligence."

"Lord Lame," Larry said.

"You just proved my point." Lane gave a loud theatrical sigh.

"The man who puts the ham in *Hamlet*," Larry said.

Lane fired a bullet at Larry's feet. "I am a theatrical genius! I'd suggest you don't anger me, or the next bullet will find itself lodged inside your 'mortal coil,' if you get my reference."

"So why the whole Skink act?" Neil asked, stalling for time. Jones and Rose must be working on some kind of plan. There were five of them, after all, against only one man . . . of course, that man did have a gun.

"I asked the delightful twins if they would allow me just a short amount of time more to make good on my loans. They refused and exerted a fair bit of argument with a knife and blackjack. I felt it was expedient to disappear."

"So you changed out of your clothes at the theater and made it look like you'd been killed."

Lane nodded. "I added some fake blood to make the scene more aesthetically convincing, of course."

"Then you dressed up as Skink and ran away," Rose said.

Lane smiled. "Skink is a persona I have inhabited for years. You see, I wished to be on the stage from an early age, but it was frowned upon in the Lane family. It was fine to watch theater, but a career as an actor? That would never do." He shook his head sadly.

Neil did his best to keep the conversation going. "So you created the Skink persona to live a double life."

"A very Shakespearean solution, in fact, don't you think?"

"Um. I'll have to take your word for that."

"I toiled in the wings for years, wilting in the shadow of lesser so-called talents." A dark shadow came over Lane's face. "It was in the pursuit of a suitable theater in which to display my brilliance that I came upon the shield. I knew then that the universe was telling me I was on the right track, that I was meant to be an heir to the great Bard himself."

"Is this a soliloquy or an epic poem?" Larry said, making a "cuckoo" sign with his finger and ear.

"But there were so many false trails. I searched and searched for more clues, for more signs of this jewel. All the while I continued my career on the stage. Then you found that note in the honey. I knew then that there were more clues, clues unlike the shield. I also knew that there was still a way to find the jewel. It was time to renew my search."

"But then the Crayfish creeps caught on."

"Those guests who accompanied me to your restaurant were not all friendly, it turns out. Some told Penny about the note. She, alas, betrayed me. I knew the Crayfish twins were casing the theater in case I tried to come back."

"And to see if you were hiding something."

"Then they saw us coming out that day and assumed we were working with you," Rose said. "So they opened fire. Lane, you owe me two side mirrors and a new paint job for my car."

"No. 'I will not lend thee a penny,' as Falstaff says. I'm afraid it is time for this play to come to a close. For me it is a comedy, but for you a tragedy. I would like to thank you for all your help, though, before I exit stage left."

"Our help?" Neil said angrily.

"You broke the code. You confirmed that with our little meeting in the theater, when you so indelicately soiled your trousers and revealed that you were on the right track for the jewel. I knew I would only have to let you go, and then I could follow you."

"What do you mean you let me go?"

Lane smirked. "Your idiot cousin didn't jimmy the lock on the theater. I let him in, and then snuck out when he went to save you. There was never any real chance of a fire. It was all theater tricks."

Neil scowled. "We would take all the risk in the final search for the jewel, and then you'd swoop in at the end."

Lane nodded. "You exceeded my expectations. I almost got the jewel at the College of Arms. If only that fool at the front desk had turned off the intercom."

Jones scowled. "You threw that poor young friend of yours in my way so you could escape."

Jones made a move toward Lane, who fired another shot into the floor. Jones stopped.

"Enough. You did help capture my enemies. I will reward you with your lives, if you cooperate. Now all you have to do is lie down on the floor while I take the jewel."

"And if we refuse?" Neil said.

Lane pointed his gun at Isabella and prepared to fire.

"No! No! I get it." Neil quickly fell to the floor.

The others did the same. "Now I would like to ask Rose to stand up and come over here, with her hands on her head."

Neil looked across the floor and saw Rose stand up.

"Very good," Lane said. "Now Neil, take the jewel from your pocket and slide it across the floor to me."

"It's not a jewel, you know," Neil said. "It's just a scrap of paper."

Lane didn't say anything for a second. "Give it to Rose."

"Rose?" Had she been working with Lane after all?

"Now!" Lane said.

Neil reached into his jacket and grabbed the rolled-up paper. It had gotten quite bent during the last few hours. He took it and slid it across the floor.

Rose bent down to pick it up, and Neil could see her wide eyes locked onto the Shakespeare signature. She seemed possessed. Then she stood up straight and Neil couldn't see her face anymore.

"Read it!"

Lane said. He seemed agitated, and his voice grew more and more shrill. "Is it worth anything? Kemp said it was a jewel!"

Rose took a second to answer. "It's a sheet from a legal document. It looks like a partial deed to the Globe Theatre. There's a list of plays by Shakespeare, and then he signed it. . . ." Rose was almost whispering now as she gazed at the signature.

Lane threw his head back and laughed. "So that's the jewel!" Neil couldn't tell if Lane was angry or happy. "The deed to a burned-down, four-hundred-year-old theater?"

"As a historical document it's priceless. It's got an actual Shakespeare signature. It lists Shakespeare as the writer of a series of plays, and then it lists them! And there's more—"

Suddenly they heard sirens wailing in the distance.

"Enough. We are leaving now. If we escape, I will let you out of the car at the city limits. If not, we will both die. Now give me the jewel."

"No. I can't let this leave the country. It's too important."

"Rose, don't be an idiot," Jones said.

"It runs in the family, I'm afraid."

"If you don't hand it to me, I'll pry it from your corpse," Lane said.

The sirens were getting closer.

"Go for it," Rose said. She turned and sprinted for the front door.

Crack!

Lane fired, and Rose fell to the floor.

"Noooooo!" Neil yelled as Rose slumped down the wall. Lane ran over and bent down, desperate to grab the parchment from her. She clutched it, gasping for breath. Neil saw to his horror that a red stain was spreading across her shirt.

"Give it to me!" Lane screamed, frantic.

Neil saw a chance to get Lane and began to stand up. He felt a whoosh past his ear as Jones rushed byhim. Neil was amazed at the catlike agility and speed of the huge man. Lane turned his head as Jones lunged, but realized too late that he was done for.

Jones knocked the gun from Lane's hand and then knocked him cold with one punch to the jaw. Now it was Lane who slumped to the floor.

Jones grabbed Rose, who was still holding the parchment in her hand. He ripped the sleeves off his own jacket and made a makeshift bandage to stop the bleeding.

"Why don't you ever listen to me?" Jones said.

Rose gave a weak smile. "I knew there was no way Lane could escape if he had to try to get the jewel off me and then get out the door."

"You idiot," Jones said. Neil ran over and handed Jones his jacket. Neil could see tears forming in Jones's eyes. Jones pressed the jacket on top of the bandaged wound in Rose's side.

Rose spoke quietly. "I knew he'd focus on the parchment long enough to give you a chance to do your gymnastic Jones thing."

Jones didn't say anything. His great frame seemed to be fighting the tears. Despite his best efforts, the red stain was clearly growing. Isabella joined Jones and handed him her shawl.

"Just stay still, *bella Rosa*. I can hear the sirens getting closer."

"There's a first-aid kit on the wall," Larry said. He ran over and grabbed it, handing Jones even more bandages. Jones ripped Rose's shirt in half and wrapped the bandages and clothing as tightly as he could around her torso. He put his enormous hand on the wound, pushing hard to help it close.

"We'll get you to a hospital," Jones said.

Rose gave a weak laugh. "'A hit, a very palpable hit,' as they say in Hamlet. But at least the jewel will stay

here in England. People will know, Jones. People will know."

"It's just a stupid piece of paper," Jones said.

Rose shook her head, her eyelids fluttered. "Some things are worth risking your life for."

Her fingers went limp, and the parchment fell to the floor. Jones hugged Rose, the red stain soaking his shirt as well.

Neil had never seen Jones cry. But his whole body now heaved with great sobs.

Then, all of a sudden, there was the screeching of tires outside and the loud hum of a helicopter. The door opened, shoving Lane a good five feet sideways as an entire team of black-clad police officers stormed inside.

The next thing Neil knew, he was lying facedown on the floor with a boot on his back.

CHAPTER THIRTY-THREE

COMMAND PERFORMANCE

The Queen insisted on the dinner, even though Neil had no heart for it. He didn't care if he got any stupid royal seal of approval. Rose was lying in a coma in the hospital. Jones hadn't left her side since the police had finally shown up at the cheese shop.

"She lost a lot of blood, and stopped breathing for a few minutes. That can do permanent damage to her body and her brain," the paramedics had said as they lifted her into the ambulance. "She will get the best care possible." Jones had climbed in with her. Everyone else had followed along in the van.

The doctors were actually keeping her in a coma to let her body heal. She would wake up eventually, if she survived, but would she still be Rose?

"You might as well finish the job and cook the meal," Jones had said. "There's nothing more you can do here." Neil wasn't sure if that was another dig, or just a statement of fact. He decided to give Jones his space and cook.

Isabella and Larry were spending most of their time at the hospital as well, which meant Neil was forced to plan the meal solo. The only plus side was that the Queen had allowed Neil to ask Angel to come help him with the actual cooking. He'd arrived on an overnight flight and was on his way to the palace.

Neil leaned against the stainless-steel counter of the kitchen and sighed. He gazed at the rows and rows of fresh cheeses, great joints of meat, capons, crabs, prawns, salmon, and oysters. There were bouquets of edible flowers and baskets of fresh vegetables and fragrant herbs.

In just a few minutes the staff and royal chef would arrive, awaiting Neil's orders on what dishes they'd be asked to make, to help realize through their hands the vision that came from Neil's brain . . . and nose.

Neil knew it was going to be a wonderful meal. He was too much of an artist to *not* do his best. To not at least try was to insult the tradition of cooking, and to insult the wonderful animals and plants that had given up their lives for the benefit of the meal.

He walked over and grabbed a knife from a magnetic rack. He began to attack the onions with a vengeance. The pungent slices fell to the cutting board as thin as paper. Neil would be baking them in meat pies with incredible pieces of chicken and plums.

The tears welled up in his eyes.

Angel walked into the kitchen and came up beside Neil without saying a word. He grabbed some garlic cloves and immediately began peeling and slicing them.

A couple minutes later they were finished, and Neil, without even thinking, hugged Angel. The tears from the onions, or the past few days, poured and they silently held each other.

Neil finally pulled himself away and wiped his eyes on his sleeve. "Nice to see you, Angel."

"I wish I were here in happier circumstances. But it is good to see you, and despite the danger, you deserve congratulations for finding the jewel."

Neil gave a brief smile. "I haven't even given it to the Queen yet. They wanted me to do it at the end of the meal, as part of the dessert. Seems weird, but apparently they are very big on ceremony here."

"You just noticed that?" Angel said with a joking smile.

"How's Chez Flambé?"

"Gary and I have done our best. He is very good with fish—amazingly good, in fact. It's a real gift. You should have tried letting him run the restaurant while we're both here."

"The Queen added some cash into the deal to cover keeping it closed, and I just don't trust Gary the way I trust you. That restaurant is my home. It's a dumpy home, but it's home."

"The man with the camera returned at least once that we know of," Angel said. "He was also taking pictures of the other buildings on the block. Gary was going to follow him once, but then there was a late rush of customers and he couldn't."

"Couldn't Nakamura do some digging?"

"It's been a rough few days for crime. As much as this is worrisome for you, there were more pressing issues back home. He did make a few calls, but 'man in dark car with a camera' wasn't specific enough."

Neil just nodded, but he was concerned. He wasn't kidding when he said Chez Flambé felt like home. He wanted to return to cooking, but this mystery man with the camera was hanging over that vision like a storm cloud.

"C'mon," Neil said, putting down his knife and putting a hand on Angel's shoulder. "I want to show you the dining hall. They've done a pretty cool job of decorating."

Neil led Angel up the stairs and into the great hall. Neil had laid out an Elizabethan-themed feast, and the royal protocol officers had answered with every bit of artwork and artifact they could find from that era.

Paintings of Tudor monarchs and other major figures hung on the walls alongside tapestries depicting the defeat of the Spanish Armada and the coronation of Elizabeth I.

A corpulent Henry VIII glared down at the diners from above the doorway. And all along the center of the dining tables were swords, clocks, shields, old theater props, and, in the middle, two large globes on ornate wooden stands.

"The head waiter told me that those globes belonged to Sir Francis Drake himself."

"They are beautiful," Angel said, admiring the wonderful script on the map and the delicately carved wood that held the globe. "And old. The inscription on the base says they were made in London in 1593."

"Just like all the other stuff on the table."

"Except for the food."

Neil smiled. "I've had it with four-hundred-year-old honey. Today, freshness is the bottom line."

"It's too bad Rose can't join us. I never met her, but she sounds like a real firecracker. I assume Larry fell in love?"

"Like a rock."

They were quiet for a few moments and then Neil clapped his hands. "Time to prep."

* * *

Dinner went off without a hitch. In fact, it was fabulous. Neil felt proud and almost cheerful. He'd called Larry between servings, asking about Rose, but hadn't heard back.

The royal family was having, by all accounts, an amazing time, not that Neil got any of the praise firsthand. Neil was struck by how formal the evening was. There was no chitchat. He was called to the carpet in front of the head table to explain every dish; then the Queen nodded and he withdrew back to the kitchens.

"What do you expect?" Angel said. "The last thing they want is the chef standing around watching them eat. Don't worry—I've been watching the plates come back, and they are all clean."

Finally, it was time for the dessert. Neil had prepared cheeses and citrus tarts and had even done some research to discover that the first Queen Elizabeth had been a fan of light spice cakes, with real gold flaked on the rose-syrup topping. He knew the current Queen would also flip for the food.

As he prepared the tricky rose syrup, he felt his brand-new phone vibrate. Perhaps for the first time in his life, he risked making an only *almost* perfect dish and stopped stirring the liquid.

"Who is it?" Angel asked, hurrying to take over.

Neil pulled the phone out and saw the caller ID. "It's Larry." Neil took a deep breath and hit answer.

Larry was so excited he didn't even wait for Neil to talk. "Neil! It's Rose! She's awake!"

"That's, that's *fantastic!*" Neil said. His fingers began to shake. He hadn't realized just how tense he was.

"Neil, she wants to speak to you. It's the first thing she said when she woke up. Isabella says Jones isn't too happy about that, so you might want to be quick."

"Larry, quit joking and put her on!"

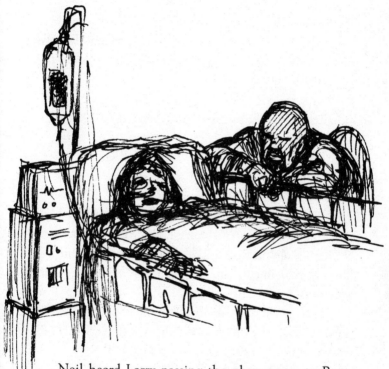

Neil heard Larry passing the phone over to Rose, whose voice was barely more than a whisper. Neil had to plug his ear to block the noise from the kitchen.

"Rose Rose? I'm so . . . happy." Neil Flambé wasn't sure he'd ever actually said that word out loud before. "Rose, are you feeling okay?"

"Don't be an idiot," she croaked.

"I think she's feeling better," Neil said to Angel.

"Do you have the parchment?" Rose said slowly. Each word seemed to take an effort, and she grew quieter and quieter. "Do you? Neil? Neil?"

"Yes. I'm supposed to give it to the Queen with dessert."

"Neil. There's more. There's more. There's mo . . ." Then she trailed off. Neil could hear Larry and Isabella saying something, and then Isabella came back on the phone.

"The doctor says she's okay, Neil. She's just so exhausted that she's passed out again. But all her signs look good."

"Maybe it was too soon to talk," Neil said.

"Sì. But she insisted. What did she say? She was so quiet we could barely hear her."

"She just said 'there's more.' But she said that back at the cheese shop, so I don't know what she means." Neil felt a tap on his shoulder. One of the waitstaff was looking very impatient, and Neil realized the desserts were already on their way out.

He hadn't tested them, and for the first time since he was in diapers, he didn't care. "I've got to go, Isabella. I wish I could be there to give you a hug."

Neil couldn't see Isabella, but he could almost hear her smile coming through the phone. "You just did. Things are good. Go get your Royal Warrant."

Neil hung up, and with a decidedly lighter step grabbed the last tray of dessert cakes from the surprised waiter and bounded up to the dining hall.

He called back over his shoulder. "Angel, it's not every day you get to wow a queen, right?"

"Exactly! Enjoy the moment." Then Angel gave Neil a big smile.

Neil entered the gilded hall bearing a silver tray of cakes in his right hand and the parchment in his left, bound in a silk ribbon. To his mild surprise, and incredible pleasure, the guests clapped as he approached the head table.

Neil noticed that even the royals were tapping their fingers against their palms.

Neil bowed and then placed the tray on the tabletop.

"'For now we sit to chat as well as eat,'" the Queen said as Neil stood back up straight. "That's a quote from Shakespeare, young man."

"Ugh," said Neil to himself. "Very fitting for the evening, Your Highness."

"And we would like to thank you for a wonderful meal. You have earned our highest honor, and it shall be conferred."

Neil bowed again. "These cakes were a favorite of another monarch, and may have been eaten by Shakespeare himself at the royal court."

"Well, you have followed in the footsteps of these great figures of our English history. And now we will ask that you confer upon us the long-sought jewel."

Neil bowed again and began to raise the parchment up. He hesitated. Rose's voice came back to him. *There's more. There's more.* He looked at the parchment. Neil had read it. He had seen what Rose had seen written on the page.

What more could there be?

Then he remembered. The smell of honey that had

first led him to the secret compartment in the box. Back at the College of Arms, Jones had been looking for lemon-based invisible ink, but Neil had smelled honey. Could honey be used to make invisible ink? To hide a message on a piece of paper?

Neil pulled the parchment back.

"Young man! What are you doing?"

"I'm sorry, Your Majesty, it's just that I need to do something first."

He ran over to a table and held the parchment close to the flame. He could smell the molecules from the honey being reactivated as the paper warmed.

"Are you *insane?*" the Queen yelled. "Stop him! Stop him before he burns the jewel!"

Neil could hear the footmen rushing toward him. Words suddenly emerged on the paper. There it was. Kemp had left one final message, hidden—words, formed into a circle. Neil stared in wonder as he read the four-hundred-year-old clue.

"'Look to the center of the earth; only there is a jewel of true worth.'" And there, in the center of the circle, was the fish-shaped key.

A guard grabbed Neil and pulled him away from the candle. Neil fell to the ground in a lump, the guards pinning his arms behind his back.

"Your Majesty. There's more! There's more!" Neil cried, his face smudged against the luxurious carpet. "Kemp hid one last clue! Rose knew it was there and now I've seen it. The parchment isn't the jewel!"

"Not a jewel? It is the signature of the greatest writer who ever lived! It is the deed to the Globe Theatre!"

Neil felt his breath being squeezed out of his lungs. "If there's one thing I've learned on this trip, it's to look at things through someone else's eyes, even if those eyes are four hundred years old."

"What do you mean?" The Queen waved a hand at the guards, who let Neil go.

Neil turned on his side, rubbing his wrists and his ribs. "Shakespeare's signature wasn't a jewel, even to Shakespeare. We think it's the jewel because it's so valuable today. Back then it was just a signature, just a signature on a piece of paper."

The Queen hesitated for a second. "You say there's more?"

"The jewel is still out there, somewhere. This isn't the jewel. It's one last misdirection from Kemp. This is just the way he hid that final clue."

The footman grabbed the parchment and took it to the Queen. "I don't see anything here but the signature and a list of plays."

"It's diluted honey. It only shows up when heated."

The Queen held the paper up to the light. "We will have to take your word for it. It is too risky to expose such a treasure to heat like that again. It appears the real jewel, then, is lost forever."

She sat down and placed the parchment on the table next to her plate.

Neil got to his feet. An idea was forming in his head. "I think I know where the jewel is hidden, Your Majesty. And I think I know what it is."

She peered at him. "Go on."

He pointed at the parchment. "On that list of plays

is a play I've never heard of, and I've had the plays crammed into my head for days."

The Queen looked at the list. "*Love's Labour's Won.* There is no such play."

"I think that's the 'more' that Rose noticed. The play is missing because Kemp stole it. What would be more precious to Shakespeare than one of his plays? Rose knew that this was more precious than a real jewel."

"And she knew about the invisible ink?"

Neil shook his head. "Rose knew there had to be a clue hidden somewhere on the paper, and I remembered the smell of honey. It turns out the honey was a central clue all along."

"So you decided to test your theory by almost burning a priceless document?"

"It's about to get worse."

"What are you talking about?"

Neil pointed to the globes on the table. "The play is in one of those."

"What?"

"'Look to the center of the earth.' Drake's own earth, his globes. That's where the manuscript is hidden."

"I hesitate to ask how you intend to test this theory."

Neil walked over the globes. "I could use a knife."

The Queen scoffed. "On a priceless antique? Never."

Neil stared intently at the globes. There had to be a way to get inside. "I am very skilled with knives," he said.

"Young man, if you think . . ."

Neil didn't hear the rest of the rant. He was staring intently at the globes.

They were both beautiful, but remarkably different.

One globe showed the earth; with all the countries Drake had visited. His path was even drawn onto the globe, along with hundreds of other navigational lines.

The other globe showed the constellations. These were represented as bears, snakes, lions, lobsters. A decorated metal arc spanned the second globe, like a rainbow in the sky.

Neil sniffed each globe carefully. He was hoping for some trace of honey, onion, lemon . . . but they just smelled like old paper and wood.

He looked at the globe that showed Drake's travels. Surely, after all the references to Drake, this was the right globe. Neil placed the point of the knife blade against the paper, and heard the Queen gasp.

Then he remembered the lobster.

He stopped. He dropped the knife.

"Your Majesty, I don't need to cut anything. I'm sorry."

"Good. Now, please step away from those treasures."

Neil shook his head. "There's another way inside."

"Preposterous!" She said, but she also seemed intrigued. The lure of the true jewel had definitely taken hold. "How?"

"Fish. Fish is the key."

"Meaning?"

"The Drake globe is a misdirection," Neil said. Misdirection had been as much a part of this mystery as food and honey. Shakespeare loved to use it in his plays. Kemp used it at every single step of the treasure hunt.

"The lobster is the real clue." Neil leaned in for a closer look at the lobster. It was almost cut in half by the equator, and the equator was a seam. And in the middle of the seam was the smallest of cracks, a tiny keyhole.

"What do you see?" asked the Queen.

"A way in." Neil began scanning the globe. "There has to be a key somewhere," Neil said, under his breath.

He ran his fingers along the wooden base and the metal arc. At the very top of the arc his finger hit a bump. It was a small pin, right over the North Pole. He squinted to get a closer look. The pin was a key, a tiny key with a fish-shaped bow.

Neil smiled. "May I?" he asked the Queen, whom he could see was now leaning in closely, holding her breath.

She nodded, wide-eyed.

Neil pinched the key. It turned, and came loose.

He carefully slid the key into the tiny slit in the lobster at the equator.

"The center of the globe. Tasteless gruel. Food." Neil closed his eyes. He gave a quick prayer that this worked.

He turned the key.

There was a click, followed by a loud snap.

Neil opened his eyes.

The globe had split in two. If he was wrong, he'd just destroyed a treasure.

He took a deep breath, and smelled the unmistakable aroma of tanned leather.

Neil leaned over. There, in the bottom half of the globe, sat a brown leather case. He reached in and lifted it carefully. Now everybody was gathered around, pressing as close as possible to see the true jewel of Shakespeare.

CHAPTER THIRTY-FOUR

THE CURTAIN CLOSES

The Queen gave them all a private tour of her palace. "It is the least I can do to thank you," she told them. Rose was even able to accompany them in a wheelchair. Neil was struck by how tenderly Jones pushed the chair through ornate room after ornate room.

The Queen could not have been more generous. Neil had asked that he not be on the front page of the papers. "It's not every day, or every five hundred years, that someone finds a real Shakespeare play," said the Queen.

"No thanks. I don't need more detective work. I need more customers." So Neil wasn't mentioned in the many stories of the museum man's great "discovery."

Well, technically, Neil did ask to be on the front page as "the greatest chef the Queen has ever met," but the story didn't compete very well with the big news.

"Besides, Neil was only part of a crack team of experts," Larry added.

Neil, much to Larry's surprise, nodded enthusiastically. "Rose is the real hero here. We were lost until we met her, and she risked her life to help us find the jewel."

"Rose will be abundantly rewarded, and her research will now carry the full support of the royal family."

Rose smiled, but beamed when she finally got the chance to handle the lost manuscript to *Love's Labour's Won.* "Can I skip wearing the gloves?" she asked. She gently touched the Bard's signature.

"There's even a whole banquet scene," she said, poring over the frantic handwritten script. "It turns out the prince is the princess in disguise, and the king is really the queen, and the cook is actually a magic fairy."

Larry lapsed into his best, or worst, thespian voice. "To quote the Bard, 'If this were played upon a stage now, I could condemn it as an improbable fiction.'"

Rose closed the leather packet carefully. "Of course, there will be skeptics. Fake Shakespeare manuscripts have shown up from time to time. But this is the real deal."

"There's one thing I don't get," Neil said. "Why was it such a big deal to lose this one copy of the play? Didn't they have others?"

Rose shook her head. "That's not the way it worked. Back then, the playwright would do the original manuscript by hand; then he'd deliver it to a printer. The printer would make a script and throw out the original."

"That's why there are hardly any Shakespeare originals left," Jones said.

Rose nodded. "None, in fact. So Kemp must have broken into the printer's shop and taken the one copy Shakespeare had of the play. Once it was gone, Shakespeare would have lost all his hard work."

"Then he had a theater prop expert make him a shield and two globes," Neil said. Rose nodded.

"I'm still concerned by the *Othello* reference," Isabella said. "The play is listed as 1604, after Kemp was dead. How could he possibly know what Shakespeare had written in that play?"

Rose smiled. "I have a theory about that as well. I think Shakespeare wrote it much earlier, and Kemp either saw it in rehearsal or maybe even at the printer's when he stole this manuscript. Shakespeare must have planned to stage the play before 1603, but then the plague hit and the theaters were shut down."

Neil sat back in his chair contentedly. "Hey, I got out of a week's worth of homework, won a royal seal of approval, and even pocketed a few pounds to buy some more equipment for the restaurant when we get back."

Angel grimaced. "I suppose it's not a good time to mention what Gary did to the deep fryer while you were gone."

Neil's face fell.

"I'm just kidding," Angel said, letting out a rolling laugh. "I've known you for a decade and you are still wound tighter than a clock."

"Ha-ha," Neil said, pulling out his phone. "Hey Angel, it's the nineteen fifties on the phone. They'd like their recipes back."

Larry spewed his tea all over the table. The Queen was not impressed. "Is that how you drink tea in the colonies?"

"It's not a total waste," Larry joked. "I'm more of a coffee man myself."

The Queen put her teacup down abruptly and smiled. "Thank goodness!" She signaled to one of her butlers. "Wooster, by all means bring coffee. I am so sick of tea."

"FAREWELL! THOU ART TOO DEAR FOR MY POSSESSING."

The light turned green. Neil Flambé pushed off and let gravity speed his bike down the hill toward Chez Flambé. The wind rustled the bits of red hair that stuck out of the holes in his helmet. Neil smiled.

He had arrived back in Vancouver late the night before and intended to rush to work right away. But his parents had refused to let him visit the restaurant until he finished at least one overdue math sheet.

"Queen or no Queen, you get some work done," his father had said, before turning his attention back to his mountain of advertising posters.

His mother hadn't even looked up from her laptop. "Yes, these globe-trotting vacations are taking away from your discipline."

"Vacations!" Neil had said, incredulous, but his parents were engrossed in their own work.

He'd done the math, grumbling the whole while, and had even phoned Larry for a few tips on quadratic equations (whatever they were), and then he'd gone to bed with visions of his kitchen dancing in his head.

And now he was cruising back to his real home. He arrived at the bottom of the hill and made a right turn.

He slammed on the brakes.

A band of yellow tape blocked off the street where Chez Flambé sat among dilapidated dollar stores and worse.

Neil parked his bike and snuck under the tape. He noticed quickly, and with a mix of anger and horror, that the front door to the restaurant was also taped up.

A man in a trench coat was standing in front of the window, jotting down something in a small notebook. He turned and saw Neil standing and staring at the door.

"Can I help you?" the man said.

Neil recognized him instantly as the man who had been taking pictures of Chez Flambé.

"That's my restaurant! What have you done to my restaurant?"

The man took a close look at Neil. "Ah yes, Neil Flambé. I didn't recognize you without your chef's clothes. My name is Charles Gray. I'm with the city."

"So?" Neil said. "Are you from the health department?"

"Um, no. My job has nothing to do with food."

"No kidding. If you knew anything about food, you wouldn't be closing down the best restaurant in the city!" Neil bellowed.

Gray shook his ears to stop the ringing. "Well, be that as it may, I am in fact from the city planning department. And this entire block has been slated for demolition." He waved his hand around to take in the ten or so buildings on either side of Chez Flambé.

"Didn't you think it might be fair to give us advance warning?"

"That's what I'm here to do today."

"Really? Explain how that works exactly."

"Well, the city has been debating for years about the need to add another entrance lane for that bridge." Gray pointed to the nearby bridge, a giant iron structure that spanned the water to the North Shore. "And this site was chosen last week as the best option."

"Because of the photos you took?"

"That was part of it, I'm proud to say." He unfurled a large blue paper and held it up on the window. He pointed at the proposed new street. It ran right over the spot where they were now standing.

"The buildings here are dumps. They should have been condemned years ago. Jackpine Street comes right down the hill, but ends a block south. All we need to do is extend it all the way to the bridge. Unfortunately, for you, that means we have to raze these buildings."

Neil was fuming. "Here's what's going to happen. I'm going to go sit in my restaurant and cook. I'm going to stay there, and if you want to bulldoze the building down, you'll have to do it with me inside."

Gray slowly rolled up the blueprint. "This area is ripe for renewal, and I'm afraid city council voted on the plan this week. It's official city policy now. And as the saying goes, 'you can't fight city hall.'"

"Just watch me," Neil said. He started to march toward the front door.

Gray called after him. "Listen, kid. It's better for everyone for this lane to get added to the bridge. And the city will be writing you a check as compensation. The amount on that check will get smaller the more you resist the future."

"Is that a threat?"

"I repeat: You can't fight city hall."

"Yeah, I got that." Neil clenched his fists.

Neil didn't care about the money. Not really. No matter what they were planning to pay him, it would never be enough to start another restaurant. Moving the stoves and fridges from Chez Flambé would cost thousands. Selling them would possibly make him a few hundred.

"You have another month before the building comes down."

"So I can still run the restaurant until then?"

"Actually, no. We're going to be shutting off the gas and water lines later today to get ready for the big digging machines. So I don't think the city would smile on you cooking in those unsanitary conditions. I would suggest using that month to salvage anything you would like to keep."

Neil didn't turn around. He heard Gray get into his car and start the engine. Neil was tempted to jump on the car, to smash the metal and glass with his fists. But he stayed still while Gray drove away.

He felt absolutely powerless. Crazed chefs had tried to steal the restaurant from him, an evil supercomputer and loony crusader had tried to blow it up, and now he was going to lose it because of a vote by people he'd never even met, including a bureaucrat with a camera. He stood absolutely still.

It started to rain. Neil didn't move. He felt the rain soak through his clothes, his socks, his shoes. The yellow tape over the door of Chez Flambé twisted and dripped water onto the ground.

His hair fell down over his eyes. He lifted his head and stared at Chez Flambé.

Maybe it was the rain, but the restaurant seemed to be hundreds of miles away. It was being washed away by the rain, flowing down the drain just like his dreams of being a great restaurateur.

The rain began to fall harder.

Neil turned around, got on his bike, and slowly pedaled back up the hill.

ACKNOWLEDGMENTS

All right, savvy readers. I know that no one ever reads these acknowledgments (except for relatives who want to make sure they are included—hi, Mom!) but this particular back page thank-you list is going to contain some worthwhile advice. I promise.

A lot of people think writers work alone, that a book is the end product of one person's effort and creativity, a story born from the crucible of the tortured artist's brain, sweat, and pain.

This is total baloney.

A book is a team effort and these acknowledgments are going to serve as a road map (of sorts) for how a book goes from an idea in my brain to the book you are holding in your hands.

So yes, it starts with me having some idea of where Neil and his gang of friends are headed to, and what enemies they will face. But then I start to do research so that I know what the world will look like. In this case, the world is London.

So I buy guidebooks. I visit London (if I can) and take pictures, write notes, etc. I rely on the amazing research done by Shakespeare scholars, mapmakers, dictionary writers, and (yes) Wikipedia.

BIT OF ADVICE #1–Do research! Even a novel needs to be real.

Only then do I start writing a first draft. I should take a moment here to thank everyone who makes fair-trade coffee available at my neighborhood supermarket as well as the musicians whose music inspires me while I'm sitting in my attic. For this book there was a lot of Gogol Bordello, Justin Rutledge, and The Tallis Scholars.

I finally get through the first draft, and then it gets reviewed and ripped to shreds by my first team of editors—my wife Laura and my incredibly smart daughters, Erin and Emily. This might be **BIT OF ADVICE #2**–always get someone to read your work who will rip it to shreds. The most useless advice you will ever get is "I liked it." Ugh.

Then I do spend a lot of time back in my attic working and reworking the plot and characters until I think they are ready to submit to my amazing editor, Julia Maguire.

BIT OF ADVICE #3–Your first few drafts stink. They do. Everyone's do. Writing is about carefully rewriting over and over.

Julia then goes through and points out the big stuff—the plot points that don't actually make any sense. Round one of the editing process doesn't even touch the (many) smaller mistakes in speliling, grammmer and uther stuf.

I go back and rewrite the book again and sometimes againandagain until we get the large issues worked out and make sure the book works with the rest of the series, and then we do a final edit.

BIT OF ADVICE #4—See #3, rinse, repeat. But also don't lose heart. And don't get angry (hard to do). Each person at each stage makes the book better.

Then the book gets sent to a copy editor who goes over everything we've gone over with a proverbial fine-tooth comb. They always find dozens of mistakes. Some in spelling, some bigger. For this book, Karen Sherman did one of the best edits ever, and I am thankful.

Many institutions are cutting copy editors from their budgets. That's because those institutions are idiots.

Of course, I also do the images for my books. So the biggest shout-out goes to Laurent Linn, who is simply fantastic at taking a rough idea from me, and pushing me to rework and rework it until it's worth putting on the cover or inside the book.

Then there are the people who lay out the book, make the paper, the glue, the ink, bind the book, package the book, transport the book, and on and on.

(There are so many more: my agent, Michael Levine, who talks to the big guns and Simon & Schuster; and people such as Jon Anderson and Justin Chanda, who arrange contracts, marketing, and so much more.)

Then there are the librarians and booksellers who get my book into the hands of readers who will get a kick out of the goofy adventures of a cocky chef who solves crimes and occasionally does his homework.

So, yes, in the end it's all about you, the reader.

Thanks!

Kevin Sylvester is an award-winning writer, illustrator, and broadcaster. *Neil Flambé and the Marco Polo Murders* won the 2011 Silver Birch Award for Fiction. Kevin was particularly pleased by this because the kids vote! *Neil Flambé and the Aztec Abduction* was the runner-up in 2012. His other books include *Gold Medal for Weird* (Silver Birch winner in 2009!), *Sports Hall of Weird, Splinters, Follow Your Money, Showtime,* and *Game Day.* He spends most of his time sitting in his attic studio, drawing and writing and listening to Neil and Larry arguing over, well, everything. He also loves to cook.

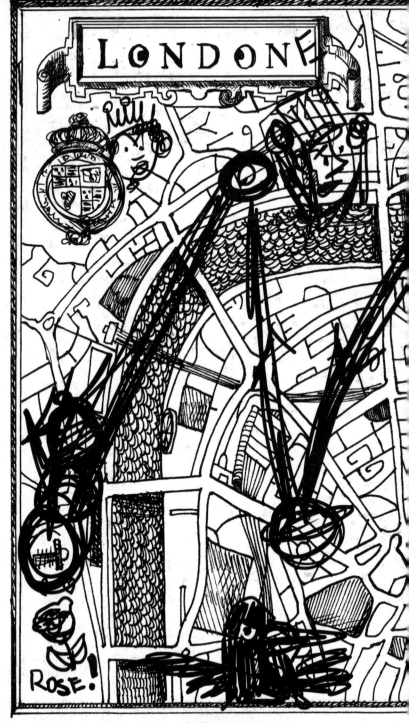

LONDON

ROSE!